Ink Flamingos

A TATTOO SHOP MYSTERY

Karen E. Olson

AN OBSIDIAN MYSTERY

OBSIDIAN

Published by New American Library, a division of
Penguin Group (USA) Inc., 375 Hudson Street,
New York, New York 10014, USA
Penguin Group (Canada), 90 Eglinton Avenue East, Suite 700, Toronto,
Ontario M4P 2Y3, Canada (a division of Pearson Penguin Canada Inc.)
Penguin Books Ltd., 80 Strand, London WC2R 0RL, England
Penguin Ireland, 25 St. Stephen's Green, Dublin 2,
Ireland (a division of Penguin Books Ltd.)
Penguin Group (Australia), 250 Camberwell Road, Camberwell, Victoria 3124,
Australia (a division of Pearson Australia Group Pty. Ltd.)
Penguin Books India Pvt. Ltd., 11 Community Centre, Panchsheel Park,
New Delhi—110 017, India
Penguin Group (NZ), 67 Apollo Drive, Rosedale, Auckland 0632,
New Zealand (a division of Pearson New Zealand Ltd.)
Penguin Books (South Africa) (Pty.) Ltd., 24 Sturdee Avenue,
Rosebank, Johannesburg 2196, South Africa

Penguin Books Ltd., Registered Offices:
80 Strand, London WC2R 0RL, England

First published by Obsidian, an imprint of New American Library,
a division of Penguin Group (USA) Inc.

First Printing, June 2011
10   9   8   7   6   5   4   3   2   1

continued . . .

The Missing Ink

"Karen Olson has launched a delightful new series with *The Missing Ink*, featuring tattooist Brett Kavanaugh. Brett is proud that she makes grown men cry. She also makes grown women laugh. I look forward to more adventures for this Las Vegas needle artist."

—Elaine Viets, author of the Dead-End Job Mystery series

"In *The Missing Ink,* Karen Olson has penned a winner, full of crisp dialogue, a red-hot setting, and a smart, sassy tattooed protagonist. Viva Las Vegas!"

—Susan McBride, author of the Debutante Dropout Mystery series

"[A] pleasantly jargon-free themed mystery. . . . Readers need not be conversant with 'street flash' or other industry terms to enjoy the setting and follow Brett down a trail of needles and gloves to the dramatic finale." —*Publishers Weekly*

"A fun read. . . . The characters are as quirky as Las Vegas itself. . . . [Brett] is both likable and down-to-earth and will have readers returning for more." —The Mystery Reader

"Olson uses the fresh setting of an upscale Las Vegas tattoo shop . . . for a fast-moving tale with quirky but affectionately portrayed characters. Although stubborn, Brett never becomes too stupid to live in her determination to solve the mystery. The tension is kept at a high pitch." —*Romantic Times*

"Fun . . . The setup is pure, the setting is flashy . . . and I expect that Brett Kavanaugh will find a devoted following."

—Gumshoe

"This one has it all with edgy characters and a tight plot."

—*Mystery Scene*

"Ms. Olson walks readers through a multiple-murder mystery, supplying clues at a steady pace. *The Missing Ink* is suspenseful, entertaining from the start, and has a touch of romance that nicely rounds out the story." —Darque Reviews

"Features the same smooth writing, insightful character development, and complex plotting as the Annie Seymour books. Brett's team at The Painted Lady is delightful, an eclectic mix of characters that adds to the fun."

—Cozy Library (cozylibrary.com)

"A winner. . . . Brett is a likable, albeit unusual heroine. I'm looking forward to seeing more of her and her zany cohorts in future books." —Fresh Fiction

"An extremely fast, extremely entertaining read. Brett is highly likable....The potential for romance in future tales is sure to keep the series fresh in novels yet to come.... Brett's work is just getting started in Las Vegas, and I can't wait to find out what happens in her next adventure."

—The Romance Readers Connection

PRAISE FOR KAREN E. OLSON'S ANNIE SEYMOUR MYSTERIES

Shot Girl

"Olson excels at plotting—with liberal doses of humor—and Annie grows more fascinating, and more human, with each novel. This one's a winner from page one."

—*Richmond Times-Dispatch*

"Easily the best one ... [Olson] step[s] up to a new storytelling level."　　　　　　　　　　　　　　　　　　　—*Baltimore Sun*

"Features the same clever plotting, great local color, and terrific personal touches that have been a hallmark of the series since it began."　　　　　　　　　　　　　　—*Connecticut Post*

Dead of the Day

"Karen E. Olson knows this beat like the back of her hand. I really enjoyed *Dead of the Day*."

—*New York Times* bestselling author Michael Connelly

"*Dead of the Day* takes the Annie Seymour series to truly impressive territory. Absolutely everything a first-rate crime novel should be."　　—*New York Times* bestselling author Lee Child

Secondhand Smoke

"Annie Seymour, a New Haven journalist who's not quite as cynical as she thinks she is, is the real thing, an engaging and memorable character with the kind of complicated loyalties that make a series worth reading. Karen E. Olson is the real thing too: a natural storyteller with a lucid style and a wonderful sense of place."

—*New York Times* bestselling author Laura Lippman

"Annie is a believable heroine whose sassy exploits and muddled love life should make for more exciting adventures."

—*Kirkus Reviews*

"[Olson's] fast-paced plot and great ending make it a perfect read for patrons who like a bit of humor in their mysteries."

—*Library Journal*

To Clair Lamb

ACKNOWLEDGMENTS

The plot of this book grew from reading tattoo blogs on the Internet. I am indebted to Bill Cohen of Tattoosday for his friendship and amazing photographs and stories of tattoos and tattooing. Ania Nowak of Aniareads gave me more insight into what it really means to be tattooed and the journey people take when they undergo body modification. Many thanks to Cheryl Violante and Angelo Pompano, my intrepid first readers, for their eagle eyes and undaunting support. Alison Gaylin, Lori Armstrong, Jeff Shelby, Patty Smiley, and Neil Smith are always just an e-mail or phone call away, ready to lend an ear. I hope I'm as helpful to them as they are to me. My agent, Jack Scovil, has stuck with me from the beginning, and I am grateful for his unwavering support and honesty. I must thank Kristen Weber, my former editor, for convincing me to write this series in the first place. When I started, I had no idea how much fun these books would be and how I would love these characters, at the same time growing as a writer, stepping out of my comfort zone and giving me more confidence. I owe that to her. And finally, to Chris and Julia, who have suffered trips to Las Vegas—dining at Thomas Keller's Bouchon, climbing the rocks at Red Rock Canyon, solving crimes at *CSI: The Experience* at the MGM—and patiently allowed me the time to create this world, you are everything to me.

Chapter 1

The picture of the flamingo tattoo was on the blog an hour before they found the body. In retrospect, I probably should've called the cops immediately.

I was working on an elaborate tattoo of a heart wrapped in the American flag when Joel Sloane, one of my tattooists, stuck his head in the door. At The Painted Lady, where we do only custom ink, we've got four private rooms for tattooing, unlike street shops that have stations out in the open.

"Brett," Joel said, nodding to my client, "sorry, but you have to see this."

I set my tattoo machine down on the counter and snapped off the blue gloves as I rose. "I'll be a minute," I told my client as I followed Joel toward the staff room. "What is it?" I asked his back.

Bitsy Hendricks, our shop manager, was standing in front of the small TV set in the corner of the staff room. When we came in, she whirled around, her eyes wide.

She pointed at the TV. Red and blue flashing lights lit up the screen, which was filled with a sea of police cruisers and at least one ambulance. Something bad had happened.

At first I was relieved it was a crime scene I wasn't witnessing firsthand. I'd gotten into a few situations in the last several months that had me up close and personal with dead bodies, and I hoped that was all behind me now.

Then I saw the picture of Daisy Carmichael on the screen, the reporter's voice-over telling me that her body was found in a hotel room.

My knees buckled a little, and Joel's arm snaked around my shoulders.

"Are they sure it's her?" I asked no one in particular. My voice sounded far away, like I was talking into a tunnel.

"Yes," Bitsy said flatly. "It's on every channel." And in case I didn't believe her, she aimed the remote at the set and clicked through all the local channels.

She was right. It was on every channel.

"Did they say what happened?" I asked.

"No, just that they found her body."

"Who found her?" I couldn't help myself. My curiosity was too strong.

"Think they said the room service guy."

As Bitsy spoke, a gurney rolled into view on the screen, a white sheet over what could only be a body. I caught my breath.

Joel tightened his grip on my shoulder, and he put his other hand on Bitsy's.

Daisy, or Dee, as she was known to her fans, was the lead singer of the band the Flamingos. They were a bit like the Go-Go's or the Bangles but with a definite edge to their videos despite the wholesome pop sound. It wasn't Lady Gaga edgy, but more an early 1980s punk look. Daisy, which was the name I knew her by, had come into The Painted Lady two years ago for the first time. She'd stumbled onto my shop by accident as she window-shopped at the Venetian Grand Canal Shoppes, the upscale stores that surrounded it. While tattoo shops weren't exactly strangers to Las Vegas, aka Sin City, this location was the result of a little blackmail by the former owner, Flip Armstrong. My clientele was a little more high-class because of it, and dropping Daisy's name now and then didn't hurt, either. When she'd first stepped foot through the door, the Flamingos were just a dream. A YouTube video discovery and two years later, they were at the top of the charts.

None of us had ever seen Daisy Carmichael socially. We'd never had dinner or drinks or even lunch with her. She only came here for her tattoos, but since she'd been here so frequently, we felt as though we had known her forever. Despite the edgy persona she portrayed to the public, to us, Daisy was a girl from Gardiner, Maine, a quiet little town where everything was within walking distance.

"... an overnight sensation on YouTube," the reporter was saying about the Flamingos as video of the band playing at the Bellagio on New Year's Eve just weeks ago lit up the screen.

That's right. They performed at the Bellagio. I frowned as I thought about that picture of the flamingo tattoo on the blog.

"She didn't call for an appointment in December?" I asked Bitsy, who kept track of all our appointments and schedule.

She flipped back her blond bob and narrowed her eyes at me. She knew what I was after.

"She didn't call. But we can't expect her to get a tattoo every time she's here," Bitsy said.

Okay, I could buy that. But I couldn't get that picture on the blog out of my head.

Since I'd had a little time to kill earlier, I'd been playing around on the Internet when I found the blog, called Skin Deep—not very original—by clicking on a link from another one. There were many blogs about tattoos these days. Some were very specialized, like those featuring science-related tattoos—one young woman had a DNA strand curling around her arm—and literary tattoos—images from books like *Lord of the Rings* and *The Little Prince* were popular—but some blogs, like Skin Deep, were more generic.

Skin Deep's latest post featured a tattoo of a flamingo. It was beautiful: long, black lines with reds and pinks and oranges. It was one of the best I'd ever designed.

Except when I'd tattooed it on Daisy, there were no colors.

I had scrolled up to the "About Me" section and read that blogger Ainsley Wainwright admired body art and the history of scarification, so felt compelled to take photographs of tattoos seen on the Vegas Strip and post them so everyone could see their beauty. Most blogs would add the stories surrounding the tattoos and where the person had gotten them. Skin Deep merely showcased the art and let that tell the story. Too bad. I could've used the publicity. Or at least a link to The Painted Lady's Web site.

"When was she last here?" I asked Bitsy. I thought of the last tattoo I gave her: a tree branch that wove its way around her arm from her wrist to her shoulder.

"October," Bitsy said without consulting the appointment book. She had a memory like the proverbial steel trap.

Since I designed her first tattoo, every time she was in town, Daisy would have another one done. I'd done ten so far. The flamingo was number eight. There hadn't been any color the last two times she'd come in.

So sometime between October and now—it was the second week of February—Daisy had another tattooist do that color.

"What's wrong, Brett?" Joel asked.

I went over to the light table, where my laptop lay. I booted it up, hooked up to the Internet, and found Skin

Deep. I pointed to the picture of the flamingo tattoo. I noticed that the picture had been posted just a little more than an hour earlier.

Joel peered over my shoulder at the computer screen.

"When did she come back for the colors, Brett?" he asked.

I shook my head. "She didn't. She can't have color. She's allergic to the dye, so she's only got black tattoos."

"So maybe it's not her. Maybe it's not yours," he suggested, plopping down next to me, his hefty frame testing the boundaries of the chair.

"It's mine," I said, pointing to the four flowers in the tip of the wing. "She wanted one for each of her bandmates. Who else could this be?"

I mulled over the picture of the tattoo. I *knew* this was Daisy.

"Is Ainsley a woman?" Joel asked, startling me out of my thoughts. I'd almost forgotten he was there, if you could forget that a man weighing about three hundred pounds was sitting next to you.

I shrugged. "Have no idea. Could be a man, too, I guess. It's sort of an androgynous name."

"So why would she"—Joel indicated the flamingo—"have gone elsewhere to get the color done?"

It was a free country; Daisy could get a tattoo anywhere she wanted. And clearly she had. But my ego wished that she hadn't. I peered more closely at the photograph. The tattoo hadn't started to get infected. If it had, it would look like a boil or a bad burn, perhaps even oozing. Maybe she wasn't even really allergic. She'd told me she'd had a reaction to the red dye in an ibuprofen tablet several years ago, which was how her doctors found out about the allergy. She said that to be on the safe side, she'd prefer to have only black tattoos.

Daisy was a canvas of black lines and curves, which made her tattoos stand out more than others, I thought.

Maybe she'd been in another tattoo shop in another city and the artist talked her into adding the color. It was possible. It was also possible to get organic inks. I'd suggested that to her, but she'd rejected the idea. Maybe someone else was more convincing.

I heard Bruce Springsteen singing "Born to Run." Glancing around the staff room, I spotted my messenger bag slung over the back of a chair. I grabbed it and pulled my cell phone out, flipping it open after noting the caller ID.

"Hey, Tim," I said. My brother, Tim Kavanaugh, was a Las Vegas police detective. I had a bad feeling about this.

"You hear about Dee Carmichael?" He didn't mince words.

"Watching it on TV right now. What happened?"

"That's what I'd like to ask *you*."

I stopped breathing for a second. "What do you mean?"

"We've got a witness who says she saw a tall redhead leaving the hotel room about two hours ago." He paused, and even if my mouth didn't feel as though it were filled with sand, I knew he wasn't done yet. I waited, curling a lock of my red hair around my finger.

"We found some ink pots and tattoo needles in the trash."

Chapter 2

I swallowed hard, forcing some saliva into my mouth so I could speak. "So you think someone saw *me*?"

"If the ink fits." He smothered a small chuckle. While it was in bad taste, it told me he didn't seriously think I had anything to do with any of this, but he had to ask.

"I've been here all day," I said. "Got witnesses, too. Bitsy and Joel and Ace, not to mention the two clients." Clients. Like the one I'd abandoned in my room to watch the news report. "Uh, speaking of which," I added, "I've got to go."

"So you didn't do her tattoo?" Tim asked, ignoring me.

Might as well tell him. "Which one?" I asked.

"What do you mean, which one?"

"Last I knew, I'd done all Daisy's tattoos, well, except for . . ." My voice trailed off.

"Except for what?"

"The flamingo. Well, I did the black part of it. A while back, actually. Maybe last year? I can have Bitsy check the records. I didn't do the color, though. She told me she was never going to have color in a tattoo because of an allergy. I don't know why she'd change her mind."

Tim was quiet a second, then asked, "How do you know, then, that the flamingo has color?"

"There's a blog. A picture on a blog."

"What are you talking about?"

"A little while ago, I found a blog called Skin Deep. There's a picture of it. The flamingo." As I spoke, I realized the implications of what I was saying. The blogger took the picture, and then Daisy was found dead. I voiced my thoughts.

"Do you know the URL for the blog?" Tim asked, his tone switching from Chatty Brother to Official Cop.

"I've got it here on my screen." I was aware of Bitsy and Joel staring at me as I recited the URL for my brother. I was also more and more aware of my client, waiting for me. I put a hand over the phone receiver and said to Bitsy, "Can you go tell Patty I'll be in shortly? That there's something I have to take care of right now?"

She was out the door before I'd finished. This was why I kept her on after I bought the business from Flip Armstrong. Bitsy was one of the most efficient workers I'd ever known, and she had institutional memory like no one else's.

As I listened to Tim tapping on his own keyboard, I scrolled down past the elaborate header decorated with Ed Hardy tattoo designs, clearly pirated from the Internet, a surprise since the blogger took pictures of tattoos and would get more mileage out of them if those were used in the design instead.

After a few seconds, Tim said, "Okay, got it." A pause, then, "So what can you tell me just looking at this?"

I went back to the picture of the tattoo, scrutinizing it a little differently now that I knew Daisy was dead.

"It's definitely mine, like I said, but before the color." I peered more closely at the screen. Maybe if I concentrated on the tattoo, didn't think about Daisy and how her life had been cut short, was more professional about this, then maybe I could be objective.

Problem was, even though the picture was pretty big,

the quality was lousy, like maybe it was taken with a cell phone camera. That didn't help the cause, because I needed to see the sharp black lines as compared to the shaded color parts, and there was nothing sharp about it.

"I would have to see it in person," I said.

"Well, that's not going to happen," Tim snipped.

"I didn't think it would," I snipped back. "But that's the only way I'd be able to tell for sure what parts are new." Even though I'd already told him.

"How many tattoos did you give her?"

"Ten," I said without hesitation. "The flamingo was number eight."

"You're sure about the number?" he asked.

"Yes," I said. "Why?"

"Do you remember what the tattoos were of?"

Off the top of my head, I recalled the flamingo, that tree branch winding around her arm, her name in Chinese characters, a portrait of Janis Joplin—her hero—a Japanese crane, Betty Boop, a peacock, the logo for the Flamingo resort, a weeping willow—she loved my Monet's garden sleeve and wanted to replicate the tree—and a rose. I rattled them off for Tim.

"You've got a pretty good memory," he noted.

"She was a special client, and I did them all in the last couple years."

"So there weren't any more?"

I wasn't quite sure what he was getting at. "No. Just the ten." And then I had a thought. "When she got the color, did she get another tattoo?" I hoped he'd say no—my ego was already bruised by that color—but instead he asked something out of the blue.

"So who do you think was impersonating you?"

"Huh? Oh, right, the redhead. I'm not the only tall redhead in this city," I said. "There are a lot of tall red-headed showgirls in Vegas."

"True, true. But who else travels with tattoo ink?"

This conversation was getting old, and I had a client.

"Listen, Tim, unless you need something official from me, I've got to get back to work. I need to pay my rent." A not-so-subtle reference to the fact that I paid *him* rent for sharing his house in Henderson.

"That's just it, though, Brett, we might need to follow up officially. Everyone here knows about you. They know you're a tattoo artist. They know you're a tall redhead. We might need proof you weren't anywhere near the Golden Palace earlier."

The Golden Palace?

"That's where she was found?" I asked. "I couldn't tell from the TV; we came into the report late. What a scummy place to die." I felt awful for the pretty girl who had more talent in her little finger than most people had all over. The Golden Palace was off the Strip. Not too far, but even a block away put you in dicey company. It was gorgeous from the outside, all reds and golds and Chinese dragon statues, but I'd wandered in there one day to see if the inside matched the outside. Absolutely not. The carpet was worn and frayed; even the slot machines were the old-fashioned kind you could still get a pot of coins out of. But no one in the Golden Palace was a winner. The gamblers were older people who came in with their Social Security checks every month and lost. They were the down-and-out who came to Vegas and stayed in the only place they could afford, and even that couldn't support their dreams.

"Daisy didn't have to stay there," I said, stating the obvious. "Did she really have a room there?"

"I'll send someone over to verify your alibi," Tim said, ignoring me, which piqued my curiosity further.

I quickly beat it down. I'd promised myself a couple of months ago that I wouldn't get involved in police business anymore, that I would curb my curiosity about things that didn't involve me.

I reminded myself, though, that this *did* involve me, if the police had to check out my whereabouts when a girl died.

There was one question, though, that was still nagging at me: "So if there were ink pots and tattoo needles, did she have a new tattoo or was it just the color in the flamingo that you think might be new?"

"How could we tell if a tattoo is new?"

She *did* have a new tattoo.

"Whatever is new will have a pinkish hue to it, sort of like a bubblegum color. And it might be a little inflamed." I couldn't help myself. "Was she murdered, Tim?"

"It's just routine, the questions," Tim said, ignoring me again. "Like I said, to make a hundred percent sure that it wasn't you in that hotel room."

"Do the police think this redhead killed her?"

"None of your business, Brett," Tim said sternly. "Remember?"

Okay, so it wasn't enough I had to remind myself that I wasn't going to get involved. Now my brother had jumped on that bandwagon.

I didn't have time for a snappy retort, though, before he threw me another question.

"Have you seen this blog before, Brett?"

I glanced down at the laptop screen, which had grown dark. I moved my finger on the pad, and the colors of Daisy's flamingo flashed bright.

"I found it through a link from another blog," I admitted. "I don't know why I didn't know about it before, because apparently they take pictures of people's tattoos on the Strip."

"So you don't know this Ainsley Wainwright?"

"No. Never heard of her. Or him. Joel and I couldn't figure out if it was a man or a woman."

"Woman," Tim said automatically.

My little nondetective antennae went up. "How do you know it's a woman?" I asked slyly.

"Never mind," he said sharply. "Don't you have a client to get back to?"

I knew when I was being dismissed, even on the phone.

"I'm sending Flanigan over to talk to Bitsy. She's got your schedule, right?"

"Flanigan? Does it have to be Flanigan?" Detective Kevin Flanigan and I had crossed paths not long ago, and it was not a pleasant experience. He always looked at me as though I were guilty of something. Even when I wasn't.

"Don't worry about it," he said and hung up.

I stared at the phone a second before setting it down. The TV was still on; Joel had stopped paying attention to me and was watching the coverage of the breaking news about Dee Carmichael. I didn't have time to join him, so I started for the door. Patty was probably wondering whether I'd ever come back.

"Brett, I know how he knew Ainsley Wainwright is a woman." Joel's voice stopped me, and I turned around.

"How?"

He pointed at the TV. "They just reported that Daisy checked into her room at the Golden Palace using the name Ainsley Wainwright."

Chapter 3

If I didn't get to Patty now, I'd have to reschedule her. I stored away what Joel said and went back to my room, where Patty was texting someone, iPod earbuds in her ears, clearly not missing me very much at all.

I'd finished outlining the American flag around the heart and needed to start with the colors. Patty was an Iraq war veteran, just twenty-nine, and she'd seen more in two years than I'd seen in my entire life. The flag was her homage to her service, the heart reminding her of humanity and the fragility of life.

She glanced up at me as I came in.

"Thought you ran away."

I sat down and pulled on my gloves. "Don't worry about me," I said, picking up the tattoo machine and dipping the needles into the red ink. I swiveled around and settled my foot on the pedal on the floor. The machine kicked in with a whir, and I put the needles to Patty's skin. She flinched slightly, then relaxed. Sometimes they can't stop flinching. Makes my job harder.

As I worked, I thought about Daisy Carmichael. Obviously, she wasn't Ainsley Wainwright. Maybe Ainsley had checked into the room and then Daisy came to visit her. Maybe Ainsley did the tattoo color. And then somehow Daisy died. Had she been murdered? It seemed a possibility. She was a young woman, younger than me by a couple of years, which would put her around thirty, maybe.

Had she killed herself? No. I couldn't buy that. Why get color in a tattoo and then kill yourself? Wouldn't you want to enjoy the tattoo for a while? Plus, she was at the top of her game, the top of her career. She always seemed like a happy person, someone who didn't take her fame for granted.

And then I had another thought. The picture on the blog was taken before the body was found, on the Strip, outside. Had she had the tattoo colored in and then gone out for a stroll on the Strip, where Ainsley snapped her picture, then back to the hotel and died?

Seemed doubtful. The sequence of events didn't make sense. And it also wouldn't explain the inks and needles in the hotel room.

I thought about the questions Tim had asked. Sounded like there might definitely be another tattoo. Maybe the flamingo had been colored in a while back, and someone gave her a new tattoo in the hotel room.

I was doing it again. I was getting way too interested in something that wasn't my business. But I couldn't help it. I was sort of involved. Tim's phone call and Flanigan's impending visit were indications that I wasn't totally out of the clear on this one.

It was possible Ainsley Wainwright was a redhead. There hadn't been a picture of her with her bio on the blog site. Thus the confusion about her gender.

I had to stop thinking about it. I pushed all thoughts aside and began to concentrate more closely on Patty's tattoo. My hand was curled around the tattoo machine, its weight familiar and comfortable. My professors at the University of the Arts in Philadelphia would probably shake their heads with disapproval that this machine had taken the place of my traditional paintbrush.

It wouldn't be such a bad idea, though, to actually teach a class in body art. Tattoos have become so mainstream, and the art has a long history that would be worth studying.

Who was I kidding? Tattooists wouldn't be considered serious artists, which was why my employee Ace van Nes felt so frustrated. He'd never felt that he was being appreciated and considered his time at the shop temporary, even though he'd been here five years now. He painted comic book versions of classic paintings, and we sold them in the shop—yet another frustration for him because he wanted to show his work in a real gallery. Right now we had Delacroix's *Liberty Leading the People*, Ingres's *Grande Odalisque*, and Millet's *The Gleaners* on the walls out front. Since we weren't allowed to have the word "tattoo" anywhere on our door—a little concession to having a tattoo shop in such an upscale place—many people wandered in thinking we really *were* a gallery, a point that Bitsy, Joel, and I kept trying to hammer home to Ace.

Although you'd be surprised how many of those people actually made appointments for tattoos once they stepped through the door, something that did not go unnoticed by Ace and didn't help our cause.

The intricacies of Patty's tattoo meant that when I was finally done, over an hour had passed. I set down the machine, wiped the last of the ink and blood off Patty's lower back, gave her a hand mirror, and sent her off to the full-length mirror in the back of the shop so she could admire her new tattoo.

I'd started throwing away the ink pots and wiping down my counter when Bitsy appeared in the doorway.

"He's here," she said, as if she were announcing the Prince of Wales.

Detective Kevin Flanigan hovered behind her, and I was glad he couldn't see the look of disdain on her face. I plastered a smile on mine.

"Nice to see you again, Detective."

Flanigan had always been a dapper dresser, but it seemed that perhaps he'd gone even classier with the Armani suit that hugged his narrow shoulders. His salt-and-pepper hair was slicked back neatly, not a tendril out of place. A few wrinkles around his eyes proved that perhaps he did smile now and then, but usually not when he spoke to me.

His mouth was set in a grim line, so I supposed he wasn't going to break his record today.

Patty tapped him on the shoulder, and Flanigan stepped aside to let her into the room. She handed me the mirror with a broad grin and said, "It's fantastic."

I saw Flanigan's eyes move down to her lower back. Her T-shirt was rolled up just under her breasts and her sweatpants had been lowered slightly so they wouldn't smudge the tattoo. A flicker of a smile, just a flicker, and then it was gone. So he was human after all. Just not with me.

I cocked my head toward him. "Can you wait just a few? I have to finish up here. Bitsy can show you the schedule; you know the drill." He'd come around checking on me before.

Without a word, Flanigan gave a short nod, and Bitsy led him to the front desk while I gave Patty her instructions for aftercare of the tattoo. I smoothed some Tattoo Goo on it, then covered it with a large bandage so her pants wouldn't chafe it. When we were done, I followed her out to the sleek mahogany desk where Bitsy would take her payment.

I indicated Flanigan should follow me back down the

hall to the office across from the staff room. Once there, I shut the door and went around the less sleek desk and sat.

"What do you need to know?" I asked bluntly.

Flanigan sat in the uncomfortable metal folding chair across from me. He leaned forward, setting his elbows on his knees, his expression blank.

"Miss Hendricks showed me your schedule for today."

"I was here all day."

"So it seems."

"So that should be that, right?"

"Not so fast."

I should've guessed. Flanigan wouldn't have come all the way out here so soon after Daisy's body was discovered just to find out whether I'd been in my shop all day. I had no idea what he was after, so I waited.

"I understand Miss Carmichael was a client of yours."

I nodded. "For the last two years. I did all her tattoos." When I realized what I'd said, I quickly added, "Except for that color on the flamingo. I did the black, but I never did color."

"Why not?"

"She told me she was allergic to red dye. Found out when she took an ibuprofen when she was younger. She was really nervous about any sort of tattoo color, because she thought she'd have a bad reaction to it." I remembered the first time Daisy had come in, adamant about not having any color. She had done her homework. The U.S. Food and Drug Administration does not regulate tattoo ink. Anything can be in it, and no one would be the wiser. There are a lot of metals and mercury, especially in red and yellow inks, and I always warn my clients that if they've got any sort of nickel allergy, they shouldn't get red or yellow. We take an elaborate medical history, like they do at the doctor's office, and make our clients sign a waiver so we're covered just in case someone has a reaction and tries to come after us.

"What would a reaction look like?" Flanigan asked, and I knew he wasn't expressing mere curiosity from the way he asked.

"It's easier to show you," I said. "Hold on." I left the room and went into the staff room, where Joel was picking at a salad. He'd been on Weight Watchers, then the Atkins Diet, and was now trying the South Beach Diet on for size.

"What's up?" Joel put his fork down, and his expression said he hoped I would stick around and keep him company. Maybe eat the salad for him so he wouldn't have to.

I grabbed my laptop and swung it under my arm. "Have to get back to the detective," I said apologetically.

"Oh, right. What does he want now?"

"He's asking about reactions to tattoos and inks." I indicated the laptop. "Figured I'd pull up some Google images for him."

"Have you ever thought about that citizens police academy?" He was totally serious.

I made a face and rolled my eyes at him as I left.

Flanigan hadn't moved, or at least it looked as if he hadn't. Nothing looked out of place, so I couldn't tell if he'd snooped while I was gone. I put the laptop on the desk and powered it up, bringing up Google and my search. When the images popped up, I turned the laptop around and showed them to him.

"Someone could get an infection because of the inks or because of a bad tattooist," I explained as he examined an image of a tattoo that we couldn't even identify because of the infection.

"So you can't tell which?" Flanigan asked, reaching into his breast pocket. He pulled out an iPhone and tapped the screen a couple times before holding it out toward me.

It looked like what we were looking at on the laptop: a distorted tattoo that was bright red with little hivelike bumps.

I frowned. "What's this?"

"This was a tattoo Miss Carmichael had."

Chapter 4

She'd most definitely had a reaction—the reaction she'd feared.

"This isn't the flamingo," I mused.

Flanigan shook his head. "You can't tell if this would be caused by the ink?"

"Can I see it more closely?" I asked.

He did one better than that. He zoomed in and showed me how to move the picture around so I could see all of it up close and personal-like. But all I knew was it was a reaction to the tattoo. I said as much as I handed him back the phone.

"Where was it?" I asked.

"Where was what?"

"That tattoo."

"Where on her body, you mean?"

I bit my lip before saying something smart-alecky. "That's right."

"On her left breast."

I knew every tattoo on Daisy's body, and as far as I knew, she didn't have a tattoo on her breast. She had them on her arms, on her upper back and lower back, on her ankle, on her wrist, on the side of her torso. But none on her breast. And none in color. Except now the flamingo and this, well, it was an abomination. And any tattooist that did that should be stripped of his inks.

Unless of course it *was* the ink.

"Why do you think Miss Carmichael would go to another tattooist if she'd trusted you to do all her other tattoos?" Flanigan asked.

It was a loaded question. I had to make sure I didn't sound bitter about being usurped, even though I was feeling rather insecure about it at the moment. If she'd stuck with me, she wouldn't have gotten such a botched tattoo. Maybe she would still be alive.

The jury was still out on how she died, though.

"Was she murdered?" I asked, ignoring his question.

"Is it possible to have an allergic reaction to the colored inks any time?" he asked, ignoring mine.

I understood what he was asking and nodded. "I'm not a medical expert on this or anything, but it's possible that she wouldn't have a reaction to the flamingo color and think that it would be okay to have another tattoo done with color but end up with a reaction on that one." That had happened with one of Ace's clients about a year ago, but he hadn't died or anything.

Flanigan put the phone back in his breast pocket "I would appreciate some help, if you will."

Flanigan asking for my help? Had something gone askew in the world? Had the earth slipped off its axis?

"I would ask you to keep your ear to the ground. If you hear of any tattoo artist who may have done this, I would ask you to call me immediately."

I forced myself not to bristle at the insinuation that every tattooist knows every other tattooist in the city. It was like insinuating that I knew every other person of Irish descent in the city just because my last name happened to be Kavanaugh.

And then I remembered Jeff Coleman. Jeff owned Murder Ink, a street shop up near Fremont Street. He *did* know everyone. He'd been working in this city his entire career and would be a better source for the cops than me. But I didn't want to tell Flanigan that. It would be easier if I asked Jeff to help me.

Jeff Coleman and I had a complicated relationship. It had morphed from totally disliking each other to grudgingly respecting each other to a weird sort of friendship. He gave me the koi tattoo on my arm, and I tattooed "That's Amore" on his shoulder, below a scar from a bullet he'd taken for me.

"I can do that," I told Flanigan, escorting him back out to the front of the shop.

He paused for a second, staring at the *Odalisque*.

"It's for sale," Bitsy piped up, ever the saleswoman.

Flanigan flashed a rare smile at her. "I'll keep that in mind." He turned to me. "We'll be in touch." And then he pushed the glass door open and went out, strolling along the canal, giving a short salute to the gondolier guiding a couple of tourists who were trying to forget that they couldn't afford a trip to the real Venice and so were living vicariously through the Venetian's illusion.

"What was that about?" Bitsy asked.

I told her about the conversation. "Neither he nor Tim would tell me how Daisy died, so I'm not sure what happened exactly. All they want to do is pick my brain about tattoos."

"Do you think that botched tattoo could've killed her? Do you think she died from the allergy?"

"I don't know," I said, although it had crossed my mind, too. "Remember Ace's client? He had that reaction the second time, not the first." I remembered my promise to Flanigan. "I'm going to give Jeff Coleman a call and see if he's heard anything about this."

"Good idea." Bitsy knew Jeff had connections. "But you might want to start a little closer to home."

"What do you mean?"

Bitsy cocked her head toward Joel's room, where we could hear his tattoo machine whirring. "He knows a lot of people, too. You know, Brett, I think he feels bad that you rely a lot on Jeff when you could just go to him."

Ouch.

"I'll do that," I promised. I was making a lot of promises today, and it wasn't much past noon.

"Oh, and the good doctor called."

She was referring to Dr. Colin Bixby. We'd been dating pretty steadily for the last month. We had a little bit of a checkered history, what with me thinking he might be a murderer at one point and him deciding that I might be a bit crazy because of that. But we kept running into each other, so we decided we'd give it another go. He'd been getting a little more serious lately—clearly an indication that either he didn't think I was crazy anymore or he did and didn't care—but while I enjoyed his company and his extreme good looks, I wasn't quite there yet.

I shrugged nonchalantly and said, "I'll call him later."

Bitsy shot me a look that told me she thought I should call him right now, but I pretended I didn't notice.

I had a couple of stencils to work on, but as I sat at the light table with my pencil in my hand, my brain started a little slide show of Daisy's appearances here at the shop. She was a petite girl, with a mop of bleached blond hair and thick black mascara and eyeliner on a face that would've been too wholesome without it. She had a quick smile and a deep laugh that didn't seem to fit with her size. When she asked me to tattoo the small flowers in the flamingo's wings for each of her bandmates, she said she owed them everything, although personally, I didn't think any of them had nearly as much talent as Daisy did.

I had started to get a little too misty thinking about her when my cell phone rang. I picked it up off the light table and saw a familiar number.

"Hey, Jeff."

"It's all over the news. She's your client, isn't she?"

"Yeah."

"I'm sorry, Kavanaugh." Six months ago, I wouldn't have heard the empathy in his voice; I'd only have heard how he never called me by my first name. Except once.

"Thanks." I thought about what Bitsy had said about Joel, but it wouldn't matter if I had two people helping me, would it? "Someone gave her a pretty botched tattoo right before she died."

"I heard it was a tall redhead."

I froze. "How did you hear that?"

Jeff chuckled. "Kavanaugh, you know better than to ask."

"Oh, that's right: If you tell me, you'd have to kill me."

"Something like that." He paused a second. "So I assume since you're answering your cell phone that you're not being held without bond. Or am I talking to you in your jail cell?"

I snorted, and he laughed.

"Okay, so you're not getting tight with some prison cellmate. Too bad. That sort of fantasy could last me awhile."

I had to totally change the subject.

"Do you know a blogger named Ainsley Wainwright?"

"I was wondering when you'd get around to that."

"So you do know her?"

"She e-mailed me about a month ago, wanted to take pictures of my mother."

Sylvia Coleman was one of the women pioneers in the tattooing business. She had retired and left Jeff the business, but she hung around all the time because she wasn't exactly the knitting and traveling type. She was covered head to toe in tattoos; each one had its own story, and I'd heard them all.

"I'm not surprised," I said. "Your mother is the stuff

legends are made of. Did she ever come by to take the pictures?"

"No. My mother refused. How did she put it? Oh, yeah: *I won't let myself be exploited in that way.*"

Good for her.

"So you've never met her?" Jeff was asking. "Ainsley Wainwright, that is."

"I never even saw her blog until today," I admitted. "Why?"

Jeff was quiet for a moment, and I waited. I started to have a bad feeling about this.

"She's got pictures of you. On her blog."

Chapter 5

Pictures of me? On a blog?

"You didn't see them?" Jeff asked.

"I only saw that picture of Daisy's flamingo, which was the latest post. It threw me for a loop. I didn't even look at anything else on the blog." I'd left the laptop in the office when I'd been in there with Flanigan. I held the phone to my ear as I left the staff room and went out into the hall.

Bitsy was sitting with her back to me at the front desk. Joel was still with a client, and Ace was who knew where. Probably at that oxygen bar, Breathe, a little ways down the walkway along the canal. He was addicted to the aromatherapy oxygen. But I supposed it could be worse.

I went into the office and shut the door. A small lamp on the desk was the only light source. I flipped up the laptop and saw it was asleep. I hit the POWER button and the picture of the infected tattoo came up on the screen.

"Have you ever heard of anyone dying from an infected tattoo?" I asked Jeff.

"No. Is that how she died?"

"I have no idea. No one would tell me how she died." There. There was the blog. I scrolled down, but didn't see any pictures of me. "Where are these pictures?" I asked.

"You have to go back a couple weeks. I thought you knew."

"Do you check this blog regularly?" I asked, hitting the link for all the posts for the past month.

"Never heard of it until she contacted my mother. It's not exactly remarkable. There are others like it. Better, actually."

I agreed.

"You haven't found it yet?" Impatience laced his voice.

"Keep your pants on," I said without thinking. Uh-oh.

"Are you sure about that, Kavanaugh?" Teasing re placed the impatience. "I could—"

"I got it." While I was glad I could interrupt Jeff, I was stunned by what I was seeing.

Under a title that read "Sin City's Famous Painted Lady," Ainsley Wainwright had posted not one, not two, but about ten pictures of me in various locations. Walking along the canal outside my shop, looking in the window at a pair of shoes at Kenneth Cole, holding a cup of gelato in St. Mark's Square, with Joel outside the Walgreens on the sidewalk.

In every picture, my tattoos were prominent: the half sleeve with the Japanese koi wrapped in a sea of greens and blues; Monet's water lily garden on the other arm; a close-up of Napoleon riding his horse up the Alps on my calf—an homage to Jacques-Louis David, my favorite painter; the Celtic cross on my upper back—why did I wear a halter top?—and she'd even zoomed in on the head of the dragon that came up over the low scoop neck of my tank top.

I felt violated.

I had not given this woman permission to take my picture and put it on this blog. I hadn't been aware of any cameras in my vicinity at any time. I would not have given permission even if I'd known. I was a walking advertisement for my shop, but I did not like the idea of being exploited.

Which was exactly why Sylvia had said no to her when Ainsley had asked to put pictures of her up on the blog.

"You take a nice picture," Jeff said, as though he knew what I was thinking and wanted to make it a little better.

It didn't work.

"Do you think I can sue her?"

"Probably not," Jeff admitted.

"Can I make her take down the pictures?"

"Probably. But you realize once something's on the Internet, it never really goes away."

"That's not exactly reassuring," I said.

"It's the truth. Listen, Kavanaugh, would love to shoot the crap with you all afternoon, but I've got a client coming in. Stop up later if you want to see how an expert really works." He barked a short laugh and hung up.

I set the phone down next to the computer as I stared at the picture of me and Joel outside Walgreens. I was in the foreground, in sharp focus; Joel was behind me, a little fuzzy. I tried to think about where the person with the camera would be to get this particular shot. Maybe the palm tree-laden median between the lanes on the Strip. How could I not notice someone with a camera? Because cameras aren't exactly a rarity on the Strip. All those tourists taking pictures of each other in front of the Duomo at the Venetian; the Eiffel Tower at Paris; the fountains at the Bellagio; the Roman columns at Caesars.

A soft knock on the door.

"Come in," I said, feeling totally deflated.

Joel's head peeked around the doorjamb.

"Are you okay?"

Was I? First I find out my friend died, and then this.

"I'm not sure," I admitted, moving the laptop around so Joel could see for himself.

He stepped inside and moved to the desk, leaning over so he could see the laptop screen. His brows knit into a frown, and he looked up at me. "What's this?"

"Apparently this blogger took pictures of me and put them up on her blog. Without my permission." The more I thought about it, the more it bothered me. Should I call Tim and report this? The cops were bound to look for Ainsley Wainwright anyway, since she took the picture of Daisy's tattoo and then Daisy was found dead. And the room Daisy was found in was booked by Ainsley Wainwright.

"This is me," Joel said, noticing the Walgreens shot.

I nodded, putting my head down on the desk. "This morning I didn't even know this thing existed. It was better that way."

I felt Joel's hand on my back, rubbing in a circular motion. "It's not so bad, Brett. At least you're all dressed and stuff. And she didn't take any pictures of you eating. That could be really embarrassing."

Got to hand it to Joel to see the silver lining in this.

Another tap on the door.

"Come in," Joel and I said together.

Bitsy's eyebrows rose high on her forehead when she saw me with my head down, Joel rubbing my back.

"Are you okay?" she asked me. "Are you sick? Do you need some aspirin?"

"I'm fine," I said, although not exactly confidently.

"Someone took pictures of her," Joel said, pointing at the laptop.

Bitsy came over to the desk and pulled the laptop to the edge so she could see.

"At least there are no pictures of you picking your nose or anything," she said. Okay, another silver lining. "It's really not so bad, is it?"

How to explain the feeling of violation?

"You know," Bitsy added, "this is a pretty interesting blog. These tattoos are really good."

She turned the laptop so we could see the tattoos she was talking about. Elaborate designs, detailed portraits, work I would be proud of if I'd done it.

"You're in good company," Joel said.

My cell phone rang. Jeff Coleman again.

"I thought you had a client," I said without any other greeting.

"Nice to talk to you again, too, Kavanaugh," he said sarcastically, then, "I forgot to tell you."

"Tell me what?"

"To read the comments."

"What comments?" A butterfly started flittering around in my stomach.

"The comments on the blog post about you. Figured you should know." He hung up.

I didn't really want to look at them. But I couldn't help myself. I reached over to the laptop and scrolled back up to the post about me and looked at the link for the comments. There were three.

I glanced up at Joel and Bitsy and then clicked on the link.

The first comment was from someone called Me-ganB: "Where is her shop?"

SkinDeep: "At the Venetian."

But the clincher was from TitforTat: "I'd stay away from there. She gave Dee Carmichael a botched tattoo that killed her."

Chapter 6

The time on the third comment indicated that it was made an hour ago, despite the fact that the pictures had been posted a couple of weeks ago. Who was Tit-forTat? There was no link attached to the name, which meant that the person was posting practically anonymously. Usually, though, anyone who commented had to fill out a form with an e-mail address that wasn't published.

I reached again for my cell phone. Tim had to know about this. He had to find this person who was accusing me of killing Daisy. Maybe this person was the redhead seen at the Golden Palace, the one who really did kill her.

Granted, I still didn't know how Daisy had died, but that was another thing to press Tim about.

"What is it, Brett?" Tim's voice was curt. He was working, and I was interrupting.

But he needed to know about this. I told him about the blog, the pictures of me, and the comment left.

"I already saw it."

"You did?"

"Don't worry about it, okay? We're on top of it."

"Have you found her yet—Ainsley Wainwright?"

"Listen, Brett, I have to go. I'm working. I'll see you

at home later, okay, and I'll fill you in then." He hung up on me without saying good-bye, much like Jeff Coleman had. If I were more insecure, I might start to get a complex or something.

"He says they're working on it," I told Bitsy and Joel.

They exchanged a look, and Joel nodded. "That's all we can do for now. I say we get some gelato. Make us feel better."

"You're not supposed to have sugar," I reminded him.

"It's a special occasion."

I couldn't help but chuckle. "It's always a special occasion," I said. "But not this time. I won't be responsible for you going off your diet." I didn't want to point out that he'd been doing a fine job of it by himself, without any help from me.

Bitsy, however, didn't have the same sort of tact.

"I saw you going into Godiva earlier," she scolded. "Chocolate and gelato in the same day? And you expect to lose weight? That's ridiculous."

Joel sighed. He'd lost some weight on the Atkins Diet, but he'd gained it all back and then some. The Weight Watchers had been worse. He hadn't even lost anything on that, just gained.

"I'm thinking about that diet where you have to buy your food. You know, the one those celebrities do those commercials for? Hey, maybe I can do one of those commercials." His face lit up as he thought about it. "I'm a regular person. If I lose weight, then regular people everywhere will feel they can, too."

I smiled. Joel, a regular person? There wasn't a more irregular person anywhere, and I mean that in the most affectionate way. Joel was large, but his heart was bigger than his body, although anyone who hadn't met him might be a little frightened. He looked like a biker, with a long blond braid hanging halfway to his waist, a barbed wire tattoo around his neck, tattoo sleeves

running down both arms, and chains holding his keys
dangling from his jeans pockets. When he opened his
mouth, though, his voice was as soft as his personality.
We weren't quite sure which way Joel swung, since we'd
never heard him talk about a girlfriend or a boyfriend,
but it didn't much matter. He was Joel, and we loved
him just the way he was.

A bell rang out in the front of the shop, indicating
that someone had come in. Bitsy scurried out the door
to see who it was.

Joel squeezed my arm. "It'll be okay, Brett. Don't
worry."

We followed Bitsy out to see Harry leaning against
the front desk. Harry Desmond had discovered us one
night when he was trying to find the Mexican restaurant here in the Grand Canal Shoppes. Since then, he'd
been hanging around. He was a victim of the recession,
told us he'd gotten laid off from his job as a blackjack
dealer at one of the casinos, so he had a lot of time on
his hands.

Today he was dressed in his usual uniform of shorts
and a bright Hawaiian shirt. He was about twenty-
five, I'd say, with a college degree in philosophy and
eighteenth-century English poetry. He wasn't qualified
to do much of anything, which was why the casino had
seemed like a good way to go. Until the layoff. Somehow
he was managing to live off his unemployment checks.

Harry always seemed to be a little stoned. Not totally,
just a little. Maybe it was the way his bright blue eyes
fixated on me as if he were seeing me for the first time.
Or the languid way he spoke, drawing out all his words
like a Faulkner novel. Or how he used his hands when
he talked, in long, slow lines, to emphasize what he was
saying.

Every tattoo shop has at least one Harry, someone
who stops in and seems to become a fixture. We hadn't

had one before, probably because we were mixed in with all the upscale shops, and until Harry arrived, I hadn't realized how much I'd missed that particular eccentricity of a tattoo shop.

Oddly enough, Harry didn't have any tattoos. He kept saying when he got a little cash in his pocket, he'd have one of us tattoo him. So far, though, no extra cash. At least not that we knew of.

As we approached the front desk, Harry looked up and grinned.

"It's the beautiful Brett Kavanaugh, the delightful Bitsy Hendricks, and the esteemed Joel Sloane," he said, bowing at the waist. "I was wondering if you'd heard about Dee Carmichael."

"We did," I said.

"I know the Flamingos' band manager," Harry said. "He's an old buddy of mine from way back."

I thought about the man Daisy referred to as The Pincher. Apparently, every time she saw him, he pinched her—either on her arm or her waist or her butt. I asked her why she kept him on, and she said she could stand a little pinching if he kept getting them gigs that continued to catapult their careers. It seemed a little much, but the guy had done wonders for Daisy and the Flamingos, so who was I to question?

"Way back when?" I probed, since Harry was fairly young to have any sort of relationship that went too far back.

"He dated my sister for a couple years when they were in high school. She's about your age, I'd say, Brett." It was the way he said it that made me feel about a hundred years old, rather than my actual thirty-two. My expression must have indicated my thoughts, because he quickly added, "I didn't mean it that way, Brett, really. I mean, you're not exactly a cougar or anything, not like Bitsy here." He flashed a quick grin at Bitsy, who was beaming, as though being called a cougar was the best thing she'd heard in a long time.

I actually thought Bitsy had a crush on Harry, but if they ever did go out, it would definitely be a December/ May sort of thing.

"In fact," Harry continued, now that he was back in everyone's good graces, "I saw Sherman last night. At Caesars. Cleopatra's Barge."

Cleopatra's Barge was a bar designed like an actual Egyptian barge. It sat in a pool of water, oars pretending to push it along as it gently rocked its customers while they sipped their cocktails and listened to whatever band had been booked that night.

Harry was still talking. "I was surprised to see him there, since, you know, the Flamingos are playing the East Coast."

He didn't seem to realize what he was saying. If the Flamingos were on the East Coast, then what was their manager doing here in Vegas? And, more importantly, what was Daisy doing here, too? She should have been safe in New York or New Jersey or wherever, rather than in the Golden Palace getting a tattoo from someone who didn't seem to know what she was doing.

Bitsy caught my eye. She'd picked up on that, too.

"So did you talk to Sherman, uh ..." I couldn't remember the guy's last name. Like I said, he was just The Pincher to me.

"Potter," Harry said. "Sherman Potter. Sure, I talked to him. Nice guy, really nice guy."

"Did you ask him why he was here and not with the band?" Bitsy asked, eager to get to the point.

Harry looked perplexed for a moment; then the grin spread across his face again. "He said he was finalizing a deal with the Golden Palace."

Chapter 7

Bitsy and I shared a look. The Golden Palace? Where Daisy's body was found? And why would he book the Flamingos into that scummy place anyway? That wasn't exactly the kind of venue the band was used to playing these days. Maybe two years ago when they were just starting out, but not now. They'd played the Bellagio on New Year's Eve; that was more their speed.

"That's where they found Daisy," Joel piped up.

"Where?" Harry wasn't too quick on the upswing sometimes. Like I said, sort of perpetually stoned.

"The Golden Palace," Joel said.

"That's right," Harry said thoughtfully as he ran a hand through his mop of brown hair, finally putting two and two together.

"Is he staying there?" I asked.

"Who?"

I took a deep breath and counted to ten. Although it wasn't as though if we drove Harry away we'd be losing a client. What was I thinking? Harry wasn't going to leave.

"Sherman Potter. The Flamingos' manager."

Harry's right eyebrow rose slightly higher than his left. "Oh, right. No, Sherman always stays in the Venetian."

He didn't seem to realize that we were in the Venetian right this very minute. But I did. And I got that little flutter of excitement that always started in my gut and spread out through my body. That little flutter that always showed up when I started asking questions Tim wouldn't want me asking. That little flutter I told myself I was going to ignore from now on.

So I didn't have much self-control.

"He stays here?" I asked.

Bitsy and Joel's heads swiveled around so fast that they looked like that girl's in *The Exorcist*.

"What?" I asked.

"You promised," Joel said.

"Not to get involved again," Bitsy added. "Wasn't it bad enough the last time?"

I didn't need reminding. It had been pretty awful, and I'd thought I was cured.

"What are you talking about?" Harry was understandably confused. I couldn't blame it on the weed this time.

Bitsy pursed her lips, then said, "Brett has this, well, um, habit."

For a second, Harry looked at me with happy anticipation. As though my habit were the same as his and maybe we could party together.

Not.

I shrugged. "So I like to snoop a little."

Joel snorted. "You're worse than Nancy Drew."

"Yeah, but I don't go looking for these things, they just seem to fall into my lap." Which was totally true, thank you very much.

"You're some sort of detective?" Harry asked, his eyes brighter than usual. "You mean, you're like a private eye or something?"

"Or *something*," Bitsy muttered.

I ignored her. "I'm not a detective," I said scornfully,

wishing I had a client coming in so I could walk away from this conversation. No such luck, however. I had at least an hour to try to explain how I managed to get myself all tangled up in things I had no business being tangled up in.

Lucky me.

"Do you want to meet him?" Harry asked me.

"Who?"

"Sherman Potter."

That flutter I mentioned accelerated.

"No, she doesn't," Bitsy said sternly.

I made a face at her. "What would it hurt?" I asked. "I mean, I did know Daisy, and I'd like to find out how to contact her family to express my condolences." As I spoke, I realized I had a perfectly legitimate reason to go talk to Sherman Potter. And from the look on Bitsy's face, she knew exactly what I was thinking.

She sighed—a deep, heavy sigh that told me I was being ridiculous.

Harry straightened himself up and put out his arm for me to take. I gave Bitsy and Joel a little shrug as I hooked my hand into the crook of Harry's elbow.

"Don't wait up," I teased as Harry and I went out the door.

They were so not happy with me. But I couldn't help thinking Sherman Potter's appearance in Vegas wasn't a coincidence.

Between Harry's outfit and my tattoos, we drew a few stares as we walked past the gondolas and tourists. Harry was a little taller than me, maybe even a little taller than Tim, who stood six feet. And as I studied his profile, I realized that because he was so much younger than me—not to mention the glassy eyes—I hadn't noticed before how good-looking he was.

A little bit of guilt bubbled up as I remembered how I'd blown off Colin Bixby's phone call earlier. Not because I thought Harry was good-looking, but one of the reasons why I'd sworn off any sort of crime entanglement was because of Bixby. What I was doing right now might not set too well with the good doctor.

He didn't have to know, did he? I mean, I really was just going to see Sherman Potter about how to reach Daisy's family.

I kept telling myself that.

Harry and I walked through the marble hallway toward the Venetian's lobby. We'd have to find out Sherman Potter's room number from the desk staff. That might not be easy.

Except I hadn't counted on Harry to come through. He stepped up to the front desk and flashed his wide smile at a dark-haired woman who truly may have been a cougar from the way she checked him out. I stayed in the background, pretending I was waiting for a free desk clerk, so Harry could work his magic.

In moments, he had taken my arm and was steering me toward the hotel elevators.

"Ninth floor," he said.

"Not the penthouse?" It slipped out before I could stop it.

Harry laughed. "Sherman likes it here, but he gets comped. So he only gets the ninth floor."

"He must lose a lot of money in the casino here," I noted as we went into the elevator. Anyone who's comped usually gambles way too much and loses way too much. That way the resort can keep him around, because they're making money off him.

The elevator doors slid open on the ninth floor, and a valet pushing a luggage cart moved into the elevator as we stepped off.

"Where to now?" I asked Harry.

He led the way down the hall, past many doors and around and around. I would get lost if I stayed here. Finally, we stopped in front of a door. Harry knocked, and we waited. He knocked again.

I indicated the DO NOT DISTURB sign hanging on the door handle. "Maybe he's still sleeping," I suggested. "We could come back later."

Harry shrugged and knocked again.

Suddenly, the door swung open, startling me enough that I stepped back.

A man wearing a flowing Chinese silk robe that was open to reveal a buff, naked torso above black silk boxers stared angrily at us.

"What do you want?" he bellowed.

"Hey, Sherm, it's me." Harry put his hand out, like it was some sort of business meeting.

Sherman Potter blinked a few times, checking out Harry before his eyes ran up and down my body. I shivered, and not in a good way. It was as though he were pinching me with his eyes. I was ready to get back on that elevator and swear off any more snooping for the rest of my life, so help me God. Sister Mary Eucharista, my grade school teacher at Our Lady of Perpetual Mercy, would approve.

But then Sherman Potter stepped forward and pulled Harry into a big bear hug.

"I thought it was the cops again. I've been avoiding them all morning."

Chapter 8

Avoiding the cops didn't sound like a very good idea. Neither did coming here, after all. But before I could backtrack to the elevators and make my escape, Harry had dragged me into the room with him and the door closed behind us.

It was a mess. The curtains were pulled shut, although a small sliver of light still managed to slip through and pooled on the floor. Clothes were strewn everywhere; a suitcase lay open near the wardrobe; stray shoes were scattered. A pizza box sat on the desk, the aroma of pepperoni and onions permeating the air. Instead of disgusting me, as it should, it made me hungry. I hadn't had lunch yet.

Two champagne flutes sat side by side next to the pizza box; a bottle floated in water that had clearly started out as ice. Their presence, and the sound of the shower being turned off, indicated that Sherman might have been avoiding the police, but he had company.

"To what do I owe the pleasure?" Sherman asked, pulling the champagne bottle out of the water and managing to pour a few drops into one of the flutes. He picked it up and raised it, as if he was giving a toast.

Harry stared at the glass, and I could see he was wishing there were more to go around.

"I asked Harry to bring me up here," I started, when it was clear Harry wasn't going to answer.

Sherman Potter leered at me. Really. Like Harry was loaning me out for the afternoon. I shook off my disgust and said quickly, "I wanted to know how to reach Daisy—I mean, Dee Carmichael's family to express my sympathies."

The leer turned into an expression of curiosity. "And you are?"

I didn't want to shake this man's hand, so I merely shoved my hands in my pockets and said, "Brett Kavanaugh. I did all of Daisy's—um, Dee's tattoos."

"Even the one that killed her?"

The voice came from behind. A tall redhead was wrapped in a very small white towel, her hair wet and hanging down around her shoulders. Her face was long, horselike, if I were going to be mean like a middle school girl, but her eyes turned her rather plain features into something spectacular: They were big and clear blue, as if she'd invested in those colored contact lenses. Which she may have.

It helped, too, that she had a spectacular body that the towel was doing nothing to conceal.

Harry looked like someone had slapped him silly. He couldn't seem to tear his eyes off her. If I were a guy, I probably would be gaping, too. But since she'd basically just accused me of murdering Daisy, I wasn't exactly her biggest fan.

"I haven't heard how Daisy died," I said matter-of-factly.

The girl, and I say that because she didn't look more than twenty-one, cocked her head at Sherman. "He said that's how she died. That's what the police told him." She cast an eye at Harry, as if daring him to say something to her.

Sherman Potter apparently had better police sources

than I did, which was bothersome, since my own brother had stonewalled me.

"I thought you were avoiding the police," I said to Sherman.

He shot me a look that told me to shut up. He didn't know me very well.

The girl sidled past me and Harry, brushing up against him so the towel slipped a little. He blushed as she adjusted it, but not before he got a glimpse of what was beneath it. I could tell he'd be good for nothing now.

"I didn't get your name," I said as she crossed the room, picked up a pack of cigarettes, and slid one out. Great. Now we'd all get secondhand smoke poisoning.

"I didn't give it," she retorted, lighting a match and putting it to the cigarette in her mouth. She blew out the match in a perfect smoke ring. If I hadn't been so grossed out, it might have impressed me.

"Might as well tell her. Everyone's going to know soon enough anyway," Sherman said to her, turning to me and saying, "She's the Flamingos' new lead singer."

Boy, he moved fast. Daisy was barely dead, and he already had a replacement. He saw the look on my face and shook his head.

"It's not what you think," he said. "Daisy told me a month ago she was leaving the band. I've been auditioning potential replacements ever since."

The word "audition" seemed to have a different definition for Sherman Potter than it did for most people.

"Congratulations." Harry finally found his voice, but he couldn't tear his eyes off the girl, who remained nameless. She was batting her lashes back at him, and there was suddenly a tension in the room that Sherman and I were not a part of. Didn't really blame her, for while Sherman wasn't a bad-looking guy, he had to be at least twenty years older than she was, and Harry probably didn't need any blue pills to help him out.

Sherman, however, was not to be usurped, and he went over to her and slung his arm around her shoulder, again dislodging the precariously held towel. She shifted it up and tightened it again, taking another drag off her cigarette.

"She's amazing," Sherman said, and I wasn't sure whether he was talking about her musical skills or another talent that we would not be privy to. "Dee was a little too girl-next-door for the Flamingos. She didn't quite fit."

I didn't remind him that Daisy had started the Flamingos on her own, that he had been the afterthought when the band had already had some success on YouTube. I didn't see the same charisma in this girl that Daisy had. True, Daisy *was* more girl-next-door, despite the goth/punk costumes, but this girl was just pure sex. Sadly, she probably would be a success.

"Do you have Daisy's family's information?" I asked, eager now to get out of here.

Sherman picked a cell phone up off the table behind him and hit a few keys. "I've got a phone number in Maine." He jotted it down with a hotel pen on a piece of hotel notepaper and handed it to me. "Will that do?"

I stuck the piece of paper in my back pocket. "I appreciate it."

"You could've just called," he reminded me.

"Would you have answered the phone?" I shot back at him.

Sherman Potter gave a short shrug. "Probably not."

The nameless girl stuck her cigarette in the top of a soda can, and we heard it sizzle as it hit the remnants of the liquid. This was way too disgusting for me. It was time to leave.

"Nice to meet you," I said politely, as my mother would want, and tugged on Harry's arm to indicate he should stop staring now.

He looked down at me as though seeing me for the first time. "Oh, right, yes, nice to meet you." And he flashed her a brilliant smile, which she returned. Again, there was that tension. It was like a bolt of lightning had struck in the middle of the room.

"Up for a drink later, Harry?" Sherman asked, escorting us to the door, eager to see us leave. Or, more likely, eager to see Harry leave.

Harry grinned and looked back at the girl, who was now perched on the edge of the table in such a way that we had a clear view of a rose tattoo on the inside of her thigh. She gave Harry a short nod and didn't make any move to adjust the towel this time.

"Always up for it," Harry said as Sherman opened the door and practically shoved us out, although I wasn't quite sure what he'd always be up for: a drink or that girl. Probably both.

"I'll be at Cleopatra's Barge again tonight," Sherman said, the door open merely a crack now. "Ainsley's singing. You can check her out."

And the door slammed shut, leaving us in the hallway.

"I think we already checked her out," Harry quipped.

But I wasn't thinking about that.

Her name was Ainsley.

What were the odds?

Chapter 9

I knocked on the door, but no one came to answer it this time. It was as though no one was home, even though we knew Sherman and Ainsley were in there.

"He wanted to get rid of us pretty quick," Harry said, his usual smile gone as he considered the reason.

I stood, uncertain what to do. I wanted to talk to Ainsley. I wanted to ask her about that blog. The one with my pictures on it. The one that had the comment about how I'd been responsible for Daisy's death. Which it seemed she might agree with, because she'd asked if I did the tattoo that killed her.

She knew who I was, and she'd been reluctant to tell me who she was. She had to be the blog's Ainsley.

"We might as well get going," Harry said regretfully.

We made our way to the elevators and back down without any conversation. I was preoccupied with Ainsley. I bet Harry was, too, but for different reasons than me.

We walked along the canal toward the shop, our strides matching step for step. Just before we reached it, though, I stopped and put my hand on Harry's arm.

"Tonight. I want to go see her sing," I said. "Are you free?"

Harry grinned. "What else do I have to do? What time?"

I didn't want to miss anything, but I did have a client coming in at eight and it would be at least a couple hours. I told myself that things didn't get hopping in Sin City until at least eleven anyway.

"Meet me at the shop at ten thirty?"

"It's a date."

And as I heard those words and saw the way Harry was looking at me, I realized what I'd just done. While I merely wanted an excuse to go over there with Sherman Potter's "old buddy," Harry might be putting a little more weight on this than I meant. And when we got back to the shop, it was clear he was.

"Brett and I are going out later," he announced to Bitsy, who was sitting at the front desk toying with her cell phone.

This was a totally bad thing. Because Bitsy can't help herself. A wide smile spread across her face. "You're going out on a date?" she asked eagerly. So much for her loyalty to Colin Bixby.

Harry nodded. "I'm picking her up here at ten thirty."

Bitsy beamed.

Now it would be all over. Joel would know. Ace would know. It could even spread as far as Murder Ink, and Jeff Coleman would find out. Bixby would hear about it. It would reach my brother, and even my mother in her retirement community in Port St. Lucie, Florida, would get the news.

"I've got, um, work to do," I said quickly, wanting to go hide in the staff room until my client showed up.

"I'll see you later," Harry said, a suggestive tone in his voice.

I nodded and didn't look at him or Bitsy, just scurried toward the staff room. I was starting a stencil when Joel and Bitsy appeared in the doorway.

"What?" I asked, irritation lacing my tone.

Bitsy grinned. "You make a nice-looking couple."

"He's had a crush on you forever," Joel added.

Before I could react to that, Bitsy spoke again. "This is why you blew off the good doctor, isn't it?" She rolled her eyes. "That relationship has been so doomed from the get-go. I'm glad you're branching out."

I had to stop her. "Harry's gone, isn't he?" I asked.

They nodded.

"Well, let me tell you what's really going on," I said, launching into the story about Sherman Potter and the Flamingos' new lead singer, Ainsley, who had to be—just had to be—the blogger who put those pictures up of me and Daisy. "And she's a redhead," I said, that small fact just dawning on me. What if she was the one who was seen leaving Daisy's room at the Golden Palace? Where her "boyfriend," Sherman Potter, just happened to be making some sort of deal?

It was all coming full circle, and I realized I should call Tim about it.

Joel had sat down at the table and was frowning at me. "You think you've got this all figured out?" he asked.

I shrugged. Seemed so.

"What's this about this girl taking over for Daisy? Did Daisy ever mention that she wanted to leave the band?" Joel asked.

"He said she told him a month ago. I haven't seen her since October." It was February now, the end of February. While it was possible she'd decided to leave the band, it still nagged at me. She'd started the Flamingos. She was the driving force behind the band. I thought about the other four girls: Cara, Melanie, Tiffany, and Josie. Where were they? Did they know about Ainsley? Did they know about Daisy?

They must know by now.

"Do you really want to go out with Harry?" Joel asked. "I mean, I could've gone over there to Cleopatra's Barge with you."

"Believe me, I'd rather go with you," I said. "It's just that I said I wanted to go and the next thing, we were going together." So it didn't exactly happen like that, but it was close. "Why don't you come with us?"

"I don't want to step on Harry's toes." He was teasing. He had to be teasing. A smile tugged at the corner of his mouth, and I was relieved. Yes, teasing.

"You can step on his toes. Please."

"Okay. I'll go, but he'll probably be disappointed when he sees me."

I didn't much care. And it would kill two birds with one stone, too, since if Joel came along, no one could say I was stepping out on Bixby. While I was uncertain about the future of our relationship, I didn't want to create trouble.

I picked up my cell phone. "I'm calling Tim." As I spoke, I punched his number into the phone.

"What is it now, Brett?" Tim never said hello, just like Jeff Coleman never said good-bye.

"Did you know that Daisy was being replaced in the band? By someone named Ainsley? And she's a redhead?"

He was silent. I'd gotten his attention.

Then, "How do you know this?"

I told him all about Sherman Potter. When I was done, I heard his short intake of breath.

"How do you manage it?" he asked.

"Manage what?"

"To get involved even when you're not involved?"

"I am involved," I said. "I mean, the redhead thing and the tattoo ink made you call me in the first place. Flanigan wanted me to keep my ear to the ground. Well, I did, and here's the information I managed to get."

He chuckled. "All within a couple hours. You're amazing, little sister. I will pass this along. But promise me, you're not going to go over to Cleopatra's Barge tonight, are you?"

I hadn't mentioned my "date" with Harry. Didn't think there was a reason to, until now. "Um . . ."

"I don't want you there. And if I see you anywhere near the place, I'll carry you out myself."

Now this was something I hadn't anticipated. "You're going to go over there?"

"We're investigating a murder, Brett. Of course I'm going to go over there."

"Murder?" I felt my heart start to pound a little faster. "So she was murdered?"

He was quiet a second, probably trying to figure out how to get around this, since he probably didn't mean to say anything in the first place but screwed up. Then, "It's looking like that, yes."

"How?"

"She had an allergic reaction to something, Brett. Anaphylactic shock. Her throat closed up and she couldn't breathe. If she'd gotten to a hospital, they probably would've been able to save her."

My brain was hung up on the words "allergic reaction."

He kept talking.

"Considering what you told us about her allergy to red dye and the symptoms and that infected tattoo, we think that's what killed her."

Chapter 10

"You *think*," I said.

"Nothing's official until the autopsy results come in, but she had an allergic reaction to something," Tim said. "So this is why you have to stay completely out of it now. You're in the clear, but this Ainsley person who now happens to be a redhead who happens to be taking Dee Carmichael's place in the band is definitely on my radar."

Seemed he had a suspect and a clear motive all rolled up into one, thanks to yours truly. But instead of feeling happy that justice would be served, I felt a little deflated. I still wanted to confront Ainsley Wainwright about those pictures of me on her blog.

I said as much to Tim.

"Don't worry, little sis. We'll cover that, too."

Like I said, all wrapped up.

It was so unsatisfying, though.

I had no way to reach Harry Desmond to let him know I wouldn't be going with him tonight. I sent Joel home when Bitsy left, because his services wouldn't be necessary after all. Ace had left earlier because he had a legitimate date. I tried calling Bixby back, but just got his voice mail. Guess I deserved that. I didn't leave a message.

I was cleaning up my room, throwing ink pots and used needles away, when I heard the bell on the door. I hadn't locked up, since we were technically still open, but when we didn't have any late clients, we would close early on occasion.

I figured it must be Harry and braced myself to explain the situation as I went out to the front to meet him.

But it wasn't Harry.

Jeff Coleman stood just inside the door, his hands in his pockets as he stared up at Ace's most recent works of art. When he saw me approach, he grinned.

"Quiet around here, Kavanaugh."

Jeff was an inch or so shorter than my own five-nine, with a salt-and-pepper buzz cut. A life lived hard showed in his face. He'd been in the Marines, served in the first Gulf War, and taken over his mother's tattoo shop about ten years ago. He used to smoke like a chimney but gave it up recently. There were some allusions to drinking and drugs, but by all appearances, he wasn't into all of that now. At least not that I'd seen.

"Let everyone go early," I said. "I'm leaving shortly myself." I glanced quickly out the glass door to see if Harry was around yet, but I didn't see him.

"Expecting someone?" Jeff asked, coming toward me.

I shrugged. "I sort of have a date. But I have to cancel."

"That's harsh, Kavanaugh. Canceling when he shows up. Why don't you just call him?"

"I can't. I don't have his number."

He frowned, but to his credit didn't say anything.

"What are you doing here?" I asked.

"Maybe I want to check out the competition," he said. "See how the other half lives."

Jeff liked to try to get under my skin about how I had a more upscale shop, where we did only custom tattoos, as compared to his street shop where he only did flash, the stock tattoos that lined the walls of his shop. I hate to admit it, but it usually worked.

Not tonight, though. I was too distracted by Harry's impending arrival.

"Really, Jeff, why are you here?"

"Maybe I'm a little worried about you. You know, those pictures on that blog. I got the sense that it shook you up a bit." He noticed I was looking outside again. "Are you expecting the doc?"

He meant Colin Bixby. I shook my head. "No."

A wide smile spread across his face. "You have a new boyfriend?"

I made a face at him.

"A new girlfriend?"

I rolled my eyes. "Just tell me why you're here."

The smile disappeared. "I was worried about you, like I said. I don't like the idea of pictures of you showing up on that blog, that someone's saying you're to blame for that girl's death."

I studied his face, looking for any sign of a joke, that he was teasing me. But he really seemed sincere. Stranger things have happened, I'm sure, but I couldn't think of any right at the moment. "Tim's on top of it," I said. "In fact, I don't even need to go out anymore— that's what I have to tell Harry."

"Harry?"

"Harry Desmond."

Jeff's expression was incredulous. "Harry Desmond? That's who your date is?"

"What of it? You know him?"

He barked out a laugh. "You surprise me, Kavanaugh."

I had no clue what he was talking about.

"What do you mean?"

"Don't tell me Harry's been hanging around here these days?"

I made a face. "He's been here almost every day for the last month or so."

"I wondered where he went."

It began to dawn on me what Jeff was talking about. "He hung around Murder Ink, too?" I asked.

"He didn't just hang around, Kavanaugh. He worked for me."

Now this was something I hadn't expected. "Worked for you? How?"

Jeff cocked his head to the side, studying me for a second. "How would you think? I own a tattoo shop. He worked for me. Do you think maybe he was one of my artists?" It came out way too sarcastically, but I didn't call him on it. I was too shocked.

"He's a tattooist? He told us he got laid off."

"Well, that's not exactly accurate. I fired his ass." Jeff's face grew dark, and I wondered what it was Harry had done. But I didn't have to wonder too long. "He botched a tattoo. Pretty bad."

My chest constricted.

"He hasn't asked you for a job?" Jeff asked.

I shook my head.

"He probably knows you'd need some background on him, and I'd tell you what he did."

"He told us he was a blackjack dealer."

"As far as I know, he never worked a casino. I wouldn't go out with him, if I were you," Jeff said.

Despite my newfound misgivings about Harry, I didn't like it that Jeff was deciding now whom I should date and whom I shouldn't. I stood up a little straighter, so I was even taller than he was, and said, "I can date whomever I want."

Jeff chuckled. "Okay, right, Kavanaugh. I forgot you're all grown up and can take care of yourself."

"That's right."

"Does he know about me?" Jeff asked.

The tone in his voice made it sound like there was something Harry *should* know, which of course there wasn't. Jeff and I didn't have that kind of a relationship. Granted, I wasn't quite sure what kind of relationship we did have, but it hadn't ever veered into any sort of romance.

He started to laugh. "You make it way too easy, Kavanaugh. You know what I mean, right?"

"He must know we're friends," I said. "He's probably been here when you've called, or someone's mentioned you. So yeah, he must know about you." Although I couldn't be sure. He spent most of his time talking to Bitsy, and sometimes I'd run across him with Ace at that oxygen bar. Until today, he hadn't really spent too much time with me, but that was usually because when he was here, I was with clients.

"So there would be no reason why when he saw me in here talking to you that he'd take off, right?"

Chapter 11

I instinctively looked out the glass door. "You saw Harry?" Jeff Coleman had powers of detection I hadn't been aware of, because I certainly hadn't seen him.

"He came around the corner, spotted me, and started back in the other direction," Jeff said.

So maybe he didn't know about Jeff, after all.

Jeff cocked his head at me again. "Ready to go? Maybe we can catch up with him, find out what his problem is."

I grabbed my bag off the front desk, and we scooted out the door. I locked it, Jeff pulled down the gate for me, and we turned left, the direction Harry had run in, according to Jeff. I couldn't see Harry anywhere, though, so I took one of the footbridges two steps at a time and stood at the top, scanning the canal and the walkway up ahead. I spotted Harry skirting around a couple of last-minute shoppers. I bounded back down the steps and grabbed Jeff's hand, pulling him along with me.

"He's up ahead," I said, then realized I was holding Jeff Coleman's hand and instantly dropped it.

Despite having shorter legs than me, Jeff kept up easily beside me, our strides in sync. It seemed that Harry didn't think we'd come after him, because he'd slowed down and we weren't that far behind him when he pushed open the door to the outside.

The door swung halfway shut by the time we reached it, but Jeff shoved it open farther and we went out into the night.

It was a crisp February night, the lights on the Strip making it seem almost like twilight.

We were right behind Harry now.

"Harry," I called out.

He stopped and whirled around, sheer shock crossing his face, his mouth open in a wide "O." He shut it again, clearly trying to get his bearings.

"Brett," he said flatly as his eyes slid over to Jeff. "Jeff."

"Why'd you take off?" I asked, standing in front of him now, my hands on my hips. "I thought we had a date." So maybe I had been preparing to cancel that date, but he didn't have to know that right now.

"I, um, well . . ." His eyes flicked from Jeff to me and back to Jeff. "I saw him in your shop. I figured three's a crowd."

"Three's a—" I stopped, looking at Jeff, wondering why he wasn't saying anything, but he was looking at me, as if I was supposed to take care of this on my own. Okay, fine. "Harry, Jeff and I are friends. He just stopped by. He does that sometimes, like you stop by the shop. He did tell me, though, that you've been a little creative with your background."

Harry cast his eyes to the sidewalk and shifted from one foot to the other. "I thought you'd kick me out if I told you."

"Damn straight she would." Wouldn't you know Jeff would decide to speak up now. "What's your angle here, Desmond?"

Nice to know I wasn't the only one he called by their last name, but it was a little disconcerting knowing that he didn't like Harry. Jeff and I hadn't liked each other in the beginning. Was this little quirk of his about my name a leftover from that time?

Harry finally stopped moving and straightened himself up. "No angle, Coleman."

Or maybe it was a guy thing.

"Brett and I had a date," Harry continued. "We were going over to Cleopatra's Barge to hear someone sing."

Jeff looked at me, his eyebrows high in his forehead, a smile tugging at the corner of his lips. "Music, Kavanaugh? Really?"

Jeff knew I was tone-deaf.

"So happens that Dee Carmichael's replacement in the Flamingos is singing tonight," I explained.

The smile came out full force. "So you were taking Harry along while you did your sleuthing? I'm hurt, Kavanaugh, that you didn't ask me instead."

I felt my face flush and hoped that because it was dark, or semidark, he wouldn't notice. "Harry knows Sherman Potter, the band's manager. He invited us."

Jeff was nodding. "Okay, then what are we waiting for? Let's take a walk."

"Not so fast," I said. "My brother told me to stay away."

"So when did that stop you before?"

Okay, so it hadn't ever stopped me before. Except this time Tim was going to be there, and I wouldn't be able to get away with it. I said as much.

"And I was going to tell Harry, here, that I couldn't go after all," I said, trying to look apologetic when Harry's eyebrows shot up in surprise.

"You don't actually have to go in, you know," Jeff said.

"What do you mean?"

Harry grinned. He knew what Jeff meant. "Brett, you can just walk through to the casino and hear the music."

"But wasn't the idea of this to talk to Sherman Potter, who will actually be in the nightclub?" I asked. "It sort of defeats the purpose."

"Your brother doesn't know me," Harry said softly.

No, he didn't.

Jeff was nodding, and even though he had warned me off Harry, he said, "That's right. Harry can go in. We'll hang out outside, and he can see what he can find out about this Ainsley."

Harry looked like he wanted to do anything except be the third wheel.

"You owe me, Desmond," Jeff said in a low, threatening tone that would've worried me if I were on the receiving end of it.

Harry pursed his lips and gave a short nod. "All right, I'm in. But only for Brett."

"Fair enough," Jeff said.

They both looked at me expectantly, until I finally shrugged and said, "Okay. Fine. But if I see Tim there, I have no idea how I'll be able to explain."

Neither Jeff nor Harry seemed to care. We fell into step along the sidewalk, sidestepping people carrying two-foot-long, thin glass containers with cocktails in them, college kids with the names of their schools blazoned across their T-shirts, and girls with low-cut jeans and high-cut tops to show off their belly rings and tattoos.

Which reminded me of something I wanted to ask Harry.

"So you hang out at my shop, and you worked for Jeff, but I'm wondering why you don't have any tattoos." Harry wore shorts and short-sleeved shirts every day, but I hadn't seen any sign of any ink. Of course he could have one in as private a place as Ainsley had her rose, and it was none of my business. But because it *was* my business, I couldn't help but ask.

Harry gave a nervous look at Jeff before answering.
"Not into it, I guess."

There was more to this than he was saying, but I
didn't press the issue. Not everyone wants a tattoo; I can
live with that. Enough people did want tattoos, though,
to keep me in business, to keep me fairly comfortable
financially, as well as my staff. Even in hard economic
times.

It always surprised me that I'd get someone in my
shop who had lost a job and was paying me from an
unemployment check. While the businesswoman in me
was happy to have the client, the woman in me wanted
to tell them to keep their money and come back when
times were better, when they'd found a job, when a tattoo wasn't going to take food or rent money out of their
pocket.

Jeff and I had had this conversation; he tended to
think we shouldn't get emotionally involved in it. If
someone were out of work and down on his luck, maybe
getting a tattoo would give him a little more confidence.
Jeff liked to think of it as his good deed.

We dealt with it in different ways, but when it came
down to it, I did the tattoo, too.

It was a little bit of a walk down to Caesars, but it was
a nice night and we walked in companionable silence.
We crossed the Strip and saw the fountains at the Bellagio start to dance. Part of me wanted to join the crowds
that had gathered, cameras on tripods, to watch. I still
worried that Tim would see me and I'd catch hell from
him.

We reached Caesars and made our way through the
Forum shops. It was as surreal as the Venetian as we
passed the Trevi Fountain, complete with a statue of
Zeus. The "sky" had darkened overhead, and I spotted
a kiosk selling brightly colored scarves. Again I was distracted and wanted to browse.

We heard the music as we got closer, but it was a familiar tune sung by deep voices.

"Beatles cover band?" Jeff asked, frowning as we approached Cleopatra's Barge.

I had moved ahead of him a little and turned toward him when he spoke.

And slammed right into someone.

I turned back, my heart pounding when I saw who it was.

Tim.

Chapter 12

He was not happy with me. Other people who didn't know him might not recognize the crease in his forehead that only appeared when he was really furious about something. But I saw it. I knew what it was. This had totally been the wrong thing to do.

"You must be Brett's brother." Harry made it worse by stepping toward Tim and holding out his hand.

Tim's eyes flicked toward Harry, then Jeff, then back to me.

"I should've known. And now you're even adding to your contingent."

Jeff reached into his front breast pocket and pulled out a pack of cigarettes, tapping one out and sticking it between his lips before putting the pack back.

"Is she here?" I asked, figuring while Tim would still be mad at me, he might actually slip up and tell me something.

Turned out, he didn't have to. Before he could answer, Flanigan came off the barge.

"Wild goose chase," he said to Tim before he spotted me standing there. "What are you doing here?"

"Keeping my ear to the ground, like you asked," I said, trying to turn the tables on him. "What do you mean, wild goose chase?"

Tim put his hand up to keep me quiet, but Flanigan, to my surprise, said, "What does it matter now?" He turned to me. "She's not here. She never showed. Neither did that manager. Are you sure they said they'd be here tonight? Because the bar manager says he's never even talked to a Sherman Potter."

"That's what he said," Harry spoke up. "He said they were going to be here. He invited us."

"That's right," I said. "I don't know what's going on."

Out of the corner of my eye, I saw Jeff Coleman taking a pack of matches out of his pocket.

"You quit," I scolded, reaching over and taking the matches and the cigarette out of his mouth. He grinned.

"Mr. Coleman," Flanigan said. "What are you doing here?"

"Wherever my sister goes, Coleman goes," Tim muttered.

I wanted to argue with him, but sometimes it was true. I didn't want to get into that. "So where are we now? Square one?"

"More than you know," Flanigan said. "Potter checked out of the Venetian shortly after your visit."

"So you have no idea where he is," I said flatly.

"We're heading out," Tim said, indicating himself and Flanigan. "If you want to stick around, be my guest."

I glanced over at Harry and Jeff. I didn't really want to have to deal with the two of them. But at the same time, I still didn't like the look in Tim's eyes, which told me that once he got me home, he would go on and on about how I had to stop getting involved in police business. He was a broken record, and maybe a cocktail might not be a bad idea before I went home to face him alone.

"I'll be home later," I said as casually as I could.

"Suit yourself." And Tim and Flanigan walked off.

"He's not happy," Jeff said softly.

"No kidding. How about a drink?" I indicated

Cleopatra's Barge, which was rocking as though it really were on the Nile, the oars slapping against the fake river.

Jeff glanced at Harry and then back at me. "I'm not going to step on any toes, here. So you two kids go off and have fun."

That was a total turnaround, and I wasn't quite sure why. Just half an hour ago, he was warning me off Harry. And now he was giving us his blessing?

He gave me a crooked smile and punched me lightly on the upper arm. "See ya around, kid." He sauntered off, without a look behind him.

I stared after him, uncertain now just what to do. I hadn't really wanted to go out with Harry. I'd only wanted to use him to get to Sherman Potter. I supposed I was getting what I deserved. At least that's what Sister Mary Eucharista would tell me.

Harry was beaming. "Glad he's gone. I can't believe you're friends with him."

"Why?" I bristled.

"Well, it's just that he's so, well, so *old*. And you're not."

"He's not that old," I said, although I wondered why I was getting so defensive about Jeff Coleman. Usually it was me who was saying disparaging things about him.

"Never mind," Harry said, seeing his mistake. "You said you wanted a drink?"

The sight of the barge rocking ·back and forth and the loud music was suddenly not very appealing. "How about somewhere quieter?" I asked.

"I know a place," he said, taking my arm.

The "place" was the bar in a restaurant on the first level of the Forum shops. It was a sleek, modern space with crystal light fixtures giving off a golden glow. Because of the hour, there were only a couple of diners; the rest of the patrons were sitting at the bar drinking fancy, multicolored cocktails that looked like something out of a science fiction flick. Fancy, multicolored cocktails were never cheap, and I thought about Harry's unemployed state and figured I would be footing the bill tonight. Since it had been my idea to get a drink, I wasn't going to quibble about it.

I slid onto a barstool, Harry next to me, and the bartender came over.

I don't usually drink hard liquor or even beer. I'm a wine girl, and I knew in a place like this I might actually get a good glass that didn't get watered down, but those fancy drinks were beckoning.

"Cosmopolitan," I said.

Harry smirked.

"What?"

"That's so 1990s." He looked at the bartender. "Two absinthes."

Okay, now I wasn't born yesterday. I knew what absinthe was, the whole crazy Oscar Wilde thing, and I knew that the last thing I needed was a possible hallucination, but the bartender had already gone to the other side of the bar to get us our drinks.

"I won't drink it," I said like a petulant child.

"You'll love it," Harry promised, his arm snaking its way around the back of my chair.

A cocktail tumbler with ice and an odd green liquid was set down in front of me. I took a sip. It tasted faintly of licorice. It was smooth, and not at all the evil drink I'd expected.

"How is it?" I felt his hand on my shoulder as he leaned toward me.

I nodded, feeling all tingly awfully fast. This wasn't supposed to be the way it happened. What did I mean by *it*? Harry was watching me, an intensity in his eyes that I hadn't seen since . . .

"Where does that dragon end up? Do you think I can find out tonight?" he whispered, his breath tickling my neck as his fingers ran up and down my arm.

I want to say that I didn't like it. That I didn't want to be there with Harry Desmond, a tattooist who botched a tattoo so Jeff Coleman had to fire him. Someone I would kick out of my own shop.

When had I finished my drink? The bartender was putting another one down in front of me, and I tried to indicate I didn't want it but he either didn't see me or didn't care.

Harry was nuzzling my neck now, little flicks of his tongue sending electric shocks through me.

And then something flashed bright in front of my eyes. Was this one of those hallucinations I'd heard tell of? I blinked a couple of times to clear my vision and saw the silhouette of a person holding up a phone. On the other side of the bar. And the flash went off again.

My whole body felt like jelly, despite the fact that my brain had kicked slightly into gear. I say slightly because there was a definite mind/body thing happening here that wasn't something I was used to. But a little neuron of sensibility flickered, and I pulled away from Harry.

"Someone's taking our picture," I said, although my voice didn't sound like it came from me at all, rather from somewhere across the room.

"It's just somebody's birthday over there," Harry whispered, his fingers gently turning my face toward him and then kissing me.

I forgot about the flash and everything else as I lost myself in his kiss.

Chapter 13

It was as though everything was illuminated, brighter, clearer than usual. All my senses were at their peak; I'd never felt like this before.

Harry pulled away and stared at me, his eyes mesmerizing. I don't know how long we sat like that, mooning at each other, not speaking, but the slap of the check on the bar next to us and the menacing look of the bartender indicated that perhaps it had been just a tad too long.

Harry picked up the check and reached into his back pocket, producing a wallet. I expected that he would now explain how he didn't have any cash on him, would I pick it up this time, but when he opened the wallet, it was full of bills. He grabbed a couple, two fifties, and put them on the bar before sliding off his barstool.

Two fifties? I didn't even have two fifties on me.

"Come on, Brett," Harry said as he helped me off the chair, his arm slung over my shoulder, his fingers still dancing on my skin.

"Where are we going?" I asked as we ventured out into the mall, which was closed up except for a couple of other restaurants and bars.

"Where do you want to go?" he asked, nuzzling my neck for a second.

Okay, I admit it. I wanted to go home with him. Probably not a good idea, although I really didn't think taking him to my house was a good idea, either. I pictured Tim waiting up for me, waiting to ream into me about my pathetic sleuthing attempt this evening. No, Harry did not need to be a part of that scene.

"Let's just get your car and see where we go," Harry said when I didn't answer him as we pushed open the doors and stepped outside.

The chilly air slapped against my face, and I knew that I was in no condition to drive. I said as much.

"I'll drive, then," Harry said easily, as though it were the only solution.

I peered into his face. He didn't seem to be feeling the way I was, although I had seen him drink his tumbler of absinthe along with me. Maybe he was used to it. Maybe he had it all the time, so it didn't affect him like it did me.

I still wasn't sure I wanted him to drive my car.

"Maybe we should take a cab," I suggested. "Where do you live?" There, I'd said it. I'd told him directly that I was willing to go with him tonight.

Harry winked at me. He knew.

We were halfway over the bridge that led to the Bellagio. The yellow lights on the Eiffel Tower and the Arc de Triomphe blinked against the black sky across the way at Paris. The pink neon signs at the Flamingo flashed.

Suddenly, I thought about Bixby.

And I stopped.

"No, I can't," I said softly.

"Can't what?"

I merely shook my head and leaned my elbows on the railing, looking down at the Strip below, watching dark shadows of people passing by, the sounds of their laughter wafting up and into my ears.

"What did you think you were going to do?" Harry asked, leaning next to me, his arm rubbing up against the Japanese koi on mine.

Maybe he hadn't really suggested anything and I'd been mistaken. Maybe I read him wrong. And I felt like a fool.

But when I turned toward him again, his lips found mine and it was happening all over again.

The flash startled me, and I pulled back, white dots in front of my eyes. "What was that?"

Harry shrugged, straightening up. "Tourists, I guess. Taking pictures." He indicated the Eiffel Tower.

I knew that. I also knew I needed to get home. "I'm going to take a cab," I announced, starting down the stairs, the outlines of the palm trees so sharp I could almost feel them cut me.

I was moving fast; Harry had to jog to keep up with me. I stopped at the corner and held out my arm like I used to do in New York City when I wanted to hail a cab. But they kept passing me, ignoring me.

"You'd do better going up to the Bellagio and having the doorman get you a cab," Harry said.

Okay, so he really *was* thinking more clearly than me. I didn't respond, just started back toward the Italian palace that doubled as a resort casino. The fountains weren't dancing now, but the lights were shimmering across the water. The wide driveway led to an elaborate entryway. All the doormen seemed to be helping actual guests.

The lights from inside winked at me, much as Harry had just moments ago, and I went through the revolving door and stepped into the lobby. Hanging from the ceiling were glass flowers of all shapes and colors, forming a mosaic that bounced against my brain like a pinball, they were so sharp and clear.

"Is it always like this?" I asked Harry as he stared, too.

"I think it was commissioned."

"What?"

"The glass flowers," he said.

"No, that's not what I meant. It's the way I feel. You know, the absinthe."

Harry grinned. "You're high. Everything is clearer than normal—it's like colors are jumping out at you. Yeah, it's always like this."

At least it wasn't just me.

I whirled around. "I have to get a cab," I said and went back out through the revolving doors.

A doorman bowed slightly, as though I were some sort of royalty, although most likely he thought I was a hotel guest, who would have as much money as said royalty if the lobby were any indication.

"Can I get a cab?" I asked him.

"Certainly, miss."

At least he didn't say "ma'am."

A yellow cab pulled up, and the doorman opened the door for me. I slid in across the seat, and just as the door was starting to close, it opened again and Harry plopped down next to me.

"Figured we could share," he said, shrugging.

"I'm in Henderson," I said.

"Henderson?" the driver asked.

Harry nodded. "You first, then I'll take it from there."

He had that wad of bills, so I supposed he could afford it. "Sure," I said, giving the driver my address.

The cab started with a jolt, throwing me against Harry. He used it to his advantage and held on to me, his lips finding mine again. I settled in against him and closed my eyes.

He was still kissing me. It wasn't a dream. I pulled away and saw the cab was outside my house. I straightened out my shirt and reached in my bag. Harry waved me off. "Go. I'll take care of it, okay?" And he kissed me again, lightly this time, before opening the door for me and letting me get out.

The cab pulled away before I got to the front door. All the lights were on. I glanced at my watch. It was almost two. Taking a deep breath, I slid my key in the lock and opened the door.

Tim stepped out in front of me. "You're home."

I tried to act nonchalant. Anything except drunk. I went into the kitchen and dropped my bag on the kitchen table. "I can stay out if I want," I said belligerently.

I heard him sigh behind me. He wasn't angry. It was something else, but I couldn't tell what.

"Why were you out drinking absinthe with that guy? And kissing him? His hands all over you?"

It was concern.

But how did he know?

"Were you following me?" I asked, anger rising.

Tim shook his head and pointed to the laptop, which was open on the table. "Take a look."

I peered at the screen. It was that blog. Skin Deep. Ainsley Wainwright's blog.

And there were pictures of me. Me and Harry. At the bar. Drinking absinthe and kissing like we would never kiss ever again. Kissing again on the bridge. Getting into the cab.

It took a few moments to sink in. Maybe because I was still high. But when it finally dawned on me, I faced my brother, my heart in my throat.

"She was following us."

Chapter 14

I remembered now. All the flashes going off. Thinking that it was tourists, like it usually is in Vegas.

"I was checking it out again, waiting for you," Tim said, "when the first picture popped in."

I looked more closely at the posts. The time they were posted. She was posting them when she took them. "Camera phone?" I asked, my brain surprisingly clear now.

"Seems that way."

I told him how I'd seen the flashes go off. He frowned. "Camera phones don't usually have a flash," he pointed out.

True. So maybe those flashes really *were* tourists. Ainsley Wainwright was much more discreet.

"So you didn't see her?" Tim asked.

I tried to think, but the absinthe got in the way. "No. It wasn't until I'd already had one drink, and, well, that stuff is pretty potent."

"Why were you drinking it at all?" Tim asked, a tiny bit of anger seeping into his tone.

"It seemed like the thing to do at the time," I said. "How was I to know she was going to be taking pictures of me drunk?"

"And hanging all over that guy," Tim added.

It was a really good thing I'd come home. It would've been far worse if I'd stayed with Harry. At least I'd had some sense tonight.

I looked back at the computer screen. "I wonder why she's taking pictures of me," I said, not wanting to get into the whole Harry thing right now. "She already took pictures of me without my knowing about it. This is sort of like stalking, isn't it?"

"Yeah, it's sort of like stalking," Tim agreed.

"But why? I never met that girl till today."

"You knew Dee Carmichael."

It took me a second, but I saw where he was going with this. "And she's dead. After pictures of her tattoos showed up on this blog." I paused. "You know, all the pictures on this blog are just of the tattoos. Not the person. You can't make out who it is, only the tattoo. But the pictures she posted earlier of me, and now these—they're of me. You can see me. My face. Not just my tattoos."

I could see by Tim's expression that he didn't know the significance of that, either.

"Should I be worried?" I asked him.

"Cautious," he said. "Be cautious." He leaned over and gave me a kiss on the top of the head. "Go to bed now, and we'll talk more in the morning. You look like you need some sleep."

Sleep was now the last thing on my mind, but he closed the laptop and shut the light out. I went into my bedroom and changed into a pair of pajama bottoms and a big T-shirt, then climbed into bed.

I must have been more tired than I thought, or maybe the absinthe was wearing off, because I fell asleep almost immediately.

Tim had left me a note on the table when I awoke.

"Had to leave. We'll talk later."

I looked out the window into the empty driveway. My

car was still in the parking garage at the Venetian. Had he not seen me get out of a cab last night? We'd been so distracted by the pictures on the blog that I'd forgotten to tell him I'd need a ride to work.

He'd made coffee, at least, so I poured myself a cup and sat at the table. The laptop was still there, so I booted it up. Maybe I shouldn't look at it again, but I wanted to. Maybe I'd get some sort of clue about why she was doing this, now that I had a clearer head after sleep and coffee.

The page hadn't even popped up when I heard the doorbell.

I got up and peered out the window. A metallic orange Pontiac sat in the driveway.

I glanced down at my pajamas and T-shirt that had a cartoon lobster on it and the words "I love Cape Cod" underneath. At least I was covered up.

I opened the door.

Jeff Coleman grinned when he saw my T-shirt, but he didn't say anything about it. He pushed his way in, and I shut the door after him.

"Tim called you," I said, my powers of deduction hard at work.

"Said you needed a ride. I'm your ride. Just dropped my mother over at the community pool." Jeff had gone into the kitchen and around the table to see the laptop. "Tsk, tsk, Kavanaugh. You really want to be doing that with Harry Desmond? He's a loser."

In the light of day and with a head clear of absinthe, I tended to agree. But then I remembered something.

"He's unemployed, right?"

"As far as I know."

"Well, he's getting money from somewhere," I said, telling him about the wad of bills in Harry's wallet.

Jeff was quiet for a second as he contemplated that. "I can check around," he said. "Maybe he's working, and we're not aware of it."

"He's always at my shop these days," I said, not wanting to get into how Jeff could "check on things." He had connections I'd be better off not knowing about.

"What's this chick's angle?" Jeff asked, changing the subject and pointing at the picture of me and Harry in the bar. "I mean, I don't get why she's all hot and bothered by you. Unless, of course . . ." His voice trailed off and a leer crossed his face.

I slapped his arm. "Get your mind out of the gutter."

"Your mind was most definitely in the gutter last night," Jeff said, his finger on the picture of Harry and me kissing on the bridge.

So sue me.

"And absinthe, Kavanaugh? Really? You should know better."

"I already got read the riot act from Tim, so leave me alone," I said, embellishing a little. Tim had been concerned, not angry. He'd told me to be cautious. "Why did you leave, anyway? I mean, you were so dead set against me going out with Harry in the first place, but then you left me alone with him."

"From the look of things, I should have stayed," Jeff said. He shrugged. "I guess I figured you're a big girl and can take care of yourself."

I hated to think how close I'd come to *not* taking care of myself last night. I'd acted stupidly, allowing Harry to buy me that drink. And then actually drinking it. I know myself better than that.

Jeff's expression changed slightly and he said, "Don't beat yourself up over it. It happens to the best of us."

"But it usually doesn't happen to me."

"We all have our moments. Really, don't worry about it. You're home, you're safe, nothing bad happened."

I cocked my head at the laptop. "Except that. I can't figure out what it means, though. Why is she stalking me?"

"Maybe she's jealous."

I snorted. "I met her, Jeff. Believe me, she can't be jealous of me."

"Are you sure about that?"

It was the way he said it that made me take pause.

"You know something," I said.

"After you and lover boy left, I went into Cleopatra's Barge."

Butterflies started crashing around in my gut. "And?"

"I met a woman there."

I rolled my eyes. "Okay, fine, be that way. I don't really want to know about your conquests."

"At least mine aren't plastered all over the Internet."

We were like squabbling kids.

"Do you want to know about this woman or not?" Jeff asked, and there was something about the way he asked that made me realize it wasn't a pickup after all.

I nodded.

"She was nursing a scotch at a table by herself. She was tall and had red hair." He cocked his head at my chest. "Even had a dragon. You know, like the one you've got."

My chest constricted, and I couldn't speak.

"We introduced ourselves. She said her name was Brett. Brett Kavanaugh."

Chapter 15

I felt myself drop into the kitchen chair. What was going on?

Jeff sat next to me, moving the laptop aside and away so I couldn't see the screen. "She wasn't you, Kavanaugh; she didn't even really look like you. Her hair was longer. She wasn't nearly as thin. That tattoo wasn't even real. It was some sort of body paint. If I hadn't been in the business, though, I might not have seen it for what it was. But she told me she was a tattoo artist, said she had a shop in the Venetian."

Someone was impersonating me. Was it Ainsley? Ainsley had longer hair than me; she wasn't as skinny. We didn't look alike, but she could've painted that dragon on her chest and fooled people who didn't know me. Was she the redhead who'd given Daisy that tattoo?

I finally found my voice. "But she couldn't be the one who took those pictures, could she? I mean, if she was with you the whole time?"

Jeff took a deep breath. "But she wasn't. We had a drink; she got a text message from someone. She said she had to go to the ladies' room. I followed her, waited for her, but somehow she got past me. I never saw her again."

"Had she been in the bar when Tim and Flanigan

were asking about Ainsley and Sherman Potter?" I wondered aloud.

Jeff nodded. "I think she was, but it was dark in there, and she was alone. Like I said, she really didn't look like you at all. I don't think they were looking for anyone like her, were they?"

Like I'd told Tim yesterday, there are a lot of redheads in Vegas. One sitting in a bar nursing a drink isn't going to raise any red flags. So to speak.

"So I don't just have a stalker, I've got someone who's impersonating me," I said flatly. "Great. What do I do now?"

"Go get dressed, and I'll take you to work," Jeff said.

"Just like that?"

"Just like that."

"I have to tell Tim."

"I already did."

Oh, that's right. They must have talked because Jeff knew to come over here and pick me up. "So is he trying to track her down, then? Is that why he left so early?"

Jeff shrugged. "Not for me to say what Las Vegas's finest do."

I stood, my legs a little shaky. I didn't much like the thought of someone running around saying she was me. Maybe even tattooing people using my name.

"Nothing you can do right now, Kavanaugh," Jeff said, standing and moving toward me.

"It's just . . ." My voice trailed off.

"I know, but you've got people on top of it."

And suddenly his arms were around me and I laid my head against his shoulder, feeling his heartbeat against my chest.

It was the first time we'd ever embraced. It wasn't anything more than just a friend comforting a friend. Or so I told myself as I pulled away, an awkwardness between us that we'd never had before.

"I'll be right back," I said, backing up and going down the hall to my room.

I sat on the bed for a few minutes, trying to wrap my head around the fact that I'd just had a "moment" with Jeff Coleman. And then my impostor crept into my thoughts, and I figured I had other things to worry about.

I pulled on a pair of skinny dark jeans and a stretchy black T-shirt with a shimmering silver skull on the front. Matched my mood. It was a little too chilly for my usual Tevas, so I pulled on a pair of black flats, grabbing my jean jacket as I went back out to see Jeff Coleman fiddling with the laptop.

When he looked up at me, I was relieved to see no acknowledgment of what had passed between us, just his usual smirk.

"There's another site."

"What do you mean?"

"This isn't the only blog."

I slid back into the chair I'd been sitting in earlier, and he turned the laptop so I could see the screen.

Instead of the now familiar Skin Deep masthead, this blog was adorned with one that was even more familiar: the flamingo I'd tattooed on Daisy's back. Next to it, in script, read, "Ink Flamingos."

Was I going to spend all day with butterflies in my stomach?

Jeff scrolled down so I could see the first and only post. The title read, "What happened?" and a picture below showed Daisy sprawled out on her stomach on dingy white bedsheets, her flamingo prominent. Her blond hair fanned out away from her face, which we could only see in profile but it was clearly her.

"Whoever took this picture did this," I whispered.

Jeff nodded. "There's more."

How could there be more? But when Jeff scrolled

down again, I saw it. The same picture of the infected tattoo that Flanigan had shown me.

"I don't want to see any more," I said, trying to shove the laptop back.

But Jeff stopped me by putting his hand over mine. "You have to know."

"Know what? That whoever put this up is a killer?"

"No, it's worse than that." He pointed to the "About Me" section in the sidebar.

As I read, I stopped breathing.

"*I'm Brett Kavanaugh, owner of The Painted Lady in Las Vegas. Dee Carmichael was a client of mine. I did all her ink. This blog is a tribute to her.*" And next to it was a picture of me. Me. Not an impostor.

Chapter 16

I went over to the phone and picked up the receiver without saying anything to Jeff. He knew what I was doing. I punched in Tim's number.

"Kavanaugh."

"There's another blog." I quickly told him about Ink Flamingos.

Tim was quiet for a second, then, "Okay. I'll check it out."

"What do I do?"

"Is Coleman there?"

I glanced over at Jeff, who was studying the blog. "Yeah."

"Have him take you to the shop. Stay there. I'll call you later."

"Tim—"

"Don't worry, okay? I've got it covered." And he hung up.

I put the phone back in its cradle and turned to Jeff. "I guess we'd better get to my shop."

Jeff indicated the laptop. "Should I turn it off?"

I nodded.

Within minutes, we were settling into the Pontiac, strapping the seat belts around us.

"You okay, Kavanaugh?" he asked before he started the engine.

I sighed. "Not really, but it'll be good to get to work and get busy."

"You do know I'm just a phone call away, right?"

It was scary when Jeff Coleman was being nice, almost too nice.

He turned the key in the ignition and the engine fired up. He backed up and started down through our neighborhood of suburban homes. Tim had bought our house when he was living with Shawna, his almost fiancée. But when she realized she was only going to get a house and not a diamond, she moved out and I moved in. I'd been living with my parents in New Jersey, but they were moving to Florida, so I needed a place to go. Tim's friend Flip Armstrong was selling his tattoo shop, I had enough money saved to buy the business, and voilà—I went to Las Vegas.

I stared out the window as we passed the strip malls and the Home Depot and the Target, heading for the highway that would take us to the Strip. The skyline was visible even from here; it was so flat until the desert hit the mountains in the distance.

I thought about Red Rock Canyon. It was a perfect time of year for hiking, and I'd been three times in the last week. But it wasn't the kind of place I wanted to go to alone if I had a stalker. Too much wide empty space up there, too many places to hide a body.

Body. Like Daisy's in that hotel room. I shivered, even though it was warm in Jeff's car.

"You okay?" he asked for the second time.

I nodded, then shook my head. "No, I guess not. I wish you hadn't lost that girl last night."

"Me, neither," he said. "I don't know how she slipped past me. I mean, I was watching that ladies' room."

An idea began to nag at me. It was plausible, and the more I thought about it, the more I was convinced.

Granted, a lot of time had passed between then and now, but you never knew.

"Let's go to Caesars first," I said.

Jeff glanced at me and frowned. "What's up?"

"I want to check on something."

"Your brother's probably been over there already, trying to find out about that girl," he said.

"Yeah, but not the way I'm going to," I said.

He gave me a funny look, but when we hit the Strip, he turned into the driveway for Caesars and found the self-parking garage. We hadn't said another word to each other.

We made our way toward Cleopatra's Barge, walking through the casino. Even though it wasn't even noon yet, the diehards were at it, slapping cards on the tables, throwing dice, punching the little PLAY AGAIN buttons on the slot machines. I was glad to see them, though, considering that Vegas was suffering from the worst economic slump in decades. Even though I hadn't lost too much business, the casinos had and the foreclosure signs were everywhere. I wondered if I shouldn't worry more, but decided I had bigger fish to fry right now.

"Which ladies' room?" I asked.

Jeff pointed to the one closest to the nightclub. "You know, Kavanaugh, it's been hours," he said.

"I need to check. My own peace of mind," I said, shrugging as I pushed the door in.

There were Roman columns edged in gold in here, too, and each stall had its own actual door. I went over to the trash receptacles first, and using a paper towel wrapped around my hand, picked up the clear plastic bag inside, scanning the contents but seeing nothing except paper towels and the occasional Kleenex.

Next I moved to the farthest stall and opened the door, looking behind the toilet and in the sanitary napkin bin. Nothing here, either.

I went to each stall, checking every corner, except for one that was being used. Whoever was in there must be wondering what I was doing. But it certainly wasn't worse than what she was doing: talking on her cell phone while she did her business.

I was washing my hands when she finally emerged. I wasn't going to go in there while she was still here. She had one of those little Bluetooth things stuck in her ear, and she gave me a nasty look as she flitted out without washing her hands, as though I'd been purposely listening to her conversation.

Like talking out loud to a person who wasn't there was supposed to be private.

When the door had shut behind her, I stepped into the stall she'd just vacated. Nothing in the sanitary napkin bin, thank goodness. I peered around the back of the toilet. Nothing there, either. So my great idea was all for naught.

I turned to leave, and the door swung shut slightly. The hook for a coat or a purse caught my eye. I hadn't checked behind any of the doors because I'd held them all open as I looked in the stalls.

Going back to the furthest stall, I quickly checked out the doors. I'd looked at all of them except two when three older women came through the door, laughing and talking. I skirted into one of the stalls and shut the door, pretending that I was here for the same reason they were.

On the back of the door hung a bag. A clear plastic bag with some paper towels in the bottom. It looked as though it were one of the plastic bags that filled the trash bins out near the sink. Someone had snagged one and brought it in here. Clearly the cleaning woman had done what I had: left without checking behind the door.

And whoever had left the bag there had dropped more trash into it: a long, red wig and a pair of stiletto heels. On top of those were more paper towels, but I wasn't sure they were there to disguise what else was in the bag. They were covered with a swirl of colors. As though someone had taken makeup off with them. A lot of makeup.

Maybe makeup that had been applied to look like a dragon tattoo.

Chapter 17

I knew I shouldn't move it. There might be fingerprints or something. Granted, since I'd touched the door, my fingerprints were there, too. And probably not the only ones that didn't belong to the woman who'd changed her appearance to get away from Jeff.

I wondered if she'd realized after talking to him that maybe he knew me, maybe he was on to her, and that's why she skedaddled.

I was also sure now that this couldn't be Ainsley, since her red hair was for real and not a wig. I'd seen her just out of the shower, after all. But somehow, thinking that my impostor was Ainsley hadn't bothered me quite as much as knowing that a total stranger was pretending to be me.

I had another new dilemma, too. I needed to get Tim over here and make sure no one moved that bag. Which meant I was going to have to camp out in here. Fun.

The women who'd come in left, laughing and looking back at me once or twice because surely I was a little nutty to be hanging in the ladies' room. No kidding.

Since there was no one else in here, I poked my head out the door and saw Jeff standing sentry not too far away.

"Hey, there," I said, not too loud, but loud enough so he turned around.

A smirk crossed his face. "What are you doing?" he asked.

I beckoned him to come closer. "I found something. I need to call Tim and have him come over here. Get the stuff."

"What is it?" He took a step closer to the door, looked like he was going to come in.

I put my hand up. "You can't come in here."

"Anyone else in there?"

"Not right now."

"Then why not?" He pushed the door in farther and stepped inside. "Wow," he said, surveying the environs. "Fancier than a men's room—that's for sure."

I didn't want to get into it.

"So where is it?" he asked,

He was here; I figured that I might as well show him, then get him out as soon as possible. I pushed open the stall door.

"Behind the door," I said.

Jeff Coleman stepped inside, and the outside door swung open. I reached for the stall handle and slammed it shut.

Two girls probably no more than twenty-five sauntered in. They wore tight jeans, shirts that rose up above their bellies to show off their belly rings, and flip-flops. They had been chattering to each other but fell silent when they saw me.

"Are you okay in there?" I asked through the door.

"Mmmm." His tone was deep, but there were women who had low voices, and as long as he didn't actually say anything, we'd be okay. And then he made some sort of sound like he was getting sick. Great. He was totally getting into his role.

The girls were staring, and I shrugged sheepishly. "Too many cocktails," I felt compelled to explain.

One of them, the one with the long brunette tresses

that had to be extensions and way too much makeup for this time of day, grinned. "Don't we know about it," she said conspiratorially. "We've been up all night partying at that Cleopatra's Barge and then some other party over at a nightclub at the Flamingo. We love Vegas. We're from Arizona. We go to Arizona State. Where are you from?"

I totally did not want to become BFFs with these two girls. I had more pressing things to worry about, like Jeff Coleman pretending to have the dry heaves in the stall and needing to call Tim to come over and shut this place down to look for clues.

But I didn't have to actually have a conversation, it turned out, because they were doing just fine on their own and didn't much care whether I answered or not. The second girl, a blonde with brown eyes and the longest lashes I'd ever seen, starting going on about some cool guy they met at "the Barge."

I pulled my cell out, not caring if I was being rude. I don't think they noticed.

"Kavanaugh," I heard my brother say.

"You have to come over to Caesars," I said. "It's really important."

"Everything's important to you, Brett."

The girls had gone into stalls now, and I stepped outside, leaving Jeff Coleman alone in there. He was just going to have to deal.

"Listen, Tim, Jeff met a woman at Cleopatra's Barge last night after we all left. She had red hair and a fake dragon tattoo on her chest and she said her name was Brett Kavanaugh."

"I already talked to him about that."

Right. He did. "I'm outside the ladies' room now, near the bar, where she ditched a wig and shoes, and it looks like that dragon was just makeup she removed with paper towels. The bag with this stuff is hanging on the back of a stall door."

"You say you're there now?"

"Jeff's in there watching it." As soon as I said it, I realized I should've lied and said, yes, Tim, I'm in there now. But it was too late.

"Coleman's in the ladies' room?"

"Please, Tim, I didn't want to move the bag. There might be fingerprints."

"You're watching way too much *CSI* these days, Brett."

"Yeah, yeah, yeah. Can you get here?"

"I'm on my way. Tell me which ladies' room."

I gave him directions to the one closest to Cleopatra's Barge and said I'd wait.

The two girls had not emerged from the ladies' room. Neither had Jeff. Since they thought I had a sick friend in there, I probably should show some empathy and go back to check on "her."

The girls were at the sinks, primping in front of the mirrors. They both looked up when I came in.

"Your friend is still in there," the brunette whispered.

I nodded. "It was a rough night." I went over to the stall and knocked. Jeff grunted. I turned back around. "You said you were in Cleopatra's Barge?"

"Cool place," the blonde said. "Met a great guy. He said he could get us into the music business."

Didn't they all? But something about that piqued my curiosity. Sherman Potter was supposed to be there last night, and as far as any of us knew, he'd never shown up. But what if he had and we just hadn't waited long enough? We were expecting Ainsley to sing, but when we found out she wasn't going to, we'd all taken off.

Except Jeff, who'd met my impostor. And when she ditched him, he left, too.

Turns out, these two girls were more than happy to tell me about their night without any prodding.

"He's the manager for the Flamingos!" the blond girl squealed.

"He said he was looking for a new lead singer for the band." The brunette picked right up where the blonde left off, and then they exchanged what I assumed was supposed to be a sad expression. "You know, Dee Carmichael died yesterday."

I nodded. I didn't want to tell them that I knew Sherman Potter. Or Dee Carmichael.

It was the blonde's turn now. "Anyway, he said he needed a new singer to take over, so he gave us his card and said we should call and audition."

Interesting. Especially since Potter had said Ainsley would be taking over for Daisy.

The brunette pulled a business card from her bag and started waving it around. "I'm going to call this morning. I mean, this could be my big break."

"Our big break," the blonde reminded her.

"Oh, right," the brunette assented, although I could tell she had no intention of sharing.

I wanted to tell them that Sherman Potter was using them, that he didn't want any more than a roll in the hay with these two girls, but it wasn't my place. They wouldn't believe me, anyway.

"It's awfully quiet in that stall," the blonde whispered to me.

I looked over, but before I could say anything, the door slammed open and Tim bounded in with two uniforms, a crime scene investigator, and a casino security guard right behind him.

Chapter 18

The girls' hands moved to their mouths, and the brunette's eyes moved to her bag. Hmmm. Bet there was something illegal in that bag.

"Where is he?" Tim asked.

I pointed to the stall. Tim sauntered over and was about to knock when the door opened and Jeff Coleman came out. "It's about time," he said. "It was a little too close in there." He winked at the two girls at the sink. "Hey there."

They stared at him, mouths wide open. Okay, so there was no girl in there getting rid of last night's cocktails after all. They'd get over it.

Tim indicated the crime scene guys should go into the stall. He turned to me as they did so, and said, "Okay, you need to tell me everything."

The girls at the sink had gathered up their things and were about to skirt out, but I stopped them by putting my hand out. "You need to talk to these girls, too. They talked to Sherman Potter last night at Cleopatra's Barge."

Tim's expression went from surprised to guilty that he hadn't stuck around long enough to pleased that maybe he'd have a couple of witnesses after all. He showed them his badge.

"I'd like to ask a few questions, if I might," he said. "I'm Detective Kavanaugh."

They giggled as they checked him out. Okay, so even though he's my brother, I have to admit that he's a good-looking guy. He looks younger than his thirty-eight years, with his freckles and boyish grin. And he's buff in all the right places, since he practically lives at the gym when he isn't working or at home.

We're actually sort of carbon copies, except I'm a lot skinnier, with more angles, and I don't have the freckles. I replaced them with the tattoos, instead.

Tim turned from the girls to Jeff. "Can you wait till I talk to them?"

Jeff nodded. "Is it okay if Brett and I get a cup of coffee? There's a buffet just off the casino."

Tim nodded. "I'll be there in a few."

I was surprised he said okay, especially since I was with Jeff, but I wasn't going to jinx the moment and tugged on Jeff's arm so we could go before Tim changed his mind.

Jeff and I walked in silence to the buffet, where we got a couple cups of coffee and settled in at a table near the door, so Tim could find us easily.

I took a few sips, thinking about Ainsley Wainwright. "The woman you met up with last night couldn't be the woman I met yesterday in Sherman Potter's hotel room," I said.

"Why not?"

"She was just out of the shower," I said. "Her hair was wet, and it didn't look like a wig to me."

"It could've been. Those wigs are pretty fancy these days."

"Maybe," I said, then remembered something. "You said that dragon wasn't real. Were you just sitting there, checking out her chest?"

Jeff smirked. "Give me a little credit, won't you?

I could tell right away. I didn't need to stare at her chest."

"A lot of guys wouldn't have a problem with that," I said.

"Yeah, but maybe I'm not that sort of guy."

I tightened my hands around my cup and frowned. I had no idea how Jeff Coleman was with women other than me. With me he was always making some sort of smart-aleck comment or teasing. I didn't remember him ever focusing on my chest or my butt or any other part of my body, except for my tattoos. The ones that weren't on my chest.

So maybe he *wasn't* that sort of guy.

But true to the Jeff Coleman that I knew, he leaned toward me and grinned. "You're never going to figure me out, Kavanaugh. Have to keep you on your toes."

I rolled my eyes at him, something I did frequently and he no longer paid any attention to. But it made me feel better to do it.

"No coffee for me?"

I looked up to see Tim standing behind me.

"It's just over there," I said, indicating the coffee bar. "Help yourself."

It was his turn to roll his eyes as he went off for his own cup.

"Why do you think my impostor ditched you last night?" I asked Jeff, watching Tim out of the corner of my eye.

"Maybe because I started asking her about her tattoos. Maybe because she thought I'd look too closely. Like you thought I should've." His eyes focused on my face as he drank from his cup.

I mulled that a second. "If she didn't recognize you, then she can't know we're friends, which means if she's going to impersonate me, she hasn't done her homework."

"Or maybe she just decided to start impersonating you. I haven't seen you in a few weeks."

True. I'd been unusually busy at work lately and didn't have time for much except work and sleep.

Work.

It was almost noon. I had to call Bitsy.

Tim slid into the seat next to me as I pulled my cell out of my bag. I held it up. "I have to call the shop."

"Why don't you go out where it's not so loud," Tim suggested, "and I'll talk to Jeff first, go over everything again, while you're gone."

I regretted my decision to call Bitsy. I wanted to hear what Jeff had to say, but then realized Tim probably wanted us separated so he could get each story without anyone interrupting. Or me interrupting, more likely.

I nodded and got up, going toward the restrooms that were in a quiet corner of the restaurant. There was actually a bank of pay phones here, which surprised me. I hadn't seen a pay phone in a long time. Since everyone had cell phones now, why would we need them?

Unless you lost your shirt—and cell phone—gambling, and you needed to call home. Or your bookie.

I punched in the number for the shop.

"Where are you, Brett?"

Right. We had caller ID now, with some new package Bitsy had negotiated.

Quickly, I told her about my impostor and how Jeff and I had come over to Caesars and found the impostor's stuff in the ladies' room.

I heard a short intake of breath. "For someone who wasn't going to get involved anymore, you sure are involved again," she said sharply.

"Hey, this time it's not my fault. Someone's wandering around impersonating me and taking pictures of me. It's creepy."

"I saw something online this morning," Bitsy said, her voice going down in volume.

I felt the panic rise in my chest. I specifically hadn't told her about my night out with Harry.

"It's that blog," Bitsy was whispering now. "It had pictures of you. What happened last night?"

I really didn't want to revisit my absinthe-laced evening.

When she realized I wasn't going to answer, she continued. "I got an e-mail. From our Web site's contact page. No indication who it was from. All it had was a link. To that blog. The one we saw yesterday."

I forced down my annoyance about how Bitsy had gone behind my back and set up an e-mail contact on the Web site. I'd asked her not to, because I didn't want anyone to have to monitor it and then deal with nutty e-mails and spam. But then something nudged those thoughts out of the way.

Someone had bothered to send an e-mail with that link. Someone who wanted to make sure I saw it. Who wanted to make sure I knew.

Chapter 19

I told Bitsy about Harry and the absinthe and that I'd seen the blog myself.

"Have you heard from Harry? Has he been around?" I asked Bitsy. I wondered if he'd seen the blog. But then again, probably not. Harry had said once that he didn't have a computer, that he'd had to sell it once he started running out of money.

Except now I knew he had money, so maybe that was a lie, too.

"Harry hasn't said anything about a job, has he?" I asked Bitsy.

She snorted. "Of course not. I think he likes being one of the jobless." She paused. "I haven't seen him around this morning, though. Usually he's here with coffee when I open up."

That was news to me. "Really?"

"Brett, you're not here as early as I am. I know you need your beauty sleep, so I always schedule your first client for noon or later. By then Harry's been here and gone, and then he comes back later. I think it's to moon at you. And after last night, well, it's pretty obvious that he's making his move now." She chuckled. "And you aren't exactly resisting, from the looks of these pictures."

I closed my eyes and took a couple of deep breaths.

"It was the absinthe," I tried lamely. But was it? For the first time yesterday, I'd noticed how good-looking Harry was, and while he certainly wasn't boyfriend material—not like the employed Dr. Colin Bixby—I admit that I enjoyed those kisses.

Colin Bixby. Uh-oh. What if he saw that blog? If whoever took those pictures sent the blog link to my shop's e-mail, what was to keep them from sending them to Bixby at the hospital?

Now I had a whole other thing to worry about.

"So when do you think you'll be in?" Bitsy was asking. "You've got a client in an hour. Joel and Ace are here, working."

I knew she threw that last bit in to try to make me feel a little guilty, and it worked.

"I'm going to finish up here with Tim and come right over," I promised. "I need a ride anyway, because I left my car over there yesterday and never went back for it."

"Can you bring lunch?" she asked.

Ah, a way to redeem myself. "Johnny Rockets?"

"I'm not sure what Joel's eating these days."

Neither was I. He bounced around too much on those diets to keep anything straight. My biggest fear was he'd turn vegan, just to avoid everything, and then we would have no clue what to feed him.

"If I have to go out again, I will," I promised.

"Right. And then we won't see you till Christmas," Bitsy said sharply and hung up.

I stared at the phone. I totally did not need attitude right now. I was under a little bit of stress. I had a stalker and an impostor, or were they the one and the same?

I wandered back out to the table where Tim and Jeff were sitting. For a second, I studied them: my brother, his back arrow straight as he took notes in his little notebook; Jeff leaning back in his seat, his arms crossed over his chest, his face unreadable as his lips moved.

Jeff was lying about something.

I wondered if Tim could tell.

I sat down.

"You didn't see this woman last night, right, Brett?" Tim turned toward me.

"No, I just wondered about how she could've gotten away from Jeff so easily. I started thinking that maybe she wore a disguise, so we came over here and found the bag of stuff in the ladies' room stall."

Tim gave me a funny look as he jotted something down in his notebook, tucked the pen in his breast pocket, and shoved the notebook in his back trouser pocket. He stood.

"Okay, I know where to reach you if we have more questions," he said and was about to walk away when I held my hand up.

"What about whoever put those pictures up on that blog?" I asked. "Well, on both those blogs. Do you think it could be the same person?" Although I wasn't sure, because Ainsley wouldn't have needed to wear a wig. But you never knew, as Jeff had pointed out.

Tim looked at me as though I had two heads. "Yes, Brett, it could be the same person. We're on top of it. We're trying to track the IP addresses—you know, the addresses that indicate which computers would be generating the information. When I know more, I'll let you know." Although from the look on his face, I doubted that. He'd tell me when he was good and ready, which meant probably when the blogger had already been arrested. Couldn't take any chances that little sister would screw up the process, now, could he?

I pushed down my irritation. I knew he was doing the best he could, under the circumstances. He wasn't a computer guy, so he had to farm this part of the job out to someone who was. That took time. I may not be a cop, but I do know some things, and not only from watching TV.

I thought of something. "Bitsy said someone sent an e-mail through our contact page on our Web site with a link to the blog. Someone wanted me to see those pictures."

Tim's frustration with me turned back into concern. "I'll tell the computer guys. They may have a way to trace that e-mail."

I nodded, and he cocked his head at Jeff. "You can get her to work, right?"

He didn't really need to. I could actually walk from here, but I was feeling really spooked with all those pictures of me all over the Internet.

Jeff seemed to be reading my mind. "I'll make sure she gets there okay," he promised.

"Thanks," Tim said. "Be cautious, remember that, okay?"

It was the only thing I *was* remembering right now.

"He's worried," Jeff said as we watched my brother walk away. "He's right, too. Someone's got it in for you. Do you have any idea who?"

I picked up my coffee mug and took a sip. Cold. I like iced coffee, when it's supposed to be iced coffee, not when it's just room temperature.

"Have you pissed anyone off lately?" Jeff asked. "I mean, besides the Las Vegas Police Department."

I made a face at him. "No, I have not," I said. "At least not that I know of."

"Well, we know it wasn't Harry Desmond taking those pictures, since he was with you," Jeff mulled.

"Why would you even consider Harry?" I asked.

"I don't like him."

"Really? Couldn't tell," I said sarcastically. "Or is it more that you're just mad I went out with him?"

A smile played at the corner of his mouth. "Why would I get mad?"

"You don't seem to like Colin Bixby very much, either."

"You think it's because you're going out with him?" The smile had come out full force now, as if he were incredulous I'd even suggest such a thing.

I put my cards on the table. "Yes. Yes, I do."

"Why?"

"You're always cutting him down, making fun of him, making fun of me going out with him. I mean, it's like you're jealous or something." I had never considered that before, but now that I said it, I wondered. Was Jeff harboring a crush on me?

"Don't flatter yourself, Kavanaugh," he said, his eyes flashing angrily. "So you're one of the few people I find I can tolerate in this city, but believe me, if I was interested in you, you'd damn well know it."

He stood, shoving his chair against the floor with a loud squeal. "Are you ready? I promised your brother I'd get you safely to your shop, and then I have to get to mine. I've got a business to run, too, if you would care to remember."

Jeff didn't even wait for me. He just started walking toward the exit. I grabbed my bag and followed him, wondering who put that bee in his bonnet. It was as though he was protesting too much, but the more I thought about it, the more I realized he was right. He wasn't the kind of guy who'd sit back and watch a woman he was interested in go out with other men. Granted, I'd never met anyone he'd dated, and wasn't sure exactly whether he was dating anyone right now. I knew he'd been married a few years back and had gotten burned pretty badly. Maybe he was just concerned I'd get burned, too, and he didn't want to see that.

Because while he might not want a romance with me,

I did know we were friends. He took a bullet for me. And if push came to shove, I'd probably do the same for him.

Jeff's back was poker straight as he strode through the Roman marketplace. Even though it was dim in here, I knew we'd get slaughtered with sunlight once we went back outside. In seconds, our steps were in sync, but he still didn't seem to want to talk.

I did, though. I had one more question.

"Why did you lie to my brother?"

Chapter 20

Jeff stopped short. "What makes you think I lied to him?"

I shrugged. "I can tell."

He gave me a funny look, then said, "That's down-right psychic, Kavanaugh."

"You did lie to him."

"So what if I did?"

"What about?"

"Nothing you need to worry your pretty little head about," he said, starting to walk again.

I hustled to keep up with him. "Maybe I want to worry about it. Because it's got something to do with me, doesn't it?"

"Exactly why you don't need to worry about it," he said, pushing the door open and letting the sunlight stream across my eyes.

I rummaged in my bag for my sunglasses and stuck them on as I followed him, not even a step behind. "You can't be serious that you're not going to tell me."

"You'll tell your brother."

"No, I won't," I said quickly, before realizing that if it was important, I might have to go back on that promise. He saw my expression change.

"There," he said, pointing at my face. "I knew it."

It was a little scary how well we knew each other.

"If you don't tell me, I'll keep badgering you."

"I'm dropping you off at your shop and leaving, so you won't have the chance."

We were bickering like an old married couple. Not the kind of thought I wanted to have about Jeff Coleman. I changed tacks.

"You didn't lie to me, too, did you?" I asked.

He studied my face a second, unable to see my eyes because of the sunglasses, then said, "No." And after a pause added, "I might not have told you everything."

"But you're going to now, aren't you?"

We stopped on the bridge I'd been on last night with Harry, when he kissed me and the flash went off. I was having some serious déjà vu, but I didn't want to seem spooked in front of Jeff, so I stood my ground, happy that the sunglasses kept him from seeing my eyes darting around behind him, worried I'd discover another camera aimed right at me.

Jeff shifted from one foot to the other, his own eyes searching out something behind me, but I didn't want to show him I was curious, so I forced myself to look straight ahead.

"The woman last night. We were talking about tattoos, and she commented on mine. But then she said Sylvia Coleman gave her a tattoo," he added.

"Your mother? She actually said Sylvia Coleman?"

"Threw me for a loop. That's what disoriented me, what I was thinking about when she went to the ladies' room."

I mulled that a second. "So she knows that I know your mother. Funny that she'd say Sylvia tattooed that dragon."

Jeff took a deep breath. "Not the dragon."

I didn't think I heard him right. "What do you mean?"

"She said my mother tattooed Napoleon on her leg. She knew it was a painting you liked."

I felt like I couldn't breathe.

Jeff kept talking, as though he didn't notice.

"She was wearing tight jeans, so she couldn't prove it. I couldn't check it out."

I wondered if she knew about the tiger lily on my side. Not many people knew about that one, because it was usually covered up by clothes. Even when I went swimming at the public pool in Henderson, I wore a Speedo one-piece. She could've seen the Napoleon tattoo when I swam, or when I wore a skirt. Although I didn't wear a skirt too often. She obviously knew about the Celtic cross on my upper back because it was in living color on that blog—my penance for wearing a halter top. I wouldn't be wearing that again. I thought about the stiletto heels in the plastic bag in the ladies' room. My footwear was not something she'd studied at length, since I usually wore Tevas or Birkenstocks. Even the flats I wore today were a rarity. Heels weren't exactly necessary when one was five foot nine.

"Did she say anything else about me?" My voice was unusually soft, as though I couldn't speak above a whisper.

Jeff moved a little closer and for a second, his hand reached out like he was going to touch my cheek. But then he seemed to realize what he was doing and pulled it back, stuffing it into his pocket.

"We didn't get much further than that," he admitted.

"Why didn't you tell Tim?" I asked. "I mean, shouldn't he know?"

His eyes skipped around behind my head. There was something else. I waited. Finally, he said, "She made a couple cracks about my mother. Unkind things. It was all I could do not to say something. I didn't exactly want to repeat what she said to your brother and then have it all be on the record."

I couldn't blame him, so I gave him a pass.

"It's enough he knows someone's out there impersonating you. What she said about my mother and the description of your tat isn't really relevant to his investigation." He paused. "Come on. Let's get to your shop. You might feel a little better once we get there."

He was right about that. Out here, I was a sitting duck. For some chick with a camera who had decided I was more interesting than she was so she had to take over my persona.

Good luck with that.

Bitsy's eyebrows rose high into her forehead when she saw me come in with Jeff Coleman on my heels.

"Just a little bodyguard duty," he quipped, flashing a grin.

Bitsy's eyes skirted from him to me. "Your client is already here. She's on the couch in back."

I was happy for the distraction.

"Thanks for the escort," I said to Jeff, wishing I could make some sort of joke or something, but my heart wasn't in it.

This time he did lean toward me, his fingers brushing my cheek. "You know the number," he said, then whirled around and walked out, a quick nod to Bitsy, who sat with her mouth hanging open.

"What's up with you and Jeff Coleman?" she asked. "It's like you two called a truce or something."

"Or something," I said absently, not wanting to get into it with her. I started back toward my client, so I could get to work, but then remembered and turned around. "Has Harry been in yet?"

Bitsy shook her head. "Haven't seen him at all. This isn't normal. I hope he's okay."

I had no idea what Harry's reaction to the pictures of us would be, but I pushed everything out of my head as I went back to greet Katie North, my client. She'd come in two days ago and wanted a butterfly on her upper back. I'd drawn up a design that she loved: a classic Monarch, with orange and black markings, its wings spread wide to make a real statement.

"Come on back," I said as I approached her. She was sitting on the black leather sofa, leafing through a tattoo magazine.

Katie jumped up with a wide grin and followed me into my room. I motioned that she should sit while I went out to get the stencil from her file in the staff room.

"You'll be facedown," I explained, showing her how the chair would lie flat, sort of like a massage table. It would be easier for me to tattoo her that way. It would also be more comfortable for her. It wasn't her first tattoo (she had the Little Prince on her upper arm), but the butterfly was a lot larger and would take longer.

Joel was in the staff room working on a stencil for one of his clients. He looked up when I came in and gave me a concerned expression.

"Are you okay? We all saw the blog with the pictures of you and Harry."

I caught my breath and bit my lip. He noticed, got up, and gave me a hug. "It'll be okay. Your brother will find whoever it is who's doing this. Don't worry."

I nodded and pulled away just as my cell phone started to ring. I still had my bag over my shoulder and I slung it onto the light table as I rummaged for the phone. I didn't recognize the number.

"Hello?" I asked tentatively, Joel watching.

"Brett? It's Harry."

"Hey there," I said, uncertain what he was calling me about, and then wondered how he got my number. Bitsy, probably. "What's up?" I tried to make my voice light, but it didn't really work.

"That's what I was going to ask you," he said.

"What do you mean?"

"Your message. You said you had something important to tell me, that I should call right away. What's wrong?"

What was wrong was that I couldn't have left him any sort of message. Because I didn't have his number.

Chapter 21

I sat, my heart back in my throat. It should just have been permanently lodged there, because it was popping up there all the time lately.

"I didn't call you," I said, forcing the words out. "Tell me exactly what the message said."

"What do you mean, you didn't call me?"

Couldn't accuse Harry of being a Rhodes scholar. "I didn't call you. Some woman is impersonating me. I bet it was her who called you. What was the number she called from?"

"Someone's impersonating you?"

Was there an echo in here? I tried not to be impatient. I needed that phone number.

"Please, Harry, the number?"

"Okay, okay, hold on." He was quiet a second; then he rattled off a number as I grabbed a pencil from Joel and jotted it down on top of one of the file folders on the table.

"Thanks," I said. "What did the message say?"

"I told you. You said it was important. I should call you right away."

"She sounded like me?" It was one thing to make herself up like me, but to mimic my voice?

"There were a lot of sounds in the background, like

she was in a car or on a bus or something, but it sounded like you, I guess." He was having doubts now. "Why do you think someone's impersonating you?"

I told him about the Ink Flamingos blog and the pictures of the two of us. "She obviously was following us around last night," I finished.

Bitsy was standing in the doorway, waving her arms around. Oh, shoot. I'd forgotten about Katie.

"Listen, Harry, why don't you stop by later and we can talk about it. I've got a client." And I hung up.

"Katie's waiting," Bitsy said.

"I know. I need to give Tim a quick call." I grabbed Katie's folder with the stencil in it as I hit the speed dial number for Tim.

"Kavanaugh."

I quickly told him about my conversation with Harry and gave him the number for the mysterious impostor as well as Harry's number, which I now had because he'd called me and it was in my phone.

"I'll get on it," Tim said, hanging up.

Katie accepted my apology for being away too long, and I pressed the stencil against her back and peeled it off carefully, leaving the markings behind that I would trace with the tattoo machine. I showed her what it looked like with a hand mirror, and she was thrilled. I told her to lie down as I pulled on a pair of blue gloves, slid a needle into the machine, and dipped it into a small pot of black ink. I spun my chair around so I had a good angle, put my foot against the pedal on the ground, and heard the machine whir to life.

As I worked, I felt my worries slip away, the tension in my shoulders ease. I lost myself in the zone, creating my art on someone's skin, carefully moving the machine with the contours of her body. When I was in art school, I'd had no idea I'd trade a stiff, white canvas for this malleable one. The black heart on the inside of my wrist, which I gave myself when I was sixteen, had been only the beginning, and I should have known then, with each painstaking and painful stab of that needle, that this was what I was meant to create.

I had someone ask me once whether I'd get into other forms of body modification, but besides the tattoos and the piercings in my ears, I hadn't considered it. Putting more holes in my body or stretching my earlobes or splitting my tongue just weren't the same to me as using my body as a canvas. I was a walking art gallery, as much a gallery as Ace's was out in the front of the shop. That's not to say I judged anyone else who might want to pursue other types of modification. That was their business and their own journey. It just wasn't mine.

I was finishing up Katie's tattoo when something else hit me about what had been going on the last couple days. Daisy was the one who'd lost her life, but somehow this had become all about me. It was wrong.

Or maybe that's what whoever did this had meant to do. Steer all speculation toward me. Did my impostor know about Tim, how he was a police detective? That Tim would probably focus on whoever was blogging about me rather than Daisy's death? Granted, Flanigan was on the case, too, as well as other police. But if it became about me, and not Daisy, then maybe she'd get away with it.

She? Had I pinned this on the woman impersonating me? What about Sherman Potter? He said he'd already replaced Daisy, saying she'd planned to leave the band. I wondered what the other band members thought about that.

As soon as Katie left with her aftercare instructions, I knew what I had to do. See where the Flamingos were playing and see if I couldn't talk to them about Daisy. If I could figure out what she was doing at the Golden Palace, then maybe I'd be a step closer to finding my impersonator.

Joel was on the laptop when I finally went into the staff room. He was in the middle of designing a tattoo. A while back, we'd had an intern who taught him how to design in Photoshop and Illustrator and he took to it easily. Ace and I had a little bit more trouble. Ace because, well, he really wanted to be a painter, and me, I didn't do so well on the computer. I liked having a pencil in my hand—or a tattoo machine.

Joel looked up as I came in.

"Done with Katie?" he asked.

I nodded, sticking my head in the fridge to see if there was anything to munch on. I pulled out a brick of cheddar cheese and a box of crackers. I cut off a little cheese and put it on a cracker and stuck it in my mouth.

"Can I have one?" Joel asked, his eyes focused on the cheese.

I made him a couple crackers and put them on a paper plate, setting it down next to him. "Going to be long?"

"Just got started," he said, indicating the screen.

The outline of a snake was weaving its way through the eye sockets of a skull. I shivered involuntarily. Despite his newfound love of computer graphics, Joel was a traditional tattooist and did mainly old-school tattoos with a slightly modern twist. So far, this one was still just old-school.

"I'll go in the office, then," I said, going down the hall. We had an old iMac desktop that had been replaced by the laptop, and I hoisted it up from its new home on the floor to the top of the desk. I had to hook it all up, which was why when Flanigan had been here yesterday I didn't bother with it, just used the laptop. I fumbled with the wires, making sure the keyboard and mouse were attached and plugging it into the socket. When I had everything where it should be, I hit the power switch.

The wireless still worked on this, and when it booted

up, I went to the Internet and did a Google search for the Flamingos Web site. I wanted to find out where the band was playing next, so I could track them down and see if I couldn't get some answers out of them.

When I clicked on the first link, a page I'd never seen before popped up. It was a dedication to Daisy, her picture and her date of birth and death, with RIP under her picture and a small button at the bottom of the page that indicated I could get to the band's Web site through that portal.

It was a touching tribute, considering that Daisy was leaving the band and had already been replaced.

But when I clicked through, I didn't get the Flamingos Web site after all.

It was the Ink Flamingos blog.

Chapter 22

I pushed the keyboard away from me and shoved back in my chair. This was getting way too creepy.

Whoever had set up the blog had a new post. I scanned it, even though I wanted to get up and walk away.

The post was all about Daisy's flamingo tattoo, how it had only been black but "I" had felt it needed a touch of color and Daisy had agreed, even though she was known for her black tattoos. There was no mention of the fact that she had an allergy.

Curious.

Where was the actual Flamingos site? Pushing aside my discomfort, I clicked back through the tribute page and to Google. Ah, there it was. Just underneath the link I'd hit.

Relief washed through me as the site loaded, the strains of the Flamingos' latest hit, "Bad Blood," in the background. I clicked on the PERFORMANCES link and found a listing of the band's upcoming gigs.

They were supposed to be here in Vegas, at the MGM, tonight. I remembered how someone had said that the band was on the East Coast. But they had played their final concert there in New Jersey at the Meadowlands last night. No indication that any concerts were canceled. No indication on the Web site at all that Daisy was no longer with the band, no longer alive.

I wondered why Sherman Potter had been here in Vegas when the band was in New Jersey last night. That didn't make much sense. Unless he had to come out here because of Daisy. How had the other girls been able to perform without their lead singer? Knowing she was dead?

I clicked on NEWS and found the latest from the local TV station: The Flamingos were due to arrive in Vegas this afternoon at two. I glanced at my watch. In about twenty minutes.

I picked up the phone and dialed information to get the MGM. When I finally got through, I asked if I could leave a message for Melanie Black. While I didn't know the other girls in the band, Melanie had come to the shop with Daisy one time and Ace had done a small tattoo on her ankle. She would recognize my name.

Reciting my name and number and asking that she call as soon as she got in, I then thanked the hotel operator and set the phone back in its cradle.

That was the most I could do. Now I had to keep myself busy, which wasn't going to be hard because Bitsy stuck her head in the door to tell me my next client was here.

Melanie hadn't called me back two hours later, and after being here every day for the last month, Harry still hadn't showed. Tim didn't call to update me.

"You're pacing," Bitsy said from her perch at the front desk, where she was arranging everyone's schedules for the next day.

"I've got a little bit of nervous energy," I admitted. "I'd love to go out for a walk and get rid of it, but I'm afraid someone's going to start taking pictures again, and it'll freak me out even more."

Bitsy made a face at me. "You know, the only person you need to worry about is Colin Bixby. No one else cares."

Nice. But she was right. And I hadn't heard from Colin since those pictures went up on the blog. Granted, he had long hours in the emergency room and probably didn't even know about them. Which meant I needed to run reconnaissance before someone pointed out that his girlfriend had been sucking face with an unemployed cabana boy. And even though this was Vegas and the desert, we were not wanting for cabana boys.

"I better call him."

"No need." Bitsy indicated a tall, lanky figure coming toward the shop.

My heart skipped a little beat as he pushed the door in. His dark hair was tousled just-so with a little bit of product; the black T-shirt showed off the stethoscope I'd tattooed on his arm; his jeans showed off a nice backside. You'd never know he was a doctor when he was off duty and a little punk and a lot bad boy.

From the expression on his face, though, I could tell that maybe he hadn't been quite as isolated the last twenty-four hours as I'd hoped.

"Can we go somewhere?" he asked, without bothering to give me a kiss hello.

Uh-oh. Definitely not isolated.

Bitsy gave me a sympathetic look as I led Colin to my room. She was no stranger to boyfriend troubles. I shut the door on her questioning gaze and turned toward Colin.

"I can explain," I said.

He held his hands up. "You can always explain. But when you go into your e-mail to see pictures of your girlfriend making out with another guy, well, there's really no need for explanation, is there?"

He was breaking up with me. I didn't blame him.

Even telling him about the absinthe wouldn't help—it would probably hurt. He knew I didn't drink hard stuff, and he would wonder why I did last night with Harry. Or maybe he wouldn't wonder.

"I guess that's it, then?" I asked, leaving the question open and hoping he'd disagree.

"I came by because I felt this had to be done in person," he said, his eyes soft and full of regret. I'd hurt him before, had promised him I wouldn't again, and here we were.

I hung my head and sighed. "I'm sorry. There were extenuating circumstances, but I understand."

"Extenuating circumstances? There are always extenuating circumstances with you." He started toward the door, but then turned back. "The only real surprise was that it wasn't Jeff Coleman. Just some stranger."

And he walked out.

Past said stranger, who had, unfortunately, arrived and was leaning against the front desk whispering with Bitsy.

For a second, I thought Harry was safe.

Until Colin realized who he was and slugged him.

Chapter 23

Colin had probably been wishing he could hit me, but it was easier to hit Harry. Because Harry really didn't know what was going on until Colin was gone, outside, walking along the canal and out of sight.

Harry rubbed his jaw. "Who was that?"

"Brett's boyfriend," Bitsy said.

"Ex-boyfriend," I corrected.

"Can't blame him," she said.

I didn't, either, but I didn't really need to hear it right now. Harry was looking at me like I should say something to him, but I didn't want to. I wanted to leave. I wanted to go home and lock the door and go to bed. But I had another client coming in, and the best I could do was turn on my heel and go into the staff room. Joel had been leaning against the doorjamb, watching, and he followed me in.

"I'm sorry," he said, rubbing my back as I sat slumped over in the chair.

I nodded. "I know. It's all my fault."

"You know, Brett, you and Bixby were on borrowed time." Joel was referring to how I'd accused him of wanting to kill me several months ago. We'd had a reprieve since then, clearly, but that had always been floating around somewhere in the background. Trust was not one of our strong points.

I remembered something. "He said he was surprised it wasn't Jeff. You know, in the pictures with me. Ridiculous." I snorted out a short laugh.

I noticed Joel had not joined in and frowned.

"You know, Brett, I'm a little surprised, too."

Me and Jeff? "You have got to be kidding me," I said incredulously. "Jeff Coleman? I mean, the guy is a, well, you know."

"What? A damn fine tattooist? A guy who took a bullet for you?" Joel's voice was soft, but his meaning was loud and clear.

Fortunately, my cell phone rang at right that very minute, saving me from saying something I might regret.

"Brett Kavanaugh?" The voice was a woman's, a little breathy, and for a second, I froze, the image of my impostor in my head.

"Yes?" I managed to squeak out.

"This is Melanie. Melanie Black. Daisy's friend."

Relief rushed through me. Melanie. Right.

"Hi, Melanie, thanks so much for calling me back."

"I don't have much time. We've got a concert tonight."

"You're going on?"

Such a slight hesitation, but one nonetheless. "Yeah. Sherman thinks we should do it for Daisy." I could tell from her tone she knew Sherman wasn't thinking about Daisy, but probably dollar signs.

"Quick question, then," I said. "I met up with Sherman yesterday. He was with someone named Ainsley. Said she's the new lead singer."

"That's right," Melanie said, and I could hear resentment. "She's singing with us tonight." She didn't want to sing with Ainsley.

"Sherman said Daisy was leaving the band, that this was all lined up before she died."

"Um, well, yeah, she sort of mentioned something, but we didn't think she'd really leave. And then suddenly Ainsley showed up out of the blue. That's why Daisy was in Vegas early. She said she had something to do here, but she didn't tell me what it was. I think maybe she might have said something to Cara, but Cara closed up tight when we heard about Daisy and hasn't talked to anyone." Melanie hadn't taken a breath the whole time she was talking and when she finished, I could hear her let it out.

"Have you talked to the police?" I asked.

"They were here this morning asking stuff about Daisy, like did she have any enemies, did we know of any problems in her life, that sort of thing."

"So none of you are suspects or anything, right?" I had to ask.

"Why would we be? We were all in New Jersey when Daisy was killed." She paused. "What do *you* know about it?"

Uh-oh. "Nothing. I hadn't heard from Daisy since October. Hadn't seen her at all."

"But they said she had a tattoo." I could hear the accusation in her tone.

"I don't know anything about that."

"I saw that blog."

Okay, so now everything was on the table.

"I don't know anything about that, either," I said. "To be perfectly honest, someone's impersonating me. The police are trying to find out who."

"Why would someone impersonate you?" Melanie asked.

I didn't want to say that I was being framed in Daisy's death. I didn't think I had to say it. But I did.

There were a few seconds of silence, then, "Do you want to come tonight?" Melanie asked. "Maybe Cara would talk to you."

"You believe me that I didn't have anything to do with Daisy?" So I needed the validation. Sue me.

"Yes. Listen, Brett, I know you were one of the few people Daisy trusted and you wouldn't hurt her. And if you can find out who's impersonating you, we'll find out who killed Daisy. So come tonight, okay?"

I hadn't seen the Flamingos perform since last spring, when Daisy gave me front row tickets. I took Joel, who has this affinity for girl pop singers: Miley Cyrus, Katy Perry, Taylor Swift. Most men might be embarrassed about that, but not Joel. He liked to put his iPod in the speaker in the staff room and play it loudly while he worked. The Flamingos were a step up from pop, but only a little step, so it was good enough for him.

"I'd love to," I said.

"When you get to the MGM, give them your name and they'll bring you backstage, okay?"

Backstage? I could live with that.

"And you can bring a friend if you want."

I hadn't wanted to ask.

"Thanks, Melanie. I'll see you tonight." As I hung up, I realized I wouldn't see only Melanie. I'd also come face to face with Ainsley Wainwright again. While Joel would kill me, I should tell Tim about the invitation and he should come with me.

I quickly punched his number into my cell.

"I was just going to call you, Brett."

"Why?"

"We found that blogger. Ainsley Wainwright."

I caught my breath. "How?"

"Some computer mumbo jumbo. I don't understand it. All I know is, we traced the IP address—that's computer talk." He paused. "It's not an exact science, and if we hadn't had a break, we would've needed a court order to track it to a specific address."

This was getting way too technical for me.

"So?" I prodded. "What was the break?"

"We knocked on doors."

"Seems like pretty basic police work."

"Yeah."

I was about jumping out of my skin. "When you finally found her, what did she have to say for herself?"

"We didn't talk to her."

"She wasn't there?"

"Yeah. She was."

I started having a bad feeling about this.

"Brett, she was dead. Had been dead for at least a couple days."

Chapter 24

If Ainsley Wainwright had been dead for two days, it meant she could've died the same day as Daisy. But then who had posted those pictures of me and Harry? I wasn't the only one being impersonated, it seemed. Tim agreed with me.

And then I had another thought. "You know, Tim, this woman Ainsley's supposed to be singing with the Flamingos tonight at the MGM. I met her yesterday. What are the odds that there are two women named Ainsley in Vegas right now? Are you sure that the woman you found in that apartment is really Ainsley Wainwright?"

"What's your Ainsley's last name?" he asked, ignoring my question.

I frowned. I had no idea what her last name was. I'd never heard it. Sherman hadn't told me and neither had Melanie.

"It *is* an unusual name," Tim admitted, "but we had a positive ID on the woman in that apartment. And we checked the computer and laptop she had there. She was definitely the one blogging."

"But not the last few posts," I said. "That would be impossible."

His silence told me he knew that.

"I'm going to the concert tonight," I said. "Melanie

says I can bring someone. Want to tag along and check out this Ainsley?"

"Might not be a bad idea. Can we get Kevin in, too?"

Right. Flanigan.

"She said I could bring one person, but maybe we can sneak him in," I said.

"If anyone can sneak anyone in, it'll be you," Tim teased.

We agreed to meet at the MGM at eight, since the concert was at nine. I put my phone down and stared at the light table, the opaque whiteness of it putting my eyes into a spin, but I couldn't look away.

"Brett?"

I had to blink a few times to put Bitsy into focus. "What's up?" I asked.

She came in and sat down next to me. "I was going to ask you."

I told her about my conversation with Tim. "So while it seems it should be over, it's really not because someone picked up the slack for her on that blog after she died." It dawned on me, too, that I hadn't asked Tim how Ainsley Wainwright had died.

"It would seem rather silly to kill a blogger just to take over the blog," Bitsy said, ever practical. "I mean, you could just start up a new blog, right?"

Which was exactly what that person had done. Ink Flamingos. The blog I was supposed to be writing.

I guess whoever was playing this game had decided that I was more interesting to impersonate than Ainsley Wainwright. I said as much to Bitsy.

She bit her lip. "But first she impersonates Ainsley Wainwright, and now she's dead," Bitsy said softly.

Her words sank in slowly, but when they did, they hit my gut like a rock. How long before I was dispensable, too? But what would the motive be? I could see writing that new blog to try to throw the blame over at me. Probably the same reason to post those pictures of Harry and me.

I thought about those first pictures, though, the ones of me on the street that were posted on Skin Deep a few weeks back. I remembered, too, how Jeff had said that Ainsley Wainwright had wanted to interview his mother and take her picture for the blog. At some point that blog was legit. And then Ainsley had died and someone else took over.

It was personal. Someone who knew me. Had been following me. Knew I had done Daisy's tattoos. A shiver shimmied up my spine.

Bitsy could tell I was spooked. "Don't go over to the MGM alone," she said. "Take Joel with you. Or have Tim meet you here and then go over with him."

Not a bad idea. But Tim wasn't answering his phone now. I didn't even get voice mail. I hated the idea of asking Joel to come with me to the MGM if he wasn't going to come to the concert, too. First it was just me, then Tim, then Flanigan, now Joel. It was turning into a party.

"I don't want Joel to think he can come to the concert," I said. "It's bad enough I'm bringing Tim and Flanigan. I don't want to push it with Melanie."

"Then have Harry escort you over." She didn't turn away quick enough to keep me from noticing the smile.

"I'm not doing anything with Harry again," I said firmly, determined not to have a repeat of last night. It had cost me my boyfriend, and I was incredibly embarrassed.

"You won't drink absinthe again," Bitsy said, "and Harry knows Sherman Potter. He could get Tim and Detective Flanigan in."

Bitsy was giving Harry way too much credit. I remembered the way Sherman Potter had looked at him when he'd first answered the door yesterday. We were lucky he even remembered Harry at all, and the way

Ainsley had been coming on to Harry, well, I wasn't sure Sherman hadn't noticed that. And if he had, he might not want his new lead singer to be performing a duet with his old girlfriend's kid brother.

No, Harry was out.

I knew what Bitsy was going to propose next, and I had to admit that it was the only thing to do.

"Call Jeff."

As I listened to the phone ring, I told myself it was merely an escort over to the MGM. Nothing more. While Joel would've had to come to the concert, Jeff wouldn't want to. Jeff was totally into heavy metal: Metallica and Tool and Creed and Alice in Chains. He wouldn't want to be caught dead at a Flamingos concert.

"Murder Ink." It was Sylvia. I couldn't help but think about how Ainsley Wainwright had given Sylvia the option of whether she wanted her body art to be featured on Skin Deep, but I'd had no choice in the matter.

"Hey, Sylvia," I said. "Is Jeff around?"

"Right here, dear. I understand you've got yourself in another pickle."

Understatement of the year. I decided to downplay it. "Not so much," I said. It was sort of true. At least this time I hadn't found any bodies myself.

"Kavanaugh?" Jeff had taken the phone.

I launched right into it, telling him about how Ainsley Wainwright was dead and I had to go to the MGM and I couldn't go alone and could he possibly come over and give me a little escort in a couple hours?

I heard a chuckle. "Can't live without me, can you, Kavanaugh?"

I was beginning to seriously regret this. Maybe I *should* have asked Harry. He would've willingly gone along. Problem was, I didn't want to give him the wrong idea. I'd most definitely been on that road last night, since the man could kiss better than anyone I'd kissed in a long time. Even Colin Bixby. But despite the obvious physical attraction, there wasn't much else there. While back in college I might have gone for the superficial relationship, I didn't want to do that now. Regardless of what Colin Bixby thought.

So, better to regret calling Jeff and asking him to be my escort than regret something a little more serious with Harry.

"I really only need a ride," I said, a little more snippily than I should have since I was asking him a favor.

"Don't get your panties in a bunch. I'll be there." And he hung up.

Again without saying good-bye.

I had asked Bitsy not to tell anyone where I was going. I didn't want Joel to feel slighted, and I was afraid Harry would try to convince me he was the best person to come with me. But when Jeff showed up, it raised a few eyebrows.

Harry looked at him like he was sizing up the competition. Great.

Jeff gave him a short nod. I'd had my jean jacket and bag waiting at the front desk, so I grabbed them and I almost made it out before I heard Joel say, "Where are you going?"

I'd had my hand on the door, but paused. "Jeff's giving me a ride," I said simply, wishing I could give him more of an answer. I'd tell him the whole story tomorrow, I promised myself as Jeff and I slipped out.

"Surprised to see Harry there," Jeff said as we turned the corner around the canal, a gondolier singing to his tourist passengers.

"Why?"

"Well, after last night and all."

I felt my face flush. He kept talking, as though he didn't notice.

"Asked around about Harry. He's feeding you a line about being unemployed."

"I knew it," I said. "I knew something was up when I saw all that money in his wallet. Where's he working?"

A smile tugged at the corner of his lips. "Here and there. Harry's got a pretty good gig for himself. He does tattoo parties."

I frowned.

"You know, Kavanaugh. Like Tupperware. Except instead of some plastic container, everyone gets a tattoo."

Chapter 25

That's why he could hang out all day at my shop. Harry was working nights, going to parties and tattooing people, making a mint, apparently.

"Why wouldn't he tell us about that, though?" I asked.

"Maybe he didn't want you to think he was any sort of competition." Jeff snorted. "Not that he is. I can't imagine who's hiring him to do these parties. They're obviously not asking for references." Jeff had started walking toward the exit again.

"Maybe he's gotten better," I ventured.

"And maybe you don't have an impostor," he said.

"You really hate him, don't you?"

"He's young and arrogant and a lousy tattooist."

"Don't hold back," I said.

Jeff pushed the door open and we stepped outside at the front of the Venetian, the Doge's Palace rising to our left, Madame Tussauds wax museum at the far end of the bridge that crossed yet another canal. We must have taken a wrong turn, because we weren't in the self-parking garage.

"Valet," Jeff said simply, reading my mind as he handed the bellman a ticket.

We moved to the side as we waited, watching the

other hotel and casino guests coming and going, both of us lost in our own thoughts. I was still reeling from finding out about Harry's party gigs. I'd done that a couple times, back in Jersey, to make a little extra cash. Usually, though, only one or two people at the party actually wanted to get a tattoo. I think they liked the *idea* of attending a tattoo party so they could tell their friends. I didn't much see the point in going if you weren't going to get tattooed, but as long as someone was willing, I made money, so I wasn't going to quibble.

It was taking a long time for the valet to get Jeff's Pontiac. I glanced over at the doors when they opened again.

Harry was coming out. He hadn't looked in our direction, just kept going straight, so he didn't see us. I tapped on Jeff's arm and cocked my head.

"Where's he going?" I wondered.

"Only one way to find out," Jeff said, taking a step toward the driveway. At just that moment, the orange Pontiac slid to a stop in front of us. The valet got out, holding the keys out to Jeff, who shook his head. "Sorry, but can you take it back?"

The valet looked confused, but Jeff pushed the keys at him. "We'll be back," he said as he indicated I should follow him to see where Harry was headed.

Harry hadn't even looked behind him, and we stayed far enough back so even if he did, he might not notice us. We passed the Walgreens and Jimmy Buffett's Margaritaville, where a kid was standing with parrots on his shoulders as a photographer snapped his picture. Just as he did, one of the birds let loose all over the back of the kid's shirt.

Jeff let out a snort of laughter but didn't stop.

Harry was walking as if he were on a mission. Didn't look one way or the other, just straight ahead. Not like me. Every time I saw a camera flash, I flinched, my eyes skirting around to make sure nothing was aimed at me. Since I hadn't noticed the night before, I wasn't sure how I'd see it this time, but at least I wasn't drunk on absinthe now.

I was getting tired. We passed Harrah's, the sounds of the casino spilling out onto the street, and the Imperial Palace, which didn't look like much since you had to walk down a sort of alleyway to get to the entrance. It was one of the older casinos, but I'd been there a while back to see the poor man's Cirque du Soleil: Matsuri, a Japanese acrobatic show that also had a magic act.

I wondered if we were walking to the MGM. Would've been easier on the feet if we'd taken the monorail.

But just as I thought we'd be walking forever, Harry veered left.

The entrance overhang was studded with lights. We hung back a little as Harry went inside and then up the escalator. When he was about halfway up, we followed.

It was the Flamingo. One of my favorite hotels and casinos because it still had that old-time feel to it, the feel of old Vegas, when Frank and Dean and the rest of the Rat Pack were kings and Bugsy Siegel felt this city in the desert was worth building and even dying for.

The black-and-white tiled floor reminded me of my grandmother's bathroom back in Jersey, and the bronze statue of the flamingo stood sentry just above the steps that led down to the casino floor.

Harry was walking through the casino, not paying any more attention to the table games or slot machines than he had to the people on the sidewalk outside. Where was he going?

We had our answer when we saw him push the glass doors open to the outdoor aviary. Somehow I didn't think he was here to check out the real pink flamingos that lived in the little watery alcove.

But maybe he was. Harry stopped on the footbridge

overlooking the flamingos and leaned his elbows on the railing, watching the birds. Jeff touched my arm and indicated I should fall back, and we moved to the right, so Harry wouldn't see us if he turned around.

"What's he doing?" I whispered.

Jeff shrugged.

"Why are we following him anyway?" While it seemed like a no-brainer back at the Venetian, the question had started to nag at me.

"You wanted to know more about him," Jeff whispered.

Okay, so it was *my* fault that my flats had given me blisters.

I was about to say something snarky when Harry suddenly straightened up and turned, not toward us, but in the opposite direction. It looked as though he was about to greet someone, but right at that moment, a wedding party moved in between us. The bride was decked out in a flowing white dress and long veil, four giggling bridesmaids in pink taffeta clung to each other, and a groom and three other young guys in tuxedos surrounded them.

I tried to see through them to whomever it was Harry was greeting, but all I caught was a flash of blond hair and a pair of jeans.

"Is he meeting up with a girl?" I asked, realizing that Jeff couldn't see any more than I could and he'd shifted a little to the right to try to get a better view.

Jeff shrugged. "Can't tell, but I think so."

So maybe she hadn't seen the blog pictures of Harry and me. After a second of feeling resentful that my boyfriend broke up with me because of Harry, I realized that Harry had been stepping out, too.

"Wonder who she is," I muttered.

"Jealous?" Jeff gave me a wink, and I knew he was teasing.

The wedding party had paused to take some pictures against the backdrop of the flamingo lagoon, but Harry and the blonde walked a little farther down the path, past the little ducks and birds and pheasants that were wandering on the grass, toward the fountain. Because night had fallen and their backs were to us, we still couldn't make out the girl's features. Jeff and I sidestepped a few people, trying to stay far enough behind so they wouldn't notice us following them.

"This is ridiculous," I finally said when another couple stepped between us in front of the little waterfall that provided a backdrop for wedding pictures. The flamingo logo of the resort was strategically placed for advertising purposes. "Why are we doing this, anyway? So he's meeting up with a girlfriend. Big deal."

Jeff nodded. "You may be right."

"I know I'm right."

He studied my face for a second, a grin spreading wide. "Is it tiring being right all the time?"

I slugged him on the arm and turned around, wincing slightly as the newfound blister caught on the leather of my shoe. Socks are underrated.

Suddenly, I felt Jeff's hand on my arm, tight, stopping me. He cocked his head back toward Harry.

The twosome was becoming a threesome.

I froze.

Ace van Nes, my employee, was laughing as he approached them. He held a case that I recognized. It was the case he used for his tattoo equipment.

Chapter 26

I could put two and two together. All that time at the shop and the oxygen bar clearly had created a friendship and possibly more. With Jeff's information about Harry's tattoo parties, it seemed likely that Ace was moonlighting with Harry.

I wanted to think that I paid him enough so he wouldn't need to do that. And anyway, what was up with all his whining about how tattooing was not his life's calling, that he was so frustrated as an artist because he couldn't express himself the way he wanted?

I took a step toward them, but felt Jeff's hand holding me back.

I could see in his face that he'd drawn the same conclusion I had, but he was shaking his head.

"They can't know we're following them," he said softly. "How would we explain that? You can talk to Ace tomorrow about this." And he indicated I should follow him back toward the building.

Once safely inside and definitely out of sight, I let out a deep breath. "That was something I didn't expect."

"You can talk to him tomorrow," Jeff said again. "We've got to get to the MGM."

But we were without a car now.

Jeff was reading my mind. "We can pick up the monorail here at the Flamingo," he said. "It'll take us straight to the MGM."

I'd been on the Las Vegas Monorail before. It ran back and forth between the MGM and the Sahara, stopping occasionally. More and more people were taking it these days, but it was still mostly tourists.

There were enough people so we couldn't sit down, but had to hold on to the silver poles in the middle of the car. It reminded me—sort of—of the New York subway, but it was a tad too clean. I noticed Jeff was checking out a girl standing close to him, long blond tresses, tasteful makeup, a tight red dress that left nothing to the imagination. Was that his type? I looked down at my own jeans and black T-shirt with the skull, my tattoos bleeding down my arms. Couldn't be more different.

Jeff caught me watching him, but instead of looking surprised, he merely winked.

I made a face at him and turned toward the guy next to me, a white kid who had aspirations to be a black rapper, wearing a wife-beater T, jeans hanging precariously around his hips, strands of gold "bling" around his neck. I bet this guy grew up in the white suburbs somewhere, had never been in a 'hood in his life.

He caught me looking at him and a leer crossed his face.

I had to stop paying attention to people. It was safer to be oblivious.

The monorail slowed at the Bally's/Paris stop. I could see the tip of the Eiffel Tower from the window, all lit up like a Christmas tree. I imagined the real thing, and wished I were there, away from all this. Would I be a coward if I left town now?

I felt the slight jolt as the monorail began to move again, and because I'd shifted my feet a little, I fell against the white rapper guy. I felt his hand cup my ass and I jerked away, my face growing hot with anger.

Before I could say anything, Jeff had the guy by the scruff of his shirtfront and had lifted him to his tiptoes.

"That's not a way to treat a lady," he growled in the guy's face, which was now even whiter with fear.

Jeff let him down with a thud, then turned to me and winked, putting his arm around me to herd me a little farther away. It reminded me of the time Tim had come to my rescue when Danny Brody had grabbed me during a game of capture the flag, his hands reaching toward my newly budded breasts.

Let's just say Danny stayed away from me after that.

The monorail slowed again at the MGM stop. Everyone filed out, the white rapper giving Jeff furtive glances as though he were afraid Jeff would come after him again. The girl in the red dress batted her eyelashes at Jeff, and I wondered if they had made an unspoken date.

"Thanks for that back there," I said as we walked from the monorail station to the MGM.

"Guy was out of line."

"It happens," I said.

"Shouldn't."

"You seemed to like that girl."

"What girl?"

"The one in the red dress."

Jeff chuckled. "What are you after, Kavanaugh? Trying to figure out my type?"

I shrugged. "I guess it's just that you've met Colin Bixby, and you knew Simon Chase, too," I said, referring to a casino manager I'd dated several months earlier. "I've never even seen you with a woman."

Jeff's face grew a little dark. He pursed his lips and stared straight ahead. "You knew about Kelly." He was referring to his ex-wife, who had been murdered. He'd wanted kids with her and found out when she died that she'd been pregnant. I'd thought that because he never talked about it, he wasn't still thinking about her. But I guess I was wrong. Hard to get over that sort of thing. Even for Jeff Coleman.

This was getting a little too personal. I was relieved to see we'd reached the entrance to the arena where the Flamingos were playing. I stepped up to the box office and told them my name.

"Melanie Black said she'd have two tickets for me," I said.

The woman barely looked at me, rummaged in a drawer, and produced a small envelope, slipping it out through a slit in the bottom of the glass barrier between us.

I took it and looked around. Didn't see Tim or Flanigan anywhere.

"Let's go in," Jeff said.

"I'm supposed to wait for Tim."

"We're late. He's probably already in there."

Jeff was right. But what was this? He wanted to go in with me?

"You can't stand this kind of music," I said.

He grinned. "Always up for something new."

I hesitated.

"What's wrong?"

Granted, Melanie had left two tickets for me; Tim was nowhere to be found. But I wasn't sure about Jeff. First, because Tim might already be in there, ticket or no, and this wasn't supposed to be a party. Second, Jeff wanting to go to a Flamingos concert was really out of character. Something was up, but I couldn't figure out what.

Jeff leaned toward me and whispered in my ear, "Your brother isn't here to go in with you, Kavanaugh. You've got someone taking pictures of you, accusing you of murdering a client. Accusing you publicly. I am not going to let you go in there alone. There must be thousands of people in there."

And one of them could be my stalker. Okay, I got it.

I handed the envelope to the usher, who fished out the tickets. And something else. He looked at it, then handed it back to me. I glanced at it. A backstage pass.

"Go down to the front and give this to the usher near the steps," he instructed.

I clutched it firmly in my hand as we made our way through throngs of people. At one point, I felt Jeff's hand on the small of my back. At least I hoped it was Jeff's. When we reached the front usher, I showed her the pass. She said something into a little walkie-talkie, then told us: "Hold on a minute."

We stood, jostled by people taking their seats for the concert. Since we were so close to the stage now, I couldn't help but notice the flowers. People had tossed bouquets and stray flowers and stuffed animals up on the stage. It was their way of paying their respects to the Flamingos. Since there was no street corner at which to leave them, the Flamingos' fans had strewn them on the stage, where Daisy was more at home than anywhere.

I felt a sob escape my throat.

"It's not your fault," I heard Jeff whisper in my ear.

I swallowed hard, and before I could answer, a big, burly, black security guard came out of nowhere. The woman usher indicated us. "That's them," she said, but I couldn't hear her because of the noise. I'd read her lips.

He barely looked at us, but a small nod of his head indicated that he might have actually heard her—or he was good at reading lips, too. We followed him up some side steps and around to the back. Before we could reach our destination, Melanie came running out toward us. The security guard stepped back, putting his hand to his ear, where he had a small headphone attached.

"What did you do, Brett?" Melanie demanded as she approached.

I looked at Jeff, then back at her, and shrugged. "What do you mean?"

"The cops. You sent cops over here."

Tim and Flanigan. I nodded. "My brother—" I started, but she put her hand up to stop me.

"They took Sherman out of here in handcuffs."

Chapter 27

herman Potter? In handcuffs? "What are you talking about?" I asked her.

Melanie's eyes flicked to Jeff.

"This is my friend, Jeff Coleman."

Jeff gave her a short nod of acknowledgment, and she looked back to me. "Come on back," she said, leading us through a hall to a door. She pushed it open, and we stepped inside.

The rest of the band—Cara, Tiffany, and Josie—turned around. They'd been facing a long mirror, putting on makeup and primping their hair.

"You actually felt you could show up here?" Tiffany demanded, brushing her long, dark locks that bounced back with a curl.

"I don't know what's going on," I said. "I really don't know what's going on with my brother arresting Sherman Potter."

"He just walked in here and read him his rights and slapped cuffs on him," Josie said. She held two drumsticks and was absently tapping her knees to music inside her head.

"What for?" Jeff asked.

All heads turned toward him, and I noticed they were all assessing him. And then dismissing him. Guess he was too old for them. I'd have to tease him about that later.

"Daisy's murder," Melanie said. "They charged him with Daisy's murder."

"But I thought she died from that tattoo," I said.

Melanie nodded. "That's right. That's what they told us, too. But I guess there were fingerprints or something. I didn't get all of it; Sherman told us to call his lawyer and make sure we went on on time."

The show must go on and all that, I guess.

"Where's Ainsley?" I asked.

I didn't think it was a trick question, but all four girls gave each other a look before Cara spoke up. "She never showed. Sherman kept calling her, but I guess she never picked up. We don't know where she is." Instead of concern, however, I heard relief in her voice. None of these girls wanted to share the stage with a stranger.

"You have to believe me. I had nothing to do with Sherman being arrested," I said.

Tiffany finally put down her hairbrush. "It would be good for you to have someone else arrested, though, wouldn't it?"

She thought I had something to do with Daisy's death. Because of that stupid blog. "Listen, I'm a victim here, too," I tried, noticing Jeff's eyes get a little wider. I'd have to talk to him about that later. I proceeded to tell them about the blog and how I'd been set up. "I had nothing to do with any of that," I concluded.

The four girls exchanged glances, as if deciding whether I was telling the truth. Finally, Cara spoke up.

"Daisy liked you, Brett. She trusted only you to do her tattoos."

I didn't know what to say. I'd been struggling with the same thing ever since I'd heard about Daisy. "This has been bothering me, too," I admitted. "But if Sherman did it, well, she'd trust him, wouldn't she?"

Another look exchanged. This one I couldn't read.

"Daisy was quitting," Josie said, the drumsticks now in her lap, still. "She was going out on her own." Her tone was sharper than cut glass. She wasn't happy with Daisy's decision. And from the look on everyone else's faces, neither were they. But Sherman Potter had someone lined up to take her place already; he'd even been using that as a line to pick up girls at Cleopatra's Barge. I didn't see why he'd have to kill Daisy. It didn't seem he really had a motive. But these girls might.

However, Cara put that idea to rest.

"I already told everyone else tonight, after they took Sherman away, that he threatened Daisy."

"Threatened her how?" I asked.

"She told me he said he was going to take her for everything she had. That he'd get her on breach of contract. She came out here early to tell him to go ahead—she was done as of right then."

So maybe Daisy had confronted Sherman Potter in that room at the Golden Palace. The one that was registered to Ainsley Wainwright. And then he'd killed her and moved to the Venetian. Ainsley, his new lead singer, must have been there, too, since she was probably the woman who the police had thought was me at first.

But how did Daisy end up being tattooed? The scenario made sense until that point.

"Did you ask Sherman about that? Did Daisy confront him?" I asked.

Melanie nodded. "We talked to Sherman not long before your brother showed up. He said he didn't threaten her, and he never saw Daisy that day. He'd been tracking down gigs for us."

"He said we didn't need her," Cara added. "That she was overshadowing us."

And it would give him a way to get his lover into the band.

"Did any of you tell my brother any of this? What Daisy told you about Sherman?" I asked, my eyes skipping from one face to the next. They all shook their heads.

"He's our manager," Josie said. "We need him."

"You need to tell my brother what you know," I said. "What if Daisy was right? You're taking his word against hers, and the Daisy I knew wasn't a liar. You can always get another manager."

None of them looked as though they believed me.

"She *was* going to quit," Josie said quietly, and by pointing out Daisy's betrayal, I could see how hurt they were. How Daisy would never be able to make it right with them.

The big security guard stuck his head in the door. "Five," he said, then disappeared.

I thought about Ainsley the blogger. Also dead. And I remembered what Tim had asked me.

"What's Ainsley's last name?" I asked.

They all looked at me as if I had three heads, but Cara said, "Wainwright. Her name is Ainsley Wainwright."

I couldn't breathe for a second. Okay, so that could not be a coincidence. And it probably wasn't a coincidence that Ainsley was conveniently missing the same day another Ainsley Wainwright was found dead in her apartment across town. Since blogger Ainsley was dead, it only figured that Sherman's Ainsley had taken her identity for some reason. But when had she taken it? Sherman Potter seemed like he'd known her longer than just a day or so, which was how long the blogger had been dead.

I needed to let Tim know what was going on, what these girls had said about Daisy and Sherman, and about Ainsley Wainwright.

Before I could take my cell phone out of my bag, though, yet another burly security guard stepped into the room and nodded at the girls. They all shuffled to their feet, Josie's drumsticks now tapping the air.

"We'll talk after," Melanie promised as they left the room.

Jeff and I stared at each other a second before that first security guard came back in. "I can take you to your seats," he said gruffly.

"I need to make a call first," I said, now pulling my phone out and punching in Tim's number. The guard didn't look all that happy with me.

"You can't stay in here," he argued.

I shrugged at Jeff, my phone to my ear, as we allowed ourselves to be herded out. It was louder out here, though, the music blasting, and I could barely hear the phone ringing. We turned a corner, and I thought I saw someone familiar up head. Familiar in that she was a tall redhead. Walking very briskly away from us, so I only saw her back.

I dropped my phone from my ear and cocked my head toward her, asking Jeff, "Look familiar?"

He didn't seem to hear me, since he was one step ahead of me, sprinting forward, but he didn't get too far before the security guard stepped in front of him.

"Can't go down there."

If looks could kill, the guard would be so dead. But he was a lot bigger than Jeff, and it seemed that he clearly meant to keep him from going farther. Jeff's mouth set in a grim line, his fists clenched, but he didn't try to get past the guy.

The security guard flicked his wrist, to indicate we were to follow him. The sounds of the arena faded as we went through a side door and down a long hallway. We hadn't come up this way, and it seemed that he was purposely leading us away from the woman we'd seen.

I felt like I was living that scene in *This Is Spinal Tap*

where the band was wandering around not able to find
the stage.

Just when I thought we would never see any other
human being again, we turned a corner and the security
guard pushed open a door.

And shoved us out into the night, slamming the door
shut behind us.

Chapter 28

Jeff and I stared at each other.

"What's up with this?" I asked, trying to pull the door open again. It was locked tight.

"It was her," Jeff said.

I knew whom he meant. The woman he'd met who'd been impersonating me. But I didn't think so. Ainsley Wainwright was supposed to sing tonight. Her debut as a Flamingo. But why would she be lurking around the arena rather than out on stage with the rest of the band? Maybe she'd shown up while Jeff and I were talking to everyone. It would make sense that she'd run from us; she probably recognized me. She probably managed to get the security guard to make sure we wouldn't see her. Having met her, I could see how she'd be able to do that. I'd seen how she behaved with Harry. She was a vixen, that one.

I put my phone back to my ear. I'd lost the call, but I redialed. It was quiet out here, so I could actually hear.

No answer.

I tossed the phone back in my bag. Jeff was surveying the door, his expression blank.

I checked out where we were: in a back parking lot. A Hummer limousine sat about fifty yards away. A chain-link fence surrounded the whole lot, probably to keep the riffraff out. Since we were on this side of the fence, I'd like to consider us anything but riffraff.

But then I saw the riffraff. And heard them. There must have been twenty or thirty of them. Young girls and guys, having a sort of tailgate party just beyond the fence. A portable iPod speaker blasted music—the Flamingos—into the still night; they danced with their arms high in the air, hands holding beer bottles that sloshed liquid as they moved. Stuck in the ground were five plastic pink flamingos, dressed up with Hawaiian leis and pink boas. One even wore a rhinestone tiara.

Fans. Who probably couldn't get tickets to the concert so they were hanging out back here, waiting for it to be over and for a possible glimpse of their favorite band as they headed to the limo.

Jeff didn't pay any attention to them as he started toward the limo.

"Where are you going?" I asked after him.

He shook his head and continued walking. I jogged to catch up with him.

"Aren't we going to try to get back in?" I asked.

He shrugged me off as we reached the limo. He knocked on the driver's side window. It came down a few inches. A pair of eyes stared out at us.

"I can't help you," a disembodied voice said ominously.

"We need to get back inside," Jeff said.

"Yeah, they all say that." His eyes flicked to the right, toward the party that was going on.

I didn't want to be mixed up in the company of those kids. And I was willing to bet Jeff really didn't want to be mistaken for a crazy Flamingo fan, either. Although if they were really fans, they would've gotten themselves tickets one way or another. I had not been above sleeping overnight on the sidewalk for a Springsteen ticket.

I shook off the thoughts. We needed to get back inside. Someone didn't want us in there for some reason, and I wanted to find out why.

Jeff was talking to the limo driver, who had let the window down another couple of inches but not enough to show his entire face yet.

"Just give them a call and say you've got trouble back here," Jeff said. He cocked his head toward the groupies outside the fence. "Maybe you could insinuate that they're storming the limo."

I could tell the guy wasn't quite sure what "insinuate" meant.

"Hey!"

The shout came from the party. Jeff and I turned to see a girl in a tight shirt and even tighter jeans holding up a camera. The flash blinded me for a second, giving me a panic attack as I thought about the flashes that had gone off the night before when I was out with Harry. If they were taking pictures, would those end up on a blog, too?

Jeff touched my arm. "It's okay, Kavanaugh. It's just a bunch of kids," he said softly.

I'd tried not to react outwardly, but I guess I was more jumpy than I'd thought.

"It's her!" This shout came from another one of the kids, a pimply, white teenager who was dressed like a wannabe rapper, like the kid on the monorail earlier.

What did he mean: It's her?

I had a bad feeling about this.

"You killed her!"

Every muscle in my body was so tight I felt like I would snap in half. They'd seen the blog. Or blogs. The ones that had me pinned as Daisy's murderer.

The limo door started to open now, and I saw a foot clad in a black patent leather shoe emerge.

"I thought you looked familiar," the limo driver said as his whole body materialized. He was tall, muscular, his fists clenched in tight balls, his jaw set firmly as his eyes narrowed at me.

I glanced around for an escape, but there didn't seem to be one. That chain-link fence surrounded us, no discernible exit. The door to the arena was still shut and locked. The fence provided a barrier between us and those kids, but this limo driver looked like he wanted a piece of me.

Jeff got in between us, shielding me.

"She's not who you think she is," he tried.

The limo driver was not to be deterred. "That's her," he said, taking another step toward us.

The kids began to chant, "Get her, get her, get her."

My heart began to pound so loudly, their voices faded. I felt dizzy, and I reached out toward Jeff to balance myself, but he brushed me off and took a step toward the limo driver, who took a swing at him.

Before I could blink, Jeff had slung the guy over his shoulder like a bag of potatoes and slammed him into the hard pavement.

The guy landed with a thud, the wind knocked out of him, his eyes circling the sky as if they didn't have a place to land.

I suppressed an urge to give Jeff a high five. He was looking down at the guy, whose feet were twitching, and then he looked up at me. "We've got to get out of here," he said, his tone urgent. His eyes moved toward the fence.

The kids were scaling it, screaming now that we were murderers. They clearly hadn't heard that the police had arrested Sherman Potter, and with this limo driver limp on the ground, they probably thought we were serial killers.

Weren't there any security guards around here? I mean, it was the MGM's arena. You'd think there would be some sort of security. I guess they figured they wouldn't need it because the door was locked and the celebrities were inside.

Sadly, though, I had become a celebrity, too, it seemed. But for the wrong reasons.

"Come on, Kavanaugh!" Jeff yanked open the door to the limo. The driver was starting to get up.

I ran around the front of the limo and opened the passenger side. I knew what Jeff was going to do, and while I wasn't sure I liked it, I didn't think we had much choice. The first kid had already landed on this side of the fence, and he was waving a pink flamingo. The one with the tiara. The kid behind him had a broken beer bottle.

Okay, time to leave.

Jeff turned over the engine and put his foot to the accelerator.

"Strap yourself in!" he shouted.

I struggled for a second with the seat belt as I watched the fence come up fast. I'd just latched the belt when I felt the impact of the Hummer against the fence. But because of its size, the limo sailed right through.

Jeff drove the Hummer along the long driveway that spit us out onto Koval Lane at Tropicana. His hands relaxed on the steering wheel as we sat at the light.

"You do know that we stick out like a sore thumb?" I asked. "Hummer limo carjacked by tattooed killer. It'll be all over the papers tomorrow. While we're sitting in jail."

"You're so pessimistic, Kavanaugh," Jeff said, and the way he said it meant he had a plan.

When the light changed, the Hummer veered right. That's when I heard the sirens.

"How are we going to dump this thing and not be seen?" I asked.

It seemed like a logical question, but Jeff just grunted something that vaguely sounded like "Trust me."

The Hummer went through the next set of lights and we turned left. And into the driveway at Excalibur.

Chapter 29

Excalibur is one of the Strip's oldest resort casinos, built like a castle, but a really fake one. It didn't even pretend to look like a real one, just a cartoon version of a castle, the kind of castle Ace would paint. It was a place to go if you wanted a cheap room or if you had a family, because kids loved the place.

"Get out," Jeff said when the valet came over. Jeff shoved the keys in the guy's hand, came around to my side, and shuffled me off into the resort.

"You're just leaving it here?" I asked.

"Why not?"

We went up the escalator to the next level. It was more fake castle in here, with fake stonework and fake balconies. A kiosk selling kitschy souvenirs was at the top of the escalators. They had a restaurant here that was supposed to be like Henry VIII's court, where you ate big turkey legs and pounded on the table for more mead. I hoped Jeff didn't want to have dinner. I didn't think I could deal with that right now.

Instead, however, he was leading me outside and toward the monorail that ran between Excalibur, the Luxor, which was shaped like an Egyptian pyramid, and Mandalay Bay, whose gold tower shimmered over the Strip. I hoped we weren't going to the Luxor, because that place creeped me out even more than Excalibur. It was way too dark inside.

"Where are we going?" I asked when the monorail began to move.

Jeff wasn't paying attention. He was leaning over me, looking down at the Hummer in the driveway at the Excalibur. It was surrounded by three police cars.

"They're going to know it was us," I said. "I mean, those kids can identify me. So can the driver. We might as well give ourselves up." Easy to say when we were gliding along the rail, passing the Luxor—much to my relief—and on toward Mandalay Bay.

"When we're having dinner, you can call your brother," Jeff said. "Explain."

I frowned. Dinner?

"I'm hungry, and I'm glad we're not at that concert." Jeff stood up as the monorail slid into the station.

The doors opened, and I followed Jeff out.

We walked down the stairs and toward the casino. As we turned another corner, a glassed-in shop distracted us. It was a tattoo shop.

"Do you know them?" I asked Jeff. I had met the owner once.

Jeff nodded, then put his arm around me to steer me away. "We don't have time to stop in."

I hadn't really wanted to "stop in." If we did, we'd have to pretend that we were out like everyone else, that we hadn't stolen a Hummer limo and abandoned it in front of Excalibur. We'd have to make small talk—oh, yes, business is quite good, how's yours—and it would be way too much effort.

No, it was better we were winding our way through the casino toward the restaurants and shops.

Jeff stopped at one of the restaurant entrances, but when I looked into yet another dark hallway, I pulled back and shook my head. "I don't think so."

"Trust me," he said for the second time that night and led me to a staircase leading down.

We were pretty high up, and to our right was what looked like a wine cellar encased in glass that stretched from the high ceiling down two stories to the bottom floor. A woman who looked remarkably like a Bond girl, wearing some sort of rappelling equipment, was scaling the glass wall as she held a bottle of wine.

"They're known for that here," Jeff said as if he saw that sort of thing every day.

When we reached the bottom of the stairs, the hostess—a tall, painfully thin woman wearing a little slip of a dress—surveyed us with pursed lips.

"I'm afraid we don't have any tables available," she said haughtily.

I took a glance around. I saw three tables that were vacant. It was most likely our jeans and tattoos that were turning her off.

Jeff wasn't about to be turned away, however.

"Tell the chef Jeff Coleman is here," he snapped.

She stood there, uncertain what to do.

"Now," Jeff growled.

She scurried off.

"Do you really know the chef?" I asked, impressed. If I'd been alone or with anyone else, I would've been back climbing those stairs and looking for another place to eat.

"Did all his tattoos," Jeff said flatly.

We watched the woman rappelling down the wine case until we heard the hostess's heels clicking on the wood floor, a fake smile spread across her face now.

"Mr. Coleman, we have a table ready right over here," she said, picking up two menus and leading the way. When we were seated, she said in a tight voice, "Richard will be out shortly." The chef, I guess.

I realized I was famished. So I didn't get to see the

Flamingos, but this was much better. My mouth watered as I perused the menu.

Jeff reached over and took it out of my hands before I was finished, though.

"Hey!"

He put the menus down. "I know what you'll like."

"Really?" I asked, my back up.

He chucked. "Really," he said. "You know, Kavanaugh, you need to lighten up."

"I've got mobs chasing me, wanting my head for something I didn't do," I said grumpily. "I think I can be wound a little tight."

"Which is why we need some wine."

The waiter hovered, and Jeff ordered an Australian Malbec and a French chardonnay. And then he said, "The chef knows what I want." The waiter nodded and shuffled off.

"I thought you didn't like wine," I said, still a little snippy but not quite as much.

"It's got its place," he said. "Now you need to call Tim and tell him what happened."

Obediently, I pulled out my phone. The hostess gave me a dirty look. "Maybe I should take it outside," I said, scrambling to my feet and spotting an elevator. Much better than those stairs. "I'll be right back."

I left him just as the waiter came with the wine. Watching Jeff Coleman taste wine was an image I figured I could live without. Too sophisticated, somehow.

Once I emerged from the elevator, I stood in the little alcove and punched in Tim's number. This time he did pick up.

"You stole a Hummer?" he asked loudly, incredulously.

"A Hummer limo," I corrected.

"What's wrong with you?"

I told him about the mob of people coming after me. The broken beer bottle. The limo driver who lunged at

me, and how Jeff had flipped him. I told him about the
security guard locking us out after we'd seen a tall redhead. I went through the story backward, until I got to
the beginning.

"You arrested Sherman Potter?" I asked. "So he really did it?"

"Where are you now?" he asked, totally ignoring me.

"Having dinner with Jeff."

"So you steal a Hummer—excuse me, Hummer
limo—and leave it at the Excalibur and then go out to
dinner? You're not having that medieval meal, are you?"

"No. We were hungry. What's this about Sherman
Potter? He killed her, right? Tell me that it'll be in
the papers and no one will come after me again about
Daisy." I really needed this to be over.

"We found his fingerprints at the scene."

I smiled. Outwardly. A woman walking by smiled
back. Maybe I'd be able to have a nice dinner after all.

"Problem is, Brett, the limo driver wants to press
charges against you and Jeff. It would be better if you
came in now and we could settle this."

Chapter 30

I didn't want to. Turn myself in, that is. And I was pretty sure I could speak for Jeff, too.

"He came after me," I said. "Those kids can tell you that."

"They said you went after him."

"You talked to them?"

"We got statements, yes. The limo driver called 911 immediately."

This wasn't good.

"If we come in, do you think we'll get thrown in the slammer or will we be able to walk out after giving our own statements?" I asked.

"Thrown in the slammer?" I could hear the amusement in Tim's voice. "Brett, if you and Jeff come in now, we can see if we can smooth this out."

"Can we have dinner first?" I asked. "I mean, I'm not sure I'm going to be able to get Jeff to agree to this so easily."

"Get a doggie bag, Brett, and get over here."

I closed my phone as I made my way back down the stairs, eschewing the elevator for a little more time to think about how to get Jeff out of here and over to the station. When I reached the table, the chef was sitting with Jeff, a plate full of assorted appetizers in front of them. Both looked up, smiling, when I approached. Jeff's smile faded when he saw my expression.

I didn't want to say anything in front of the chef, so I shook his hand and listened to his description of the appetizers. When he came to the foie gras, I pushed Tim's admonishing voice out of my head and reached for it, savoring its smoothness and washing it down with a little Malbec. Jeff watched me with a touch of a smile at the corner of his lips. I made a face at him and finished the foie gras, noticing that he'd already had a piece.

When the chef went on to make his rounds among the other diners, I leaned forward and whispered, "We have to go to the police station."

"Why?"

I told him about the limo driver. "Tim seems to think that we can settle this quickly, if we go right now."

Jeff indicated the appetizers. "But we've just started dinner."

"I tried that excuse, but he wasn't buying it."

He leaned back in his chair and studied me a second. "I'll meet you there, if you really want to go now."

There was no use in trying to talk to him about this. I'd told Tim.

"Dinner could be at least two hours," I said, aware that my resolve had lost a lot of steam. "I really don't want to end up getting arrested or anything."

Jeff grinned. "Your brother is an LVPD detective. You really think you'll get arrested?"

I felt my face flush as anger rose in my chest. "You think that's some sort of GET OUT OF JAIL FREE card? Having a detective for a brother? He'd be so quick to throw me in jail, you have no idea."

Jeff's eyes settled on my face, and I squirmed a little. Then he said, "Okay." He motioned for the waiter. "Can you wrap up our meals for us? We have to go. Please tell the chef we're sorry."

The waiter looked a little flustered, but scurried off.

"Thanks," I said softly.

"You'll thank me when you can finally eat your dinner," he said.

We only waited a few minutes before the waiter came out carrying fancy to-go bags tied with ribbons. They looked like Christmas packages, not a five-star meal. I poured myself another quick glass of Malbec and downed it. Jeff grinned. "We could take that, too."

Vegas, home of the open container.

We left the bottles on the table. Somehow showing up at police headquarters with open bottles of wine didn't really seem like the right thing to do.

Once we reached Mandalay Bay's entrance, we realized something. We didn't have a car. Sure, we could take the monorail back to the Excalibur, walk the footbridge over Tropicana Boulevard to New York New York, walk the other footbridge to the MGM, then take the monorail from there up to Harrah's and fetch Jeff's car from the Venetian valet, but it would probably take us longer to do that than it would've to finish our dinner.

So we had the doorman get us a cab.

I was reminded a little of last night, when Harry and I had gotten that cab, and that flash going off. But there were no flashes tonight, I was with Jeff Coleman, we weren't drunk on absinthe, and I was pretty sure he was going to keep his hands to himself.

He was looking at me with an amused smile. "Taking a trip down memory lane, Kavanaugh?"

I wished he couldn't read my mind quite so well.

The bags with the food were tucked at our feet, the smell wafting up. That piece of foie gras hadn't been enough. My stomach growled, and Jeff reached over and pulled out a container, opening it to reveal perfectly cooked rack of lamb. He pulled one out by its bone and handed it to me.

"Bon appetit."

We munched on the lamb.

"Your friend's a great cook," I said, my mouth half full.

"I know."

The police station came up a lot faster than I expected. The cabdriver, to his credit, made no comment about our destination or the fact that we were having a gourmet meal in the back. We shoved the empty container back in the fancy bag and scrambled out; Jeff handed the cabbie some money. I tried to pay him for my half, but he waved me off.

"Don't worry about it."

"But I didn't pay for dinner, either," I said, realizing then that I hadn't seen a check come to the table.

"Don't worry about it," he said again, pushing the door to the station open and letting me go through first.

Once we identified ourselves, we were led upstairs by a uniformed cop. He'd done a quick double take when he saw me—Tim and I were virtual carbon copies of each other—but then basically ignored me.

Tim was waiting in an interrogation room. His eyebrows rose high in his forehead when he saw the bags. Jeff put them on the stainless steel table and opened them, taking out one of the plastic containers.

"Steak?" he asked, lifting the top off.

The scent of charred meat drifted into the air, and my stomach growled again, despite the rack of lamb. Tim's stomach didn't growl, but he looked longingly at the steak.

"Maybe later," he said, having much more self control than I did.

Jeff sat, pulled out a plastic fork and knife, and began to cut up the steak and eat it as though we weren't in a police department interrogation room but back at that fancy restaurant. Tim looked at me, and I shrugged.

I wasn't Jeff Coleman's keeper, regardless of what Tim thought.

"So what's going on with that limo driver?" I asked. "Is he really pressing charges?"

"He says Jeff assaulted him."

Jeff kept on eating.

"Only after the guy started coming after me," I said, recounting the scene, explaining how the driver had said I was a murderer.

Something in Tim's expression made me take pause.

"Have you been on a computer since I talked to you on the phone?"

I frowned. "What, are you kidding me? I was at the restaurant. Jeff and I caught a cab and came over here. Why would you think I was on a computer?"

Tim sighed. "Someone posted on that Ink Flamingos blog. The one that you're supposedly writing."

I caught my breath. This was not going to be good.

"It said you're going to get away with murder, because you planted Sherman Potter's fingerprints at the scene."

Chapter 31

It was possible that whoever was impersonating me actually *had* planted those fingerprints. But it certainly wasn't me. I said as much to Tim.

"I know that, but it throws a wrench into everything. Because now Potter's lawyer is shouting about how he was framed, and this blogger is saying she did it, and now he's demanding that Potter be released immediately because he's falsely accused."

"The fingerprints are his, though, right?"

Tim nodded. "But that doesn't matter. There's someone out there implying that he *was* framed."

And that someone was me. Or someone posing as me.

I started to worry that I was going to end up arrested for all this. "Am I in trouble, Tim?" I asked, my voice so soft I could barely hear it myself.

Jeff's head shot up, and he put down his fork. The steak was history.

"She was with me the whole time," he told Tim. "She didn't post anything on any blog."

Tim nodded. "I know that. But it's possible Potter will get released based on that."

"So we'll have the real murderer wandering around," I muttered, "but everyone will still think it's me." I had another thought. "Do you think Potter has an accomplice? Someone who posted that blog while he was in here just so he *could* get out?"

Tim ran a hand through his hair, exasperated. "It's possible. Or whoever's writing that blog really is the murderer and is setting Potter up."

"Can't you trace that blog back to whoever is posting?" Jeff asked.

"I'm not a computer guy," Tim said. "But we've got people on it."

Which basically meant: I have no idea. That was not reassuring. At least, though, I didn't seem to be a suspect, but I didn't like that someone was out there, impersonating me.

Which reminded me . . .

"What about Ainsley Wainwright?" I asked.

"She's dead, Brett," Tim reminded me.

I made a face at him. "I know that, but this new lead singer for the Flamingos, well, the band told me her last name is Wainwright, too. And I'm almost positive I saw her at the arena. She's a redhead, too. What if she's the one posting on the blog? What if she picked up the slack for the dead Ainsley Wainwright?"

"You saw her?"

I closed my eyes and could see the red hair. "Yes," I said, although I wasn't a hundred percent sure.

"Potter said he hasn't seen her since this morning. Said she never showed for the concert tonight."

"That's right. That's what the girls said, too. But then when we were leaving, I'm pretty sure I saw her. And then that security guard led us outside and shut the door behind us." The more I thought about it, the more I thought it had to have been Ainsley. And she was probably in on it with Potter. She'd been on intimate terms with him. Which made me think of something else. I quickly told him about what the girls in the band had told us, how Sherman Potter had threatened to take

Daisy for all she was worth and how Daisy had come out here early because she was going to confront Sherman about that.

Tim was jotting it all down in a little notebook. Jeff was strangely quiet, just listening and watching. The food containers were packed neatly into the bags again.

A small knock sounded. Tim reached over and pulled the door open to let Detective Kevin Flanigan in. Flanigan nodded at Jeff and me and indicated he wanted to talk to Tim. Outside. Out of earshot.

They left the room and shut the door behind them. Jeff leaned back in his chair and swung his legs up on top of the table, like he owned the place.

"I saw her, too," he said.

That's right. He'd said so earlier.

"Why didn't you say anything to Tim? Back me up?" I asked.

"Because you wouldn't shut up," he said, a smile tugging at the corner of his mouth.

I made a face at him. "You could've interrupted. It's not like you haven't done that before."

"You are so easy to get to," he said, chuckling.

Tim and Flanigan came back in, saving me from having to say something I might regret.

"You're free to go," Flanigan said.

"The limo driver won't press charges?" I asked.

"No, but you'd better get out of here before he changes his mind."

Jeff pushed his seat back and stood up. I started for the door, then turned around. "We don't have a car. We took a cab over here. Our cars are at the Venetian."

Flanigan nodded at Tim, who said, "Okay, I'll take you over there. I'm off shift anyway." From the way he said it, I wasn't so sure about that. I remembered how Flanigan wanted me to keep my ear to the ground. Tim could grill me further at home. I was tired, though, so he wouldn't get too much out of me. Not that I knew anything more anyway.

I was so exhausted I nodded off in the car. Jeff nudged me a little when we got to the Venetian, and I realized my car was up in the garage and it was late and I didn't want to go up there alone. Tim was one step ahead of me.

"I'll take you up to your car, and you can follow me home," he said.

Jeff took his packages, even though I didn't think there was any food left, and got out of the car. He leaned in the window and said, "I'll check in with you tomorrow," and went off to find the valet who'd bring him his car.

Even though the food was gone, the scent lingered. My stomach growled.

"Jeff ate all our food," I muttered as Tim drove his Jeep into the self-parking garage. "Fourth level," I directed.

It was after midnight now, but there were still plenty of cars in the garage. They probably belonged to the gamblers who were trying their hands at the tables and slot machines. I spotted my red Mustang Bullitt up ahead. I'd been a little leery of driving the car after I found the body of Jeff Coleman's half brother in the trunk. But my love for my car superseded any creepy feeling I might have—that, and the fact that I didn't want to spend any money on a new car right now. Unbeknownst to Tim, I was trying to save up for my own place.

I'd been living with him for two years now, and I'd started to think that it was time. Time to grow up and be a little more independent. I'd been checking out condos and townhouses up in Summerlin near Red Rock Canyon; if I were going to live anywhere, it would have to be at the foot of those magnificent mountains. But so far, I hadn't told anyone of my plans. My mother would say it was silly—why not just stay with my brother, unless I was going to get married. Tim would get those little lines next to his eyes as he stressed out about how he'd pay the mortgage. But I knew something. I knew that he really didn't need me to help with that. He was just being cheap. Jeff would say something smart-alecky, and I didn't want to deal with him. Bitsy and Joel, well, I should tell them, but I was settled into the idea of just doing it and then springing it on everyone like a surprise.

Our neighborhood was dark and quiet when we pulled into the street. The front of the house was a gray shadow. When we turned into the driveway, the headlights illuminated the banana yuccas in the front near the door.

The garage door was gaping open.

Tim slammed his brakes on, and I was glad I wasn't following too closely. I watched him scramble out of the Jeep. I was close on his heels.

We stood, looking into the garage, but nothing looked out of place, and I didn't notice anything missing. We exchanged a look, and Tim motioned with his hand that I should stay behind him as he pulled his gun out of his hip holster and crept toward the door that led into the house.

I noticed now that that door was open, too. He put out his hand and mouthed, "Stay here." I didn't much like the idea of staying in the open, dark garage, but I could see his point. So I stayed as he disappeared into the house.

A few minutes later, I saw the lights flicker on and heard Tim's voice as he spoke into the phone. I scurried into the house, which didn't look any the worse for wear. Maybe whoever had broken in had heard us drive up and took off before taking anything. I started toward the back of the house and my bedroom, but Tim actually reached out and took my arm, keeping me from going farther. He hung up the phone.

"Don't go down there."

I didn't like the sound of that. "What's wrong down there?" I asked, my voice sounding as though I were talking in a tunnel.

"You can't go down there," Tim said, his jaw tight.

I broke away from him and ran down the hall. I stood in the doorway to my bedroom and felt my chest constrict. A plastic pink flamingo sat on top of my bed, which was splashed with what looked like blood.

Chapter 32

It's red paint, Brett," Tim said, but it was cold comfort. Moving out had totally seemed like a great idea, but now the thought of living alone scared the daylights out of me.

"Who would do this?" I asked, staring at the flamingo, which wore a rhinestone tiara. That looked familiar. "Those kids. At the arena. They had one of those, with a tiara on it," I whispered.

Tim's head was bobbing up and down. "Okay, good, that's good to know. We got their names and statements about what happened over there, so maybe we can track this down."

Hated to play devil's advocate here, but it struck me: "What if the one who did this left? Left before giving a statement?"

For a split second, I saw something cross his face that indicated he'd had the same thought, but then his expression shifted into neutral.

"We'll get him," he said simply as he put his phone to his ear and went back to the living room.

I couldn't stop looking at it. But I couldn't go any farther than the doorway. No way was I going in there. Not even to make sure it was red paint and not blood. And not only because the cops would be coming in here to dust for prints and do all that stuff cops do when investigating a crime scene.

Tim reappeared at my side and I jumped.

"Sorry," he said. "How about calling Bitsy and seeing if you can crash over there tonight?"

Best idea he'd had in ages. "Don't you need me to make a statement or something?"

He shook his head. "No. I think you'd better go somewhere safe."

His tone made me take pause. Somewhere safe? As though I wasn't safe here, in my own house? He was back on the phone now, disappearing again. It was like a bad magic trick.

I took a deep breath and pulled my bag around my shoulder, where it still hung. I stuck my hand in, finding my phone and flipping it open.

"What's wrong?" Bitsy sounded like she was wide awake, thank goodness. I hadn't wanted to wake her.

I told her what happened. "Tim wondered if you couldn't put me up for the night," I said.

"No problem, no problem. Are you coming now?"

I realized I didn't want to drive. I didn't want to get in my car and drive over there. Because whoever had done this could follow me, like that person who posted those pictures on the blog had followed me.

"Yes, as soon as I can," I said, figuring I'd ask Tim if he could get me a police escort. I hung up and found him putting his phone on the table in the kitchen. The sound of sirens echoed in the distance.

"My ride?" I asked, trying to joke, but not really succeeding.

He came over and put his arm around me, pulling me to him and hugging me tight. "I'm sorry," he whispered. "We'll get him, whoever he is."

I knew he would. This was his house, too, which meant

even though I was the one with the red paint on my bed, this was personal for him, too.

"Coleman's coming to bring you to Bitsy's," he said when he pulled away. "I would take you, but I need to be here."

Jeff? "But he went home," I said.

"Don't worry about it," Tim said. "He's glad to do it."

I settled into the Pontiac and strapped the seat belt around me. Jeff hadn't said much, even though Tim showed him the mess in my bedroom. I watched his profile as he pulled out of the driveway.

"You'll have to tell me where she lives," he said.

Bitsy's condo was down past the university. I gave him the address, and we drove in silence. I tried not to think about what was going on, but it was swirling in my head, threatening to turn me into a crazy person.

"You're not okay, are you?" Jeff asked, breaking the silence.

I shook my head. "Not really." I had another thought. "How did he know where I live?" My heart started to beat faster.

Jeff was watching me out of the corner of his eye as he drove. "You should take a few days off. Maybe get out of town."

I didn't want to run away. I didn't want to abandon my business to my employees who pulled more than their own weight. I couldn't look like a coward. Even though it was an incredibly appealing idea at the moment.

I heard him chuckle. "I guess that would be too much to ask of you," he said, reading my mind.

I didn't really want to talk anymore. I wanted to get to Bitsy's and see if I could sleep a little.

Once we got there, Joel was hovering in the doorway to welcome me. He pulled me into a big bear hug before

I could even say hello. When he finally stepped back, he grinned. "We're going to have a sleepover."

I appreciated the thought. That my friends were here for me. But it wouldn't make everything go away.

Jeff dropped the small overnight bag that Tim had packed for me on the floor. Bitsy picked it up and disappeared down the hall. Joel looked from me to Jeff, then mumbled something about a glass of wine and went toward the kitchen. Jeff and I stood, facing each other, that weird awkwardness back.

"You're in good hands," Jeff said.

Why was everyone treating me like I was some sort of china objet d'art that would crash to the ground and break into tiny pieces?

Oh, right. Because that's the way I felt.

I took a deep breath and tried a smile on for size. I'm not sure it worked, because Jeff took a step closer, his expression unreadable. I wanted him to crack a joke, call me by my last name, tell me to stop being so serious all the time.

Anything except what he did next.

He kissed me. Right there. Right in Bitsy's hallway.

His lips were warm and soft and nothing like I ever would've imagined, if I'd ever imagined something like this happening. I closed my eyes and felt his hands settle gently around my waist, pulling me closer.

I let him.

I kissed him back.

I'm not exactly sure why. Maybe it was the surprise of it all. Maybe it was because it felt good. Because he made me feel safe.

Slowly the kiss changed; it became a little more urgent, more passionate, and I felt myself slipping away, losing myself in it.

When he finally pulled away, I couldn't catch my breath. But in a really good way. I opened my eyes, almost surprised to see it had been Jeff Coleman who'd made me feel that kiss in all the right places, all the way to my toes. He stepped away, the familiar grin back. "See ya, Kavanaugh," he said jovially, as if that kiss had never happened. As if it was somehow all mixed up in my head with the flamingo with the tiara on it, two things that were just too weird to even be based in reality.

And then he went through the door and was gone.

I stood there for a few minutes, not quite sure what to think.

Bitsy, however, was not at such a loss.

"It's about time," she said flatly, seemingly appearing out of nowhere. "Come on. Joel's got the wine poured."

If I hadn't been a total mess before that kiss, now I really was. Because I couldn't make sense out of it. I allowed myself to be led into the living room and given a glass of red wine. I hardly tasted it.

Bitsy noticed.

"Don't get nuts about this, Brett," she said. "I mean, we've all known for a long time how you two felt about each other."

I finally found my voice. "But how do we feel? I mean, we're friends. This isn't right. Why did he do that?"

"Because the man's been in love with you since the get-go, that's why," Joel spoke up. "You've just been too stupid to notice."

Stupid. Yes, because I still didn't buy it. "He just wanted to distract me," I tried. "From everything that's been going on." I remembered how he'd said he wouldn't have sat around and let a woman he was interested in go out with other men. This was a ruse. It had to be.

Bitsy's phone rang, and she picked up the handset off the coffee table. "Hello? Oh, hi, Tim." She listened for a few minutes, then put the phone down and reached for a laptop on the side table.

"What's up?" Joel asked, replenishing everyone's wine.

She shook her head and pointed to the screen. It was Ink Flamingos again. I looked away. I didn't want to see anything else.

Joel caught his breath, and curiosity took over. I leaned in and took a peek.

Another picture. This time it was of the flamingo on my bed.

Chapter 33

"**O**kay, so we know that whoever took this picture and is posting on this blog is the one who put that flamingo there," Bitsy said.

"But who is it?" Joel asked. "Who could get into their house?"

That was a question that had been swirling around in my head since I'd seen the garage door open. The only person I knew who'd ever broken into our house was Jeff. But it couldn't be Jeff. Could it?

I hadn't realized I'd spoken out loud.

Bitsy and Joel frowned.

"Jeff wouldn't do that," Joel said.

"I didn't think he'd ever kiss me, either," I said.

"It's stupid to even think it," Bitsy said, taking a sip of her wine. "No, it's someone who's close, though."

"Why is someone trying to scare me? Why is someone trying to pin Daisy's murder on me?" I asked.

As I spoke, I realized that those were the key questions. If we could figure out who had it in for me, then we'd have our murderer. At least I'd hope so. Problem was, I didn't think I'd made anyone angry enough so they'd try to frame me like this. Except maybe Tim. But he wouldn't do it. He was my brother. And a cop.

As I started thinking about people close to me, I disregarded Bitsy and Joel, who were sitting here with me, Bitsy now unwrapping a hunk of cheese and putting out crackers.

What about Ace? Which reminded me . . .

"You guys know Ace is moonlighting?" I asked.

"Doing what?" Joel asked.

"Tattoo parties, I think."

"Why would he do that?" Joel asked, slicing off some cheese and sticking it on a cracker. So much for his diet. I thought about the cheese and crackers we'd had earlier at the shop and felt guilty for enabling him.

"What are you talking about, Brett?" Bitsy asked, pouring more wine.

I told them how I'd seen Ace meet up with Harry, and he'd had his case with him.

"But why would you think he's doing parties?" Joel asked.

I'd forgotten to tell them what Jeff found out. "Harry does tattoo parties. He's not completely unemployed, like he's told us."

Bitsy and Joel frowned.

"You mean, he's been lying to us?" Bitsy asked.

I nodded. "Seems that way. I noticed he had a lot of money on him last night when we were out, and Jeff asked around, found out."

"He's a tattooist?" Joel asked, incredulous.

I told them Harry's history with Jeff. "But I didn't realize Ace knew, and clearly he didn't tell either of you, either," I finished.

We all mulled that a few minutes as we ate our cheese and drank our wine in silence. And then we all looked up at the same time.

"Ace is close," Joel whispered, voicing what we were all thinking. "He knows everything about you. He knew everything about Daisy, because she always came to the shop. He's a tattooist. He knew Daisy was allergic. Daisy might have trusted him."

I didn't even want to think about it. I couldn't think about it. It was absurd.

Wasn't it?

"You both know him better than I do. He's kept his distance with me, but I'd only thought it was because he still thought I was an outsider. Because you all had been working for Flip for so long, and then I came and bought the shop and he had a new boss. And then there was all that stuff with Charlotte." Charlotte had been a trainee in our shop, and she and Ace had had a relationship. But Charlotte got into some stuff that she shouldn't have, and I had to let her go. I didn't think Ace ever forgave me for that.

But would that be reason enough to set me up like this? To create that blog? To break into my house and splash red paint around?

I'd like to think that one of my employees was not that crazy.

But the more I thought about it, the more I wondered.

"Where was Ace last night?" I asked Bitsy.

She knew what I was asking: Was Ace working last night or was he out of the shop, taking pictures of me and Harry and then posting them on a blog?

Bitsy bit her lip and took a swig of wine. This wasn't good.

"He left early. Not long after you did," she admitted. "His last client canceled. Or so he said. I didn't talk to the client, but Ace said he'd intercepted a call earlier when I was out getting lunch."

So he had opportunity. And maybe motive.

"Where was he when Daisy was killed?" I asked. Flanigan had come by the shop to find out where I had been, not anyone else.

Bitsy shrugged. "I would have to check. I think he was there, but I'm not a hundred percent sure. And then he does disappear sometimes, but usually to that oxygen bar."

We stared uncomfortably at each other, not wanting to think the worst but thinking it anyway.

Finally I shook my head and said, "Listen, it can't be Ace. It's ridiculous to think that."

Bitsy started clearing up the cheese and crackers. "You're right. It's late, and our imaginations are running away with us. Ace is a good guy. He's a little impulsive at times and gets a little too high on his horse about that so-called art he creates. He's not a murderer." She snorted. "Maybe we should all just go to bed. We'll have clearer heads in the morning."

I helped her bring the wineglasses in while Joel pulled out the sofa bed. I wondered about sleeping arrangements, if Joel really was staying over, too.

"Joel's going to be in the spare room," Bitsy said when I asked. "I'd put him on the sofa bed, but I'm afraid it might not be sturdy enough. If you get my drift."

I did, and I said I didn't mind. I started to go back out into the living room, but she caught my arm and stopped me.

"I know you're uncertain about Jeff," she said.

I opened my mouth to say, well, I wasn't sure what I was going to say, but I didn't have to because she put her finger up to stop me.

"He's a good man," Bitsy continued. "He's got his own business. He's settled into the community. He's got a healthy relationship with his mother. He cares about you. You could do worse. In fact, you've done worse."

I hated hearing it in such black and white terms, but she was right. I just wasn't sure I was ready to take my relationship with Jeff to another level. Although that kiss had been a real surprise. In more ways than one.

She took her hand off my arm and patted it. "Think about it. He won't push you; you know that. He'll back off if you want. But I wouldn't make any rash decisions just yet."

I didn't think I could, with this stalker blogger out there somewhere. I pushed Jeff Coleman and his kiss out of my head, although admittedly, it lingered somewhere in my subconscious; it wouldn't go away altogether.

I pulled on my pajama bottoms and big T-shirt, brushed my teeth, and went back into the living room and crawled under the covers. The sofa bed was surprisingly comfortable, sans that metal bar that usually cut into someone's back. As I closed my eyes, I heard something familiar. A little dinging sound.

A text message on my cell phone.

I grabbed my bag off the plush armchair next to the sofa and took out the phone. When I looked at the display, I caught my breath, my hands beginning to shake as I read the message.

"Brett, I know you did this to me. You won't get away with it."

I checked the display again. It was Daisy's number.

Chapter 34

I put the phone down and pulled my legs up to my chest, my arms around them, my head down on my knees. I needed to call Tim, who was no doubt still trying to clean up the mess at our house, but I felt as though I'd fall apart if I let myself go. Literally let myself go. So I sat there, rocking slowly, trying not to think about the person who was trying to make me crazy.

The light in the hall went on, and Bitsy's shadow appeared.

"What's wrong, Brett? I heard something."

Couldn't get anything past Bitsy.

She came in and sat down on the edge of the bed. I cocked my head toward my phone where I'd tossed it, and she picked it up, hitting one of the buttons so that the display shone like a Christmas tree. She read the text, her eyes wide.

"What is this? Who sent this?"

I shook my head, unable to speak.

"Did you call your brother? Someone's got Daisy's cell phone. I didn't know she had your number."

We'd exchanged numbers at one point, and I keyed her number into my phone. I supposed she'd done the same thing.

Joel lumbered out, wearing a big terrycloth bathrobe.

"What's up?" he asked, and Bitsy handed him the phone.

When he read the message, he came around and sat in the armchair, leaning over to rub my back. He'd been doing that a lot lately.

What was wrong with me? I was acting like some sort of victim. Which, of course, I was, but this was ridiculous. I pulled my arms away from my legs and reached for the phone, punching in Tim's number.

"You okay?" he asked when he answered.

I told him about the text message.

"You're sure it's from her number?"

I was acutely aware of the four eyes watching me. "Yes. It's her number."

"No one saw a cell phone in the hotel room where she was found," Tim said thoughtfully.

So whoever killed her and wanted to frame me could've taken it and planned this. Or taken it and decided just this very moment, hey, here's another way to make Brett Kavanaugh insane. As if the blog pictures and Ink Flamingos weren't enough already.

This really was personal. But who on earth hated me this much?

Or who wanted Tim and the cops to concentrate on who was harassing me and not on who actually killed the poor girl?

I voiced my thoughts, and Tim grunted.

"I need your cell phone."

Great. I'd had to give up my car in the past, but this was a first. "When?"

"Morning. Can you drop it by for me at the station?"

I thought about the hassle I would have with the wireless company about getting a new number, after all their promotions about how you can take your phone number with you whenever you get new service or a new phone.

I said okay and hung up, Bitsy and Joel still watching me.

"You're creeping me out," I said, irritation lacing my tone.

"Like we're any creepier than that," Bitsy said, indicating the phone.

"Okay," I sighed. "Sorry. I'm on edge. I have to bring Tim the phone tomorrow, so I guess we can all get some sleep." I picked up the phone and shut it off, so I wouldn't get any more messages from the dead.

They shuffled off to their respective beds, and I lay in the dark, staring at the ceiling, not sleeping until about an hour before I had to get up.

The three of us were in Bitsy's car. This was not an easy feat. Bitsy was the only one who was comfortable in her Mini Cooper. Joel had squeezed himself into the front seat, "squeezed" being the operative word. I was in the back, all folded up across the backseat, my knees almost hitting the ceiling, my head grazing it.

It was like a clown car.

Bitsy had fed us bagels and coffee, and we were on our way to pick up more coffee before we dropped off my cell phone to Tim and then went to the shop. The text message from the night before seemed a long way away in the light of day. The only good thing about it was that it pushed Jeff Coleman's kiss way to the back of my mind.

The kiss. Right. Something else I'd have to deal with. Or not. Knowing Jeff, he wouldn't mention it. But what if he decided to do it again?

I noticed we weren't headed in the right direction.

"Where are we going?" I asked.

Bitsy and Joel had been mumbling something this morning when I'd gotten out of the shower, but I was afraid they were talking about me and I didn't want to know. So I'd ignored it. Now, however, it seemed that maybe they'd been hatching a plan.

"We've been doing a little thinking," Bitsy said.

Uh-oh. That might not be the best thing.

"And we thought that we should try to find out a little more about this blogger, you know, the one who's been . . ." Joel's voice trailed off.

He didn't need to finish the sentence, because we all knew what Ainsley Wainwright had been up to. Except that she wasn't the one doing it. I said as much.

"That's why it might be a good idea to poke around a little," Bitsy said. "Go back to the beginning. See who might want to impersonate her, and then decide to impersonate you."

It wasn't a bad idea. I'd been so wrapped up in me that I hadn't thought about her. It might be a good thing to concentrate on someone else for a little while. It would take the pressure off.

"So what's the plan?"

"We go to her place. Start there."

"How do you know where to go?" I asked. Bitsy seemed very sure of the direction we were heading.

"I did a Yahoo! People search. Gave me her address, so then I Google-Mapped her."

Always thorough, that was Bitsy. But it made me wonder why the cops hadn't done that. Or maybe they had. Maybe that's the way they finally found her. That's right. Knocking on doors, Tim had said.

Ainsley Wainwright lived in an apartment building off Fremont Street, in a rather run-down area. The white stucco, three-story building had faded to gray. The windows were covered with bars, even on the third floor. The parking lot was in the back, so Bitsy turned in and parked. We scrambled out of the car as well as we could, and I was happy to stretch my legs out.

The entrance wasn't locked, so we let ourselves in.

The hallway smelled like old gym socks and cigarettes. I wrinkled my nose and said, "So which apartment?"

Bitsy was already halfway up the stairs. Joel and I shrugged at each other and followed.

The crime scene tape had been torn, and it hung in two pieces on either side of the door. Looked like we weren't the only ones who were going in uninvited.

Bitsy reached into her bag and pulled out a pair of latex gloves.

"What are you doing?" I hissed.

"I thought we might need them," she said, handing some to me and Joel as well before she put her hand to the doorknob and turned.

To our surprise, the door easily swung open. Bitsy looked up at me, raised her eyebrows, and stepped inside.

That's when we heard the footsteps come up behind us.

Chapter 35

"I wish you people would go away," a voice said.

I turned around to see a young woman with short, spiked, bleached blond hair and wearing extremely short denim shorts and a tank top standing on the landing.

It took me a second, but I finally figured "you people" meant she thought we were cops. Right. The latex gloves.

"Didn't you get everything already?" she continued. "And when are you going to catch her killer? I mean, on TV they catch the killers right away." Her eyes flickered at me, narrowing slightly. I felt as though she recognized me, knew about the blog, that she, too, thought I was guilty.

"This isn't TV," I heard myself saying, still keeping up the charade that I really was the cops. The girl's expression changed a little then—maybe she was having second thoughts about me, maybe she wasn't quite so sure about me now.

Tim would totally kill me for this, and I wondered if they would cart him off to prison or decide it was justifiable homicide.

"Did you know Miss Wainwright?" Joel asked her.

Sadness crossed her face. "She was amazing. So nice to everyone."

Of course she was. All victims were saints after they

were dead, weren't they? Sister Mary Eucharista would say so.

"She was beautiful, too," she said. "She had red hair, like yours," she added, looking at me. "But her hair was long."

I absently ran a hand through my short hair.

The young woman was frowning. "You sort of look like her, though. Weird."

I knew I didn't look like the Ainsley Wainwright I'd met in Sherman Potter's hotel room. She was a lot more voluptuous and had that long horse face with those spectacular eyes. What had this Ainsley Wainwright looked like?

Suddenly there seemed to be an overabundance of redheads in Vegas. And at least one other who wasn't a redhead but wore a wig to pretend to be me.

I had a real need to go inside now, see if I could find a picture or something of this Ainsley Wainwright, but I was unsure about leaving Joel out here alone with this girl. I mean, she was young, yes, but not stupid. She'd soon figure out that this large tattooed man with the long braid down his back and chains in his pockets wasn't a cop. Unless she was more used to narcotics undercover officers. But then again, if they were undercover, she wouldn't necessarily know they were cops.

Oh, he'd figure out how to deal with her. I nodded at Joel in what I hoped looked like a very professional way and went through the door.

The apartment was fairly Spartan but not very clean. Piles of newspapers were stacked in one corner; books spilled off shelves onto the floor. Kitschy little items lined the mantel of the faux fireplace: snow domes from the Flamingo and Caesars, shot glasses from the Bellagio, New York New York, and the MGM. You'd think because she lived here she wouldn't buy the souvenir stuff.

I didn't see any photographs.

Bitsy was in the bedroom, and I joined her in there. She wasn't touching anything, just looking around.

"The cops were here," she said, indicating the fingerprint dust.

"That's their job," I said, even though I didn't have to. I was too distracted by the bed.

The sheets had been taken off it, and the mattress lay bare on the frame. I'd had no idea how Ainsley Wainwright had died—Tim hadn't felt compelled to tell me— but I had a bit of a clue now. A large red stain was in the middle of the mattress.

"Do you think she was shot or stabbed?" Bitsy asked matter-of-factly.

I shrugged, not really wanting to speculate.

"I wish we could clean up," Bitsy said. Sure she did. Bitsy liked everything in order, and this room was no less messy than the living room. A laundry basket was bleeding dirty clothes; the closet doors hung open to reveal scattered shoes and clothes hanging haphazardly on hangers; the two dressers were topped with stray costume jewelry.

I went over to the closet and checked out the clothes. They were plain: T-shirts and jeans and longish skirts. Nothing flashy. I wondered out loud what Ainsley Wainwright did when she wasn't blogging.

"She worked for a dentist," Bitsy said, holding up a piece of paper she'd taken off one of the dressers.

Looking closely, I saw it was a pay stub from a local dental group.

"Maybe we'd have better luck going there and talking to them," Bitsy suggested. "Maybe you could get your teeth cleaned or something."

"Or maybe you could."

"Or maybe Joel could."

We both started cracking up a little over that, sending Joel to a dentist just to get information.

"We're grabbing at straws," I said when I caught my breath. "And I'm doing exactly what I said I wouldn't do ever again. Why did you talk me into this?"

"We have to clear your name." She was totally serious.

"But that's for Tim and the cops to do."

"Well, they're not doing a very good job of it, are they?" she asked.

No, they weren't. Couldn't argue with that.

I told her I was going back out to the living room. She nodded, staring at the bed.

The books on the floor bothered me for some reason. I leaned down and sifted through them. She sure liked romances, historical and contemporary. The covers were adorned with bare-chested young men who needed haircuts and thin, willowy young women with their cleavage hanging out all over the place.

I started stacking them in neat little piles next to the bookshelf. There, that looked better.

I spotted a stray book that had fallen behind another one on the shelf and pulled it out, ready to stack it along with the rest. But something was stuck inside it.

I yanked it out and turned it over.

Here was the picture I'd been looking for. But it wasn't what I expected.

"What did you find there?" Bitsy asked, hovering over me as I sat on the floor.

I held it up and she took it, a long, slow whistle leaving her lips. "You're kidding me. Why didn't the cops find it?"

"It was stuck in this book." I showed her how it had been crammed into the binding. "They might have gone through these, but maybe since it didn't just fall out, they missed it."

I could still hear Joel talking to that young woman outside. Hmm. That was interesting. When I got closer to the doorway, I heard him say, "You know, I could do both of you."

Now that sounded a little too kinky for me, but I needed to talk to her, so I announced my presence by clearing my throat. They both looked up, and the girl grinned at me.

"He says he can tattoo me and my girlfriend for a discount," she said excitedly.

The mystery of Joel's predilection remained.

While I wasn't sure about the discount thing, I couldn't worry about it now. I held out the photograph to the young woman. "Is that Ainsley Wainwright?" I asked.

She stared at the picture for a second before saying, "Yes, with her twin sister."

Chapter 36

I'd suspected as much. The two women in the picture were identical, and one was most definitely the Ainsley I had met in Sherman Potter's hotel room. But since Tim said the dead girl in here was identified as Ainsley, and the paycheck stub Bitsy had shown me inside had indicated that the woman who lived here and worked for the dentist was, in fact, Ainsley, then for some reason her sister was using her name.

"Do you know her sister's name?" I asked the young woman.

She shook her head. "No. I never met her." But her eyes skittered around the hall, wouldn't meet mine. She knew something she didn't want to tell.

"Ainsley never mentioned her?"

She shrugged, still evasive.

I wasn't going to get anywhere with her. I pocketed the picture.

The young woman frowned. "That's not yours," she said with a pout.

"Evidence," I said, snapping off my gloves.

Bitsy had come out now.

"Ready?" I asked.

She nodded, looking up at Joel, who was handing the

girl one of his business cards. Great. Now she knew for sure that we weren't cops.

"I told her how I moonlight on the side," Joel said with a wink.

Oh, like that would make a difference when she showed up at the shop and we were all there, working.

Whatever.

I needed to get out of here and bring Tim my cell phone and now this picture. But wait. I hadn't thought this through. Where would I tell him I got said picture? Now I was in a pickle. Because I couldn't tell him I'd been here and found it in a book.

For a nanosecond I thought I could tell him I got it from one of the girls in the band last night and had forgotten about it. But why would they have it? They didn't even like Ainsley. Or whatever her real name was.

There really was no place I could say I got it. Except here.

And I had no idea how to bring up the fact that Ainsley Wainwright had a twin sister without showing him the picture.

I was stuck between that rock and hard place.

As we squeezed ourselves back into the little Mini Cooper for the ride to the police station, I told Bitsy and Joel my dilemma.

Bitsy snorted. "Why don't you just tell him that you found it in that Hummer you and Jeff stole last night, and you forgot all about it because there was a flamingo with a tiara covered in red paint on your bed?"

This was why I paid her the big bucks. Because she came up with ideas I would never have thought of. Granted, it was still a little weak, but if I played it right, Tim would be none the wiser.

"Do you think for sure that she's the one impersonating you?" Joel asked.

I thought for a moment, not certain. While the young woman at the apartment building said I looked like Ainsley Wainwright, I knew I didn't, but Jeff said the woman he met didn't look at all like me. But that woman didn't really have red hair, because she'd left it behind in the ladies' room.

"I'm not sure." I thought about meeting the other Ainsley in Sherman Potter's hotel room. Her sister must have been dead by then. Did she know?

"I still don't understand why someone would do this to you," Joel said.

That was the million-dollar question, wasn't it? Because even though this felt personal, I didn't know Ainsley Wainwright. I had never met her. And it had been a fluke that I met her sister when she was with Sherman Potter. I'd never met him before, either, although Daisy had told me about him. So why? Why would anyone go to all that trouble to set me up? To set up that fake blog? To take my picture? To put a flamingo on my bed? To text me, pretending to be Daisy?

I still had way more questions than answers. I wondered if Tim could help with the phone issue.

"What are you going to do about Ace?" Joel asked.

Now that was a tough one. We'd pretty much charged and convicted him last night, but in the light of day, it wasn't quite so easy. I wanted to give him the benefit of the doubt.

I shrugged. "I need to ask about the moonlighting."

"Do we have rules against that?"

The way he asked made me wonder if Joel hadn't been moonlighting, too. "No," I said, "but if you want to, it might be best to tell me or Bitsy so at least we know."

That seemed to satisfy Joel, who was probably having the same issues with our discussion last night as I was. Bitsy, I noticed, was oddly silent.

Tim wasn't at the police station, and no one would tell me where he was. Flanigan wasn't there, either. I could assume they were out somewhere together, since they'd seemed a bit joined at the hip lately. Maybe they had a lead on the case.

Listen to me. I sound like I watch too much TV.

I didn't leave my cell phone with the sergeant, like he suggested. There was way too much possibility that it would get lost or something, so I took it with me when we left for the shop.

Ace was hanging around out front when we showed up. He was holding a white box that caught Joel's eye. The gate was still down over the glass door.

"Lost my key," he said apologetically.

I didn't like the sound of that. If he'd lost it, then someone could find it and get into the shop. Since my house had already been broken into, I didn't want the shop suffering the same fate.

"You'd better find it," I snapped sharply.

"I'll launch a full-blown search in my apartment later," Ace said, an edge to his tone that indicated I might have held back a little. I'd never talked to him like that before, and immediately I could hear Sister Mary Eucharista reminding me that everyone's innocent until proven guilty.

I unlocked the gate and pulled it up and out of sight, then unlocked the door and let everyone in. We all headed to the staff room, where Bitsy and I stashed our bags and Ace put the box on the table, breaking the tape that held it shut.

"Pastries," he announced.

We all leaned over to check them out. They were from Bouchon, a bakery downstairs that was affiliated with the fancy Thomas Keller restaurant of the same name up on the eighth level of the Venetian Grand Canal Shoppes. Bouchon pastries were something special.

I peered over at Ace, feeling even guiltier. He had taken one but hadn't started nibbling on it yet.

Joel hadn't waited that long. His was already half gone.

My pastry would have to wait. I needed to talk to Ace now. I gave Bitsy and Joel a look, and they got the message so they filtered out. Ace was following them when I said, "Ace, can I talk to you a minute?"

He paused at the door, flipping back his dark hair. He was incredibly handsome in a Greek god sort of way. Everything was symmetrical, even his tattoos, down to the fleur-de-lis on the tops of his hands.

"What's up? I told you I'd look for the key."

"It's not about that. I know you'll find it." I sounded a lot more confident than I felt. "Are you moonlighting?" Might as well get it out in the open right away. Didn't want to pull any punches.

Confusion crossed his face, then dismay. But he didn't want to admit it. "What are you talking about?"

I might as well come clean. "I saw you last night. At the Flamingo. You were there with Harry Desmond. You had your case."

He frowned. "So what of it?" A little more belligerent now.

I sighed. "I know Harry does parties. He used to work for Jeff; do you know that? And Jeff fired him."

All pretense left his face. "He shouldn't have, you know. Fired him, I mean. Harry's a good tattooist. I told him he should ask for a job here."

Like I'd hire him after what Jeff told me. After the other night. I felt myself blush a little as I thought about those kisses, how I'd almost gone home with him. And then out of the blue I thought about Jeff. I struggled to push the thoughts away and keep my focus on the matter at hand.

"Jeff fired him for a reason," I said, making my voice

all professional-like, the blush gone now. "I'm not sure you want your name associated with his, considering. And he never even told me that he's a tattooist. So how could I hire him? He lied to us, said he got laid off at one of the casinos. It was all one big fabrication."

Ace slumped a little, running a hand through that perfect hair. I could see he was debating something with himself, then finally he spoke.

"Today's my last day."

Chapter 37

I didn't think I heard him right. "What?"

Ace sighed. "I'm quitting."

I hadn't meant for this to happen. "Why?" I managed to sputter, totally thrown off. "Not because of this?"

"I need more time to devote to my painting," he said. "And I can make a lot of money at those tattoo parties."

A lot? How much? I wanted to ask, wondering if this wasn't a ploy. "Do you want a raise?" I asked, worried about what he'd demand. He made less than Joel, which was only right, because he hadn't been with the shop as long, starting only a year before I bought Flip out, whereas Joel had been with Flip from the start, about ten years. I couldn't possibly give Ace more and have it all be fair. And while business was still good, the recession had hit us a little, and I didn't want to overextend and have to give everyone raises.

Ace shook his head. "No. I just want to leave. This isn't my thing anyway; you know that. I really need to concentrate on my art."

I thought about his comic book renditions of famous paintings. We'd sold a few, but not enough to warrant a full-time gig.

"I'm going to try to set up an exhibit," he continued.

"I need to establish myself, and I can't do it here. Harry says—"

Little red lights went off in my head. "Harry? What does Harry have to say about this?"

"He says he knows someone who owns a gallery, who might want to set up something for me."

Harry certainly knew a lot of people, didn't he? First, it was Sherman Potter. Now it was some gallery owner. He'd infiltrated himself into our lives here at The Painted Lady in more ways than one. Maybe it was time to tell him to stop coming around. We were doing better before he showed up on our doorstep.

Bitsy popped into the staff room door. She cocked her head at Ace. "Your client's here."

He gave me an apologetic look and sidled past her toward his room and his client. Bitsy frowned at me.

"What's going on?"

I told her.

She didn't believe it, either. "What does he mean, he's going to concentrate on his art? The man will starve." Bitsy, always the realist, had never been one to mince words.

I nodded. "You're right. But there's something else at play here." I told her about how Harry was encouraging it. "Maybe we need to discourage his presence here," I finished.

"You can tell him now," she said. When she saw my expression, she added, "He came in while you were in here talking to Ace. But I'll warn you, he's got a surprise for you."

A surprise? For me? I didn't need any more surprises, thank you very much. I followed Bitsy out to the front of the shop, where Harry was draped over the front desk as if he owned the joint. A huge vase of red roses sat on the desk. When Harry saw me, he straightened up and grinned.

"For you, milady," he said in a mock English accent, waving his hand in front of the roses as if he were a game-show hostess showing off the latest model of refrigerator for a lucky winner.

I didn't feel so lucky.

"You didn't have to," I said, stumbling over my words, since they were not the ones I wanted to utter. I wanted to tell him he was crazy, that he needed to go away. Now. But somehow, in the presence of those flowers and his lopsided, charming smile, I lost my resolve. Why did he have to be so affable that it was difficult to kick him out?

I glanced around for a little support, but Bitsy had disappeared. She probably didn't want to see the bloodletting. If there was, in fact, any bloodletting at all.

Harry was talking. "Ace told me you're having a tough time of it. That blog, those pictures . . ." His voice trailed off as a flush crept up his neck. He was embarrassed about it, too.

I finally found my voice. "Harry, this was really nice of you. Thank you."

"And then your boyfriend broke up with you. All because of it," he continued.

I didn't want to be reminded of Colin Bixby. Another failed relationship. It was a good thing I'd never mentioned him to my mother. She would've been so excited about the prospects of a son-in-law who was a doctor, and then so disappointed—again—that it didn't work out.

I shook my head. "Don't worry about me," I said, forcing a smile. "It's not your fault; you didn't need to do this."

Jeff Coleman had been convinced Harry Desmond was the devil incarnate, but I wasn't so sure. Except for one thing . . .

"Ace tells me you've been encouraging him to give up his job here and have a gallery show with his paintings."

Harry cast his eyes to the floor for a second; then he looked back up at me. "He's really talented, but I didn't think he'd leave the shop. I'm sorry. It's just that I know this guy—"

I put up my hand to stop him. "You know a lot of guys, Harry," I said. "Do you really think it's someone who can help Ace, or is it a scam?"

Something crossed his face, but I couldn't read it.

"No scam, Brett," he said, putting up three fingers. "Scout's honor."

The door opened, and my first client of the day walked in. She grinned at me, and I turned away from Harry for a second to tell her to go to my room and I'd be there in a second.

"Harry, I've got to go," I said.

His face broke out in a wide grin as he reached into the vase and pulled out a single rose and handed it to me. I had no choice but to take it.

Harry walked out through the glass doors.

"Why is it when I want to dislike him, he's just so nice?" I asked when Bitsy appeared by my side. Being a little person, she tends to surprise me that way some times.

"You should have laid into him. Told him not to steal your employees for his own purposes," Bitsy admonished.

"He bought me roses."

"You don't have any backbone. You should've left it to me. At least I didn't make out with the guy, giving him the wrong impression."

She was totally serious.

"He got me drunk on absinthe. It wasn't my fault," I said, although not too convincingly. Sister Mary Eucharista was rapping me on the knuckles and reminding me that I could've said no to that absinthe. No kidding.

I needed to get to my client, who was sitting in my

chair, bopping her head to her iPod tunes. So much for providing magazines to pass the time. I sat in my swivel chair on wheels and slipped a new needle into the tattoo machine. I set out the little pots of ink. As I did so, I realized I'd left her stencil in the staff room. I got up, taking off the one glove I'd managed to pull on.

"Just a sec," I said. "Have to get your stencil."

She gave me a short nod, the wires from the iPod dancing as she moved.

My cell phone started ringing as I grabbed the manila folder with the stencil in it. I pulled it out of my bag and saw it was Tim.

"You didn't leave your phone," he said without saying hello.

"I didn't want to leave it with just anyone. I asked for Flanigan, too," I said.

"Well, it doesn't matter anyway. We found Daisy Carmichael's phone. And the text she supposedly sent you was on it."

Butterflies started crashing into the sides of my stomach. "Really? Where did you find it?" I wasn't a hundred percent sure I really wanted to know.

"In Ainsley Wainwright's apartment."

Chapter 38

Okay, so this was a bit freaky. And now I was in a bind, because I needed to tell him about the picture, how there were two of them. Might as well hold off as long as possible.

"When did you go over to her apartment, then?" I asked. "I mean, I got that text last night, so did you go this morning?"

"That's right."

They must have been there before we got there, because we didn't see a cell phone anywhere.

I couldn't stall forever.

"You know Ainsley Wainwright has a twin sister, right?" I asked.

Silence for a second, then, "Yes, I do know that. How do *you* know?"

"So you know? Don't you think this twin sister is the one who's behind all this?" Keep talking and maybe he won't realize I'm not answering his question.

"Why don't you let us do the investigating, Brett. And how do you know about the twin sister?"

So he wasn't going to let me off the hook.

"I found a picture."

"You found a picture? Where?"

I thought about how Bitsy said to say I found it in the

limo, but it seemed a bit far-fetched, and why hadn't I told him about it yesterday? I was stuck.

"You're not going to tell me?" His voice echoed in my head, and then I had it. I wasn't going to tell him. Simple, right? Maybe not so much. "I hope you're not doing anything you're not supposed to be doing, Brett."

"Are you going to find her today? So I can stop looking over my shoulder?" I couldn't keep the worry out of my voice.

Tim sighed. "We're on it, but still stay cautious. Can you get Jeff to take you home later?"

I felt something snap. "Why Jeff? I mean, why not Joel or Bitsy? Why does it have to be Jeff?" Yes, the lady was protesting too much, and it didn't escape Tim.

He chuckled. "It can be anyone you'd like. I just thought—"

"Well, don't think. I've got a client. I've got to go." I punched END on the phone, although it didn't have the same satisfying feel as slamming a phone receiver down.

I grabbed the manila folder and started toward my room. I was still clearly having issues with Jeff Coleman and the fact that he'd kissed me. Or more, that I'd kissed him back. And liked it.

I pushed the thoughts aside and went back to my client, putting myself on autopilot, forcing a smile.

I was glad to know I could still work. In fact, work was a way to forget about what was going on. As long as I was in my room, the familiar weight of the tattoo machine pressed against my hand, I felt as though I had no troubles.

Too bad I couldn't hole myself up in there for the next couple of weeks, or at least until Tim found Ainsley Wainwright's twin sister. I had begun to wonder if she wasn't responsible for pinning Daisy's murder on Sherman Potter and trying to frame me as well. Although setting two people up for the same crime seemed a bit overachieving. And then there was the little fact that her sister was murdered—even though Tim hadn't told me officially, the red stain on the mattress was more than a clue. She wouldn't kill her sister, would she? So someone else must have.

I couldn't be thinking about all this while I worked. Shea Collins was a science major at the university, and she wanted a tattoo of the bones of her spine along the bones of her spine, from the top of her neck down to her lower back. She was a skinny girl, and it was a little dicey working with the uneven canvas. Also, because it was very bony, it was a lot more painful for her than having a tattoo on a fleshy part of her body. She choked back sobs, and when I offered to make the design simpler so I could be done more quickly, she adamantly refused. I had no choice but to keep going.

My hand had started to cramp up a little after an hour, and I turned off the machine and set it down on the table behind me. I surveyed the design and was pleased. I handed Shea a box of Kleenex.

"How about if we finish this up another day?" I asked. "How about the end of the week?"

She nodded, blowing her nose.

After I smoothed some Tattoo Goo on the outline I'd managed to get done and covered up the new tattoo so she could put her shirt back on, Shea and I went out into the front of the shop, where Bitsy was leafing through the appointment book. She looked up when we approached. I explained how Shea needed to come back. Bitsy nodded, then said softly, "That girl is here."

"What girl?"

"The one Joel talked to this morning. At Ainsley Wainwright's apartment. He said he'd give her a discount. What sort of discount would be appropriate?"

I had no idea she'd really show up here, and from the look on Bitsy's face, Bitsy hadn't expected it, either.

"I'm not sure," I said.

"She did help us," Bitsy reminded me.

Had she? Oh, right. She had told us about the twins. But that was about it. I had a thought. If she was getting a discount on a tattoo, then she should cough up a little more information. I said as much to Bitsy, who concurred.

"She's in the back with Joel, who's doing up a design for her."

We'd told her we were cops. Unless she was stupid, she couldn't still believe that.

"Did she bring that friend with her? The one she mentioned."

Bitsy shook her head. "She's alone."

I left Shea with Bitsy and strode down the hall toward the waiting area in the back. The black leather sofa clashed in a nice way with the blond laminate flooring. A glass coffee table held a variety of tattoo magazines and a couple of our portfolios, so clients could get an idea of the kind of work we did.

Joel was sitting next to the girl on the couch, his pad open, his pencil frantically sketching. The girl was pointing, showing him what she wanted.

I cleared my throat, and they both looked up. Joel smiled. "Brett, this is Terri."

I stepped forward to shake her hand, but she didn't make a move toward me. I waited for her to say something about how we'd impersonated Las Vegas's finest, but she merely nodded. I hoped she wouldn't make some sort of citizen's arrest or complaint. I didn't need Tim on my case again.

I wondered again if she thought I was a killer, like the blogs said. So far no clients had mentioned it. Maybe they didn't read the blogs. I could only hope.

Terri's eyes were running up and down my person, though, checking me out. I shivered slightly, uncomfortable under her gaze. It was almost as if she were a guy. Uh-oh. Maybe she played for the other team. This was definitely awkward.

I pushed through it, though, and shifted from one foot to the other, finally asking, "I was wondering if you could tell me a little something about Ainsley Wainwright. I mean, if you live in the same building, you must know her, right?"

She hesitated a second before shrugging. "Sure. But you probably only want to know about that blog, right?"

Okay, she did know about it. I nodded.

"She liked tattoos. She had a bunch of them, but not where you'd notice." Terri flashed a little knowing smile. Hmm. Maybe they were closer than I thought. But that also made me think. When I'd met Sherman Potter's Ainsley, the only tattoo I'd seen was the one on the inside of her thigh. If she'd had others, I would've seen them, considering how small that towel was. So she must really be the sister.

"You said you'd never met her sister, right?" I asked Terri, who had lost interest and was now paying more attention to Joel's drawing.

"No," she said.

"What can you tell me about the blog?" I asked, when I realized she wasn't going to say anything more.

"She loved doing that."

I'd hoped for a little more, but Terri didn't seem inclined to elaborate. I changed tacks.

"She worked at a dental group?"

Terri nodded. "She was a hygienist."

"Did she have a boyfriend or anything?"

"Some guy showed up last week. Never saw him before. Tall, dark hair, looked like he worked out, older guy. He had a long nose. It didn't seem to go with his face."

Terri had just described Sherman Potter. What was

he doing there? He was involved with the sister, not the blogger. Or had he known both of them?

"I'm done." Joel put his pencil on the table and lifted up the notepad.

I stopped breathing. It was a flamingo. He shrugged at me. "This is what she wanted."

I stared at Terri, who was admiring the sketch. "I love it," she said. "It's perfect."

I wanted to put a ban on flamingo tattoos. A sign out front that said NO FLAMINGOS HERE. Joel knew what I was thinking, and his eyebrows rose high in his forehead as if to tell me to chill.

I forced a smile. "It's nice," I said and went back to the front of the shop to leave them alone to figure out the particulars and see when Terri could come back for the actual tattoo.

Bitsy's mouth formed a little "o" when she saw my face, but the phone rang, interrupting any question she'd had, and she picked it up. "The Painted Lady," she said, all signs of emotion wiped from her voice.

"Hold on a sec," Bitsy said, putting her hand over the receiver and frowning up at me. "There's a problem."

I waited.

"This is your next client. She said she got a message from you saying you had an emergency and wouldn't be able to keep her appointment. She wants to reschedule. What's up?"

I had no idea. Because I hadn't called her.

Chapter 39

I took the phone from Bitsy.

"Jenny? It's Brett."

"Oh, is everything all right?"

"I'm not sure. When did I call you to cancel?"

Silence. I could hear Jenny wondering why I was asking, then, "Maybe about an hour ago. I had my phone off because I was in class." She paused. "What's going on?"

Exactly what I'd like to know, too. "I didn't call you, Jenny. I'm sorry. It wasn't me."

"It sounded like you."

My impostor strikes again. "I can keep your three o'clock, if you can still come in," I offered.

"I'll be there," she said, relief in her voice.

"Okay, great. See you in an hour," I said, and hung up. I turned to Bitsy, who'd been hanging on every word. "I want Tim to catch that woman and lock her up."

"But how did she know Jenny was coming in? How did she know her phone number to call her?" Bitsy asked.

Good questions. Wished I had the answers.

"Only way to know was the appointment book," Bitsy pointed out.

I knew what she was thinking.

"Where's Ace?" I asked reluctantly. Ace had access to our appointments.

"He went out for lunch, but remember, she said a woman called her," Bitsy reminded me. "So it couldn't have been Ace."

Not Ace, maybe, but a friend of his? Did he know Ainsley Wainwright? Or her sister? I didn't hang out with Ace after work; I had never been as close with him as I was with Bitsy and Joel.

Bitsy anticipated my next question. "He wouldn't sabotage the business, Brett. No matter how he felt about it or you."

None of this made any sense. I waved my hand in the air and shook my head and went into the staff room. I sat at the light table, grabbed Jenny's folder, and pulled out her stencil. I still had a little work to do before she came in, and now, because of that phone call, I wanted to make it up to her, so I added more detail to the rosebush that she wanted on her side.

I saw Joel walking Terri out, and then I heard Bitsy and Joel talking; the phone rang, but I shut it out, concentrating on the roses.

"Brett?" Bitsy stood in the doorway.

"Yes?" Jenny couldn't be here yet; it was still too soon.

"It's another one."

"Another one what?"

"Another client. Said she got a phone call, wanted to make sure you were okay after the accident."

A lump stuck in my throat. "What accident?"

"She says you called, said you were in an accident and would be canceling all your appointments for the rest of the week. She's worried about you."

I couldn't breathe. What was going on?

"Ace is back," Bitsy added softly. "Do you want me to ask him about this, or will you?"

I didn't think I could form a coherent sentence at the moment. Finally, I took a deep breath and said, "I will. Please tell my client that I was not in an accident, that I'll be able to keep her appointment."

"I'll send Ace in." Bitsy disappeared, and I was still staring at the doorway when Ace appeared.

He wore a frown. "What's up?"

I indicated he should come in and sit down at the table, where I joined him. I licked my lips, uncertain how to start.

Finally, "I have to ask you something, but please don't take it the wrong way. It's just that someone's been impersonating me, sending me text messages from dead people, breaking into my house and leaving plastic flamingos on my bed."

"That blog," Ace said, his voice low, his eyes dark.

I nodded. "Right. That blog. Well, now someone is calling my clients and telling them I was in an accident, that I can't make their appointments. And the only place to find those clients' information is in the appointment book."

Ace stared at me, confusion slowly replaced by understanding. His eyes flashed. "You think it's me?" he asked incredulously.

"I have to ask everyone," I said. "Not just you. I just need to make sure it's no one here."

"You're mad that I'm leaving," he accused. "So now it's my fault." He stood up, his hands clenched into tight balls.

I stood, too. We were about the same height, both of us almost six feet. "No, Ace, I want you to stay. I want to talk to you about what I can do to convince you to stay."

"So you do it by accusing me of taking your client list and telling them not to come for their appointments?"

I totally screwed this one up, because now I could see

it in his face. He had nothing to do with this. I was way off base on this one.

"I'm so sorry," I said. "I just had to ask." I tried again. "But please reconsider your decision."

He shook his head. "No, this pretty much seals the deal for me." And he stormed out.

I sank back down into the chair and put my head in my hands. This was not working out the way I wanted. Whoever was doing this was responsible, and I had to stop her.

"Guess that didn't work," I heard Bitsy say.

I looked up over my elbow and saw her coming toward me. I shook my head. "No, it was pretty awful."

"He's packing his stuff up now."

"I made a mess of all this."

"No, someone's messing with you. Bad. You should call your brother about this one."

Bitsy was right. I did need to call Tim, but he knew so much already and still hadn't found Ainsley Wainwright's sister. There was no guarantee that he would ever find her, that this would ever stop, until my life was totally ruined and I was hiding under chairs all the time.

I heard my cell phone ringing in my bag. What now?

I reached over and grabbed it, hesitating a little when I saw the caller ID. Jeff Coleman.

"Hey, Jeff," I said, trying to sound casual. "What's up?"

"What's wrong?"

"Why would you think something's wrong?" I asked. Not as though he couldn't hear the tension in my voice.

"Give it up, Kavanaugh; then I'll tell you my news."

He had news. Hmmm. I quickly told him about the impostor now canceling my clients. When I was done, he said, "Oh."

"That's it? Oh?"

"What do you want from me? To say that someone's out to get you, that it's all one big conspiracy?"

I tried to hear the teasing in his voice, but I couldn't. For once. Immediately I grew suspicious. But before I could respond, he spoke again.

"Because it *is* one big conspiracy."

Huh?

"Sherman Potter's out."

"Out where?" Butterflies began crashing into the sides of my stomach.

"Out on the street. And he's on the move."

Chapter 40

On the move? "How do you know this? Did you talk to Tim?" I asked.

"Potter ponied up the bail. Did a little business with my neighbor."

Goodfellas Bail Bonds. Right next door to Murder Ink.

"How did you find out?"

"I *am* on speaking terms with Sonny."

"Sonny?"

He gave an exasperated sigh. "Sonny owns Goodfellas. He stops over occasionally when it's slow, although I haven't seen him too much lately. I think the crime rate's going up."

I didn't need Jeff Coleman's opinion about social issues. "He just happened to tell you about Sherman Potter?"

"No, Kavanaugh. I asked him directly. I figured Potter would need a bondsman—why not ask around?"

So at least I knew one of Jeff's sources now. "Seems a little convenient that Sherman Potter went to the guy next door," I said.

"Sonny hangs out over near the police station, just in case. He happened to hear about the Flamingos' band manager. Let's say Sonny enjoys a little notoriety, and he has a thing for celebrity clients." Jeff paused. "Are you finished giving me the third degree, or do you want to know where Potter's off to?"

Oh, right. Sherman Potter was "on the move."

"Let me guess," I said, remembering something. "He's on his way here. To the Venetian."

Jeff was silent a second, then, "Give the girl a gold star. How do you know that?"

I didn't want to tell him that Harry had told me Potter always stayed at the Venetian when he was in town. Instead I said, "You're not the only one with sources, you know."

I heard a low chuckle, then, "You could go keep an eye on him."

"I could, but I've got a client coming in." I glanced at my watch. Jenny would be here in a few minutes. I couldn't back out now, considering. "You could come over and spy on him, though, until I'm done."

"You remember that I've got my own business to run."

"So I guess no one's keeping an eye on him for now." My tone was flippant, but it was hardly the way I felt. I did want to see what Sherman Potter was up to, but more than likely he'd hole himself up in his room and order room service or something.

Bitsy stuck her head in the door and mouthed that Jenny had arrived.

"Listen, Jeff, I've got to run. I'll call you when I'm done, okay?" and I hung up without saying good-bye.

My head was totally not into the tattoo. I kept having to shake myself out of thoughts about Sherman Potter. He was so close. I could track him down and demand to know about Ainsley, *his* Ainsley: Who was she, where was she, why did he go visit her sister?

I couldn't finish the tattoo today, since it was too big, but I managed to get the black outlines done. It reminded me of the tattoos I'd done on Daisy, and I felt my mood go even further south.

Jenny was happy, though, when she came back into the room after checking out her new rosebush in the bigger mirror in the back. She grinned and gushed about how wonderful it was and how soon could she come back for the color?

I sent her out to Bitsy so she could make her next appointment as I started to clean up, throwing away the disposable ink pots and needles, wiping down the chair with antibacterial spray. It was busywork as I plotted out how I was going to go about finding out which room Sherman Potter was in. The last time, I'd had Harry with me, and he'd turned on his charm with the woman at the front desk. This time, I'd have to figure out how to charm them myself.

Unless Potter liked the same room every time. People who came here had a lot of superstitions, and it was possible that if Potter stayed here every time, staying in the same room might be part of his ritual. I scoured my brain trying to recall what room number it had been, which floor. And then I had it. I stood up straighter and smiled, proud of myself for being so clever. Sister Mary Eucharista was whispering that I shouldn't count my chickens, but I was never that good at math anyway.

I passed Ace's room on my way to the staff room, glancing in but seeing nothing missing except Ace. Had I really driven him out?

I didn't want to think about that now. I had more pressing things on my mind. I could concentrate on talking Ace back later. After I found my stalker/impostor. After this whole nightmare was over.

I grabbed my bag and slung it over my shoulder. Bitsy frowned when she saw me.

"Where are you going? Are you going to pick up some food?"

Even though five o'clock might be dinnertime for some people, it was a bit early for those of us at The Painted Lady. We were usually having dinner at seven or later. I shook my head. "I won't be too long."

"You need to call Jeff first." Bitsy waved a little pink message slip in my face. "He called about half an hour ago."

"He knew I was with a client," I muttered as I stared at the slip, which merely said, *Call Jeff.* I pulled my cell phone out of my bag as I pushed the glass doors open and stepped out into the illusion that is the Venetian Grand Canal Shoppes. The gondoliers' oars slapped against the water in the canal, making a little *pft pft* sound. Music wafted toward me from St. Mark's Square just over the footbridge, and I could imagine the dancers in their Renaissance costumes performing for the tourists.

Jeff picked up on the first ring. "What took you so long?"

"Rosebush. Big one. On her torso on the side."

"Little clichéd, huh?"

"Like your flash isn't boring," I snapped back.

"Touché." He was quiet a second, then, "So what are you up to now?"

"I'm walking through the shops to the hotel," I said. "I'm going to find Sherman Potter."

"You don't have to bother."

I stopped short, and an elderly couple almost crashed into me. They gave me a dirty look as they scooted around me. I stepped to the edge of the walkway.

"What do you mean?" I asked.

"He's not at the Venetian anymore."

He said it like he knew it for a fact. Which meant . . .

"You came over here," I said.

"That's right. And he left."

I sighed.

"I know you're disappointed, Kavanaugh," Jeff said, "but don't despair."

Don't despair? What, was he reading romance novels these days?

"I'm following him."

"You're following him?"

"Is there an echo in here?"

I totally didn't need his crap. "Do you have any idea where he's going?"

"Yes."

"Yes, where?" This twenty-question thing was getting a little old.

"He's pulling in right now. I have to hang back a little."

"Pulling in where?" I closed my eyes and took a deep breath, counting to ten so I wouldn't explode.

"The Golden Palace. The hotel where they found your friend's body."

Chapter 41

"I'm on my way," I said, turning around to go to the parking garage.

"I've got it covered. Stay where you are."

"I'll be there in a few," I said, tossing my phone into my bag.

It only took me about six minutes to get to my car and find my way out of the parking garage. As usual, I turned left, so I'd go down to Koval rather than up to the Strip. I could take Tropicana past New York New York, although it was rush hour now and the traffic was backed up at the light at the Strip. As I inched forward, I glanced down to the left and saw a long row of cars waiting in that direction, too. The airport was mere minutes away, and the infamous Las Vegas sign was down that way. The city had finally created a rest stop at the sign, complete with parking spaces, so people wouldn't have to risk their lives to take their picture under it.

It dawned on me as I finally sailed through the light that trying to find Jeff at the Golden Palace might not be the easiest feat, the only saving grace the fact that he drove a bright orange metallic car. Which begged the question: How on earth could he tail anyone in that and not be seen? Except I kept forgetting that despite his declarations otherwise, I suspected he'd been some sort of covert operative in the Marines during the Gulf War. Not to mention that he was a sneaky sort of person. Someone I absolutely wanted on my side while trying to track down my impostor.

I turned into the Golden Palace's driveway and drove around the parking lot only once before I spotted the orange Pontiac. It was the only one I saw, so it must be Jeff's. I'd never seen another car that color anywhere.

I parked next to the Pontiac, got out, and locked the doors, swinging my bag over my shoulder and wondering where I might find Jeff now. As I started to pass the Pontiac, a hand shot out of the back window and grabbed me.

I froze; the fingers wrapped around my forearm were tight as a vise. My heart began to beat so fast I could barely hear anything over it.

Except something did get through.

"You're late."

I looked down to see Sylvia Coleman's face peering out at me. Her white hair was piled high on her head, little rhinestone butterflies clipped throughout. As if she needed any more adornment than the body art she sported.

"What do you mean, I'm late?" I asked.

She released her grip and pulled her hand back inside the car, the door opening just seconds later. She stepped out, her small figure looking much taller than it was because of the way she held herself.

"Took you long enough."

"Traffic. What are you doing here?"

"Waiting for you."

Okay, so that one was a no-brainer, but it still didn't answer my question. "No. I mean, Jeff brought you along? Who's at your shop?"

"No one. We closed up. We don't do a lot of business anyway until later."

After the kids were out partying and decided to get tattooed. I understood. They were close to Fremont Street, which had a little different clientele from the one I had over at the Venetian.

She still hadn't answered my question, though, and I wanted to know why Jeff would've brought her along on his spy mission. But knowing Sylvia, we could go around and around on it and I'd never get an answer, so I merely asked, "Where's Jeff?"

"He said to wait for you."

"So that's why you're here?"

"He knew you'd come, and that someone would have to meet you."

He knew that, did he? I hated it that he knew me so well, that he knew I wouldn't stay put even when he said I should. But then, most people knew that about me, so it didn't make Jeff Coleman any more special than anyone else. So there.

Sylvia swung a cheetah-print tote bag over her shoulder, tucked her hand in the crook of my elbow, and said, "Let's go find the bad guy."

We weren't that far from the Golden Palace entrance, and as we approached, I could see the familiar facade made up to be like a Chinese palace, with golds and reds swirling about in columns that stretched up over our heads to meet in an entryway that looked like those friendship gates you'd see whenever you went to a Chinatown.

We went under the gate and crossed over a driveway to the revolving doors.

"I hate those things," Sylvia muttered. "You go first." She let go of my arm and gave me a little nudge toward it.

I stepped inside, and she crowded behind me, holding

on to my waist as we took baby steps around until we reached the other side. I took her arm and helped her through.

The Golden Palace kept the Chinese theme here in the lobby of the hotel, with gold and red sashes looping above the front desk. All the employees were wearing Chinese-style clothes: the men wore blue Mao jackets; the women wore bright red dresses with Mandarin collars. But despite the attempt to mimic the theme hotels on the Strip, the Golden Palace couldn't erase the telltale signs that it wasn't even a second-rate resort, rather more like third or fourth. White orchids sprung from plastic vases that looked as though they were picked up at the local Walmart, undermining the attempt at elegance, and a large gold Buddha whose paint was peeling stood sentry in the middle of the lobby. Another problem was that no one working here was Asian. Couldn't they find any Asians in Vegas? Couldn't they steal them away from the Chinese restaurants?

Maybe that was the start of the Golden Palace's problems.

I glanced around but didn't see Jeff anywhere. "I wonder where they'd go," I mused.

"Maybe to the casino." Sylvia pointed up to a red sign with gold script, pointing out the direction we had to walk to get there.

I wasn't sure, but we didn't have any clues to where we should head, so why not? Sylvia's hand found its way back to my elbow, and I had to slow my pace a little so our steps could be in sync. She was almost a foot shorter than me, although pretty spry when she had to be. She swam every other day at the pool in Henderson, where I swam in the summer months when it was too hot to go hiking up at Red Rock.

We'd reached the casino now, and it was more of the

same here: reds and golds and buddhas scattered among the table games and the slot machines. I took a glance around but didn't spot Jeff anywhere. But I did see someone familiar: Harry Desmond.

He was walking briskly through the casino like a man on a mission, his eyes focused straight ahead, his hands in the pockets of his plaid Bermuda shorts.

"What's *he* doing here?"

I whirled around to see Jeff Coleman standing behind us.

"No clue," I said. "Where's Sherman Potter?"

Jeff studied my face for a second before answering, and I wondered if he was going to stonewall me, but finally he said, "He's upstairs. In a room."

"But he has a room at the Venetian. Doesn't he?" I asked.

Before he could answer, Sylvia piped up. "I'd love to stand here all day, but I'm hungry. Can we go get something to eat?"

I didn't want to point out the obvious: We weren't here to eat, but to see what Sherman Potter was up to. Find out whether he was behind everything that had been going on the last few days.

But Jeff didn't seem quite so focused on that right now. "Sounds like a plan," he said to Sylvia.

Huh? He'd gotten me all the way out here, and now we were just going to eat?

We were standing outside a restaurant. The sign said to wait to be seated, but Jeff took his mother's arm with one hand and grabbed my hand with his other one and led us into the restaurant anyway. He nodded at a waitress, who came over with menus; Jeff pulled out a chair for Sylvia, who sat, and then he turned to me.

I plopped down into the chair before he could do anything chivalrous. He raised one eyebrow at me.

"I can seat myself," I said.

"I see that," he said, a smile tugging at the corner of his mouth. I ignored it.

There had only been two chairs at the table, and he grabbed one from another table and pulled it over, closer to me than to his mother. I resisted the urge to give myself a little more personal space. I didn't want to hear his sarcastic comments.

"So while we're sitting here," I said after we'd all ordered coffee and Sylvia ordered a slice of lemon meringue pie, "will Sherman Potter take off on us?"

Jeff shook his head and leaned back in his chair. "No."

"And how are you so sure about that?"

"He put a DO NOT DISTURB sign on the door."

"That doesn't mean anything."

"It does when he's gone in there with a woman."

I sat up a little straighter. "What?"

He let the smile come out now. "Figured that'd get your attention."

"Who is she?" I asked.

"Please?"

I took a deep breath but didn't say anything.

"Okay, Kavanaugh, if you must know. She's a tall redhead."

Chapter 42

It had to be Sherman Potter's Ainsley. I said as much, and Jeff nodded.

"The room was in her name. Wainwright."

I frowned. How did he know that? He saw my expression and smirked.

"I told you, Kavanaugh, I have my ways."

Instead of getting irritated as usual, though, I remembered how Daisy had been found in a room that was reserved for Ainsley Wainwright. I reminded Jeff of that.

"And since Ainsley Wainwright is dead, the girl you saw must be her twin sister."

"She's got a twin?" Jeff asked.

Oh, right, I hadn't told Jeff about that yet. I nodded.

He chuckled. "How on earth do you know these little tidbits of information, Kavanaugh?"

"If I told you, I'd have to kill you."

He laughed out loud.

I rolled my eyes. "Maybe we should go up there," I suggested. "Maybe it's time to find out what's going on."

"You think they'll tell you?" Jeff asked, taking a drink of his coffee.

Who knew? But it would be better than sitting here, doing nothing.

Jeff stood up. "Okay, let's go."

What?

"Let's go up there," he said. "Let's find out what this is all about."

I thought he was joking, until he put his hand under my elbow and pulled me up. "Come on."

I looked over at Sylvia, who was still eating her pie. She waved a hand at us. "I'll hold down the fort here. I might try the peach pie next."

Sure. Why not? Jeff and I walked out of the restaurant and toward the lobby.

"You're sure they're up there," I said.

"I saw them go in."

"So tell me how you found out the room was in her name."

Before he could answer, a young, petite blonde scurried toward us, a big smile on her face. As her eyes flicked to me, the smile faded slightly; then it blossomed again when she looked at Jeff.

"Do you need any more help?"

So that's how he'd done it—how he'd found out the room was in Ainsley's name. He had a mole at the front desk. A woman who clearly had the hots for him. What was it with women who worked at hotel front desks? Were they really so easily swayed by a flash of a smile that they'd give up room information? Although frankly, I could understand giving up information to Harry. He was young and had those swaggering good looks. But Jeff?

For the first time I attempted to see Jeff Coleman through another woman's eyes. We'd started out antagonistically as competitors, when he was all caught up in his ex-wife's murder and I helped him out, and then we slowly, very slowly, became friends. So I'd never looked at him objectively before.

I knew what he looked like, of course. He was a little shorter than me—not that that bothered me, and it was obvious it didn't bother him, either—with a salt-and-pepper buzz cut, maybe ten years older than my own thirty-two years. The lines in his face showed that he'd lived hard at some point, not to mention the cigarettes, but they gave his face some character, I realized. He'd bulked up a little bit in the last months, as though he'd been working out, but I never said anything because I knew he'd twist it all around and say something all smart-alecky about it. But looking at him now, I saw a different Jeff, a guy who was in good shape, good-looking in a rugged sort of way, actually, someone I might have noticed if I hadn't been so competitive and he hadn't been so annoying to start out.

And I felt a flush crawl up my neck when I thought about that kiss again. I had liked it more than I was letting on to myself.

Which was probably why I felt a sudden flash of—dare I say it—jealousy as this young, cute woman batted her long black eyelashes at Jeff and he flirted back.

The emotion caught me by surprise, and I caught my breath. And wouldn't you know it, Jeff was on to me. He winked at me before turning back to the blonde. I'd totally missed her name, but it's not as though I'd ever need it.

"We've got a singer in the nightclub here tonight," she was saying, clearly an invitation. For him, not me. She hadn't given me another look.

"Anyone I know?" he asked. His voice had gotten softer, and there was a distinct Southern lilt to it now. Great.

I wasn't in the mood for idle chitchat. I shifted from one foot to the other, but almost fell over when she answered.

"The Flamingos' new lead singer. She's doing a solo gig."

"Ainsley?" I croaked.

It was as though she'd just noticed I was there. "No, not Ainsley," she said, frowning. "It's Ann. Ann Wainwright." She studied my face for a second, then said, "I know you, don't I?"

Uh-oh. I hoped she didn't read the blogs. Or the newspapers. I tugged on Jeff's shirtsleeve. Time to go.

Fortunately, he agreed with me. He nodded at her and said, "I'll see if I can make it."

"She starts at eight."

"Okay," he said, as if he'd really show up, and then we turned toward the elevators. One was opening just as we approached, so we hopped in.

"So at least we know Ainsley's sister's name now," I said. "But why not reserve the room in her own name, since that's the one she's using tonight? Didn't you say the room was reserved under the name Ainsley Wainwright?"

Jeff shook his head. "I never said that. I didn't get a first name. Just the last."

"Losing your touch?" I teased.

He shrugged, his eyebrows rising slightly in his forehead, his lips curving into a sly smile. "What do you think?"

"Okay, so you made quite the impression on that little thing back there," I said.

"All for the cause, all for the cause."

The elevator doors slid open. We were on the nineteenth floor. It was shabby up here; a moldy odor hung in the air. The carpet was gray, but I couldn't tell if that was the original color or whether it was supposed to be white but had gotten dirty. Jeff took my arm and led me to the left, pointing at the room numbers on a sign.

"Down here."

The hallway was a maze of turns. It felt as though we were walking blocks. The odor grew stronger the farther away from the elevator we got.

"You got a little jealous back there, didn't you?" Jeff teased.

I didn't answer.

He stopped at a door, a DO NOT DISTURB sign dangling from the knob. "This is it." He reached out and put his knuckles to the door, but as he knocked, the door moved. He gave it a little push and it opened.

We exchanged a glance.

"Wasn't closed properly," he said, as if setting up our explanation to the police as to how we ended up breaking and entering. Tim would not be pleased, regardless.

I hung back as Jeff put his head around the door. I could see the corner of an unmade bed, sheets in a pile on the floor at the foot of it, a leg hanging over the side.

"Stay here," Jeff whispered as he went farther around the door.

I didn't want to be out here all by myself, so I followed him, but stopped when I saw the naked man sprawled across the bed.

And the tattoo of a flamingo on his arm.

Chapter 43

It was Sherman Potter. And he wasn't merely sleeping.

Jeff was hunched over the body, studying the flamingo tattoo, which was not nearly as colorful as Daisy's had been when she died.

"It's not new," he said.

I leaned over his shoulder and studied it, too. Jeff was right: This tattoo was not new at all. It actually looked like it was a lot older than the Flamingos, because the color was faded, the lines not so sharp anymore. I wondered if Sherman Potter had given the band its name from the tattoo he sported. Daisy had never said anything about the origin of the band's name, although I'd always assumed it had come from her.

Jeff was no longer paying attention to the tattoo, but scanning the body.

"What are you doing?" I asked, wondering if we should cover the man up. It wasn't exactly dignified to be letting it all hang out like that.

"Looking for a cause of death," Jeff said.

Okay. Sounded reasonable.

I thought about how Daisy had been found in a room in this very same hotel just a couple of days ago. It could not be a coincidence that now Sherman Potter was here, too.

A redheaded woman was seen leaving Daisy's room, and Jeff had seen a redheaded woman come in this room with Sherman Potter.

That could cast doubt on whether Sherman Potter was responsible for Daisy's death, but it was pointing every finger at Ann Wainwright. I wondered why Ann had been using her sister's name.

I glanced back at the tattoo, then looked around the room. Sherman Potter had traveled light, since I didn't see a suitcase or any clothes except the ones that were scattered on the floor. A hotel room key card lay on the desk. Maybe he really was staying at the Venetian and this was just some sort of afternoon delight. Well, until he died, of course.

I heard a familiar tone. My cell phone. A text message. I reached into my bag and pulled it out, reading the screen.

My hand started to shake, and Jeff gently took the phone from me, looking at the message.

It was a picture text, with a picture of Sherman Potter's flamingo tattoo. The one we were looking at right this very moment. And a message that said, "You keep giving me good reasons to blog."

"She put it up on the blog," I whispered. "What else did she put there?" Was she watching us now? Did she see us come in here?

"We could go down to the lobby and see if we can use a computer in the business office to find out what's up." Jeff's tone was matter of fact.

"We need to call Tim," I said, although I wasn't too sure how he'd take me finding yet another dead body.

Jeff knew what I was thinking. "How are you going to explain to your brother that you happened upon poor old Sherman Potter? It's breaking and entering."

"The door was open," I said after a moment.

He grinned. "That's right. But considering that you're

already on the hook for Daisy Carmichael and there's another flamingo tattoo in the picture, maybe you'll just want to phone this in anonymously."

It was tempting. I didn't need Tim telling me yet again that I shouldn't get involved. But I couldn't do it. I had to tell him. Because the guilt would eat me alive. Sister Mary Eucharista had taught me well.

"Didn't think so," Jeff teased, but I could hear something in his tone that indicated he agreed with me.

I took the phone out of Jeff's hand and punched in Tim's number.

"What is it now, Brett?"

His tone made me wish I hadn't felt so guilty.

"Well, there's a bit of a situation," I started.

"There always is with you," he said. "Spit it out."

I told him about finding Sherman Potter, and he caught his breath.

"What is it with you?" he asked. "I mean, how do you do this? It's like you're some sort of murder magnet."

Great. Exactly what I wanted to put on my résumé. Not.

"Just get over here, okay?"

"You haven't touched anything, have you?"

I glanced at Sherman Potter's naked body again and shivered. "No. Nothing."

"Stay put." And he hung up.

Jeff had wandered into the bathroom, and now he emerged. "On his way?" he asked.

I nodded.

"She took a shower. There are wet towels on the floor."

"Maybe he took one," I suggested.

"His hair's not wet, and it doesn't look like the sheets under him are, either."

"Who died and made you a CSI?" I asked.

He rolled his eyes at me—something I usually did,

so it was interesting the other way around—and said, "I suppose you think you're the only one who knows her way around a crime scene."

"Maybe we should buy those little flashlights like they've got on TV. Then we could look under the bed and see if there are any more clues."

Jeff laughed out loud. "And then we'll find out it was Mr. Plum in the dining room with a candlestick. Let's go down to the business center and wait for your brother," he suggested, moving toward the door.

"I told Tim I'd stay put," I said.

"We're not leaving the hotel—we're just checking on something. We'll come right back." He didn't wait for me, went out into the hallway.

His argument made sense, so I followed him out. He pulled the door shut tight, locking Sherman Potter inside.

We wandered the hallway maze until we found ourselves at the elevators. Jeff pushed the DOWN button. I could hear the whir of the elevator, but it didn't stop for us.

"So, Kavanaugh," Jeff said, leaning against the wall, his arms crossed over his chest. "Are we going to talk about it?"

I knew what he was referring to, but I played stupid. "What?"

"This thing between us."

"What thing?"

"You know. We've got a thing."

"We do not have a thing," I said, and the elevator doors opened.

We stepped inside, and we were trapped together for the moment. I couldn't get away.

But he didn't say anything. Not until the elevator doors opened to the lobby. As I started out, he touched my arm and said, "We *do* have a thing." And then we stepped into the lobby.

I totally did not need this right now. I did not need Jeff Coleman to start getting all relationship-y on me. If that was what he was doing. I couldn't quite tell. It was so like him to dance around this, to make me start thinking about it. I shrugged it off. I didn't have time. I had a stalker, an impersonator, I'd just found a dead body, and I had to sort all that out first.

Jeff led the way to the front desk without saying anything else, which I was grateful for. I was also glad to see that the little blonde was nowhere in our vicinity. Maybe she'd gone off shift. One could only hope.

I wasn't paying much attention to Jeff, until I saw him slide a key card across the desk to the young man in a Mao jacket. Immediately red lights started to go off in my head. Had he taken Sherman Potter's room key? He turned slightly and caught my eye, winking. Of course he had. He took the key card. This was so not good.

The young man was now pointing around the corner. He handed Jeff back the key with a smile.

"I can't believe you did that," I said in a hushed tone as we approached the glassed-in business center.

"We needed a key to get in," he said matter-of-factly. "We couldn't have if we didn't have a key."

Just as he slipped the key card into the slot on the business center door, I heard a voice from behind us.

"What are you doing?"

Chapter 44

We'd forgotten all about Sylvia. We'd left her with her pie and coffee and said we'd be right back. We'd lied.

Jeff shuffled her into the room with us. "Sorry," he said, "but something came up."

"I would hope so, otherwise why would you leave an old lady alone?" she said.

No one else was in the business center, and Jeff ignored Sylvia as he slipped into a chair in front of an old PC and clicked on the Internet icon.

"What are we doing in here?" Sylvia asked.

"Checking a blog," Jeff said. I was glad he kept it simple; I wasn't quite sure just how much to tell her.

"You can't do that at home or at the shop?" she demanded.

Jeff waved his hand to shush her as the Skin Deep blog popped up on the screen. I peered over his shoulder, but no pictures had been posted since the ones of me and Harry. I looked away. I didn't want to be reminded.

"What were you doing, kissing that boy?" Sylvia asked me.

I shrugged. "Momentary lapse."

"Induced by absinthe," Jeff added.

"You were drunk?" Sylvia frowned. "My dear, never kiss a boy when you're drunk. He'll get the wrong idea."

No kidding.

Jeff was typing, and then another page came up on the screen. I cringed slightly, because it was "my" blog, Ink Flamingos.

And there it was: Sherman Potter's flamingo tattoo.

I hate it when I'm right about the wrong things.

Jeff scrolled down to see if there was any text, but there wasn't. It was like on Skin Deep, just a picture with no title. Just like the one of Daisy's tattoo on Skin Deep.

"At least she didn't have pictures of us up there," Jeff mused.

"Maybe she doesn't know he's dead," I suggested. "She could've taken it any time."

Jeff pointed at the time on the screen. It had been uploaded fifteen minutes ago. "And what was it the text said? That you keep giving her good reasons to blog? Like the first dead body, and now this one?"

He didn't have to rub it in.

"Let's go back upstairs," I said. "We have to meet Tim." Somehow it seemed more urgent right now.

"If he doesn't see us up there, he'll probably call your cell," Jeff said absently. He was back to Skin Deep, now looking at the picture of Daisy's flamingo. He'd clicked on the picture and it came up in a separate window, much larger than it was on the blog.

I still couldn't figure out why Daisy agreed to have color, although from what Flanigan said, it wasn't this particular tattoo that killed her. It was that second time she was exposed to the allergen. But it still nagged at me that she'd gone somewhere else, to another tattooist, for this work, and not to me. Yeah, it was an ego thing.

"Are you looking for something in particular?" I asked.

"This is interesting," he said softly.

"Interesting how?" I asked.

He turned to Sylvia. "What do you know about this?"

"What do you think?" she asked belligerently.

"I didn't notice this before. Maybe because it was smaller, but I can see it now," Jeff said. "And maybe you should explain." He was still talking to Sylvia.

"What didn't you notice? What needs explaining?" I asked.

Both sets of eyes turned to me.

"Do you want to tell her?" Jeff asked Sylvia.

"Someone better tell me, and fast," I said.

Sylvia patted my arm and smiled as though I were a moron for not picking up on whatever it was they saw.

"I started a tradition a long time ago that in every tattoo I'd hide a little 'mi' for the name of the shop within the tattoo. You know, my signature," Sylvia said. "No one knows," she added with a little smirk, "but it's the way we can keep track of our tattoos. When I turned the shop over to Jeff, he continued with it."

Clever.

Sylvia's finger moved on the screen, and suddenly I saw it. The initials were there. In the pink plumes of the flamingo.

"What?" I asked, turning to Jeff. "*You* colored her flamingo?" I hadn't seen the initials the first time because I hadn't been looking for them, and they were so small I wouldn't have noticed them if they hadn't been pointed out. Like the flowers in the tips of the wings that I'd done.

Jeff shook his head. "Not me." He looked at Sylvia, who'd puffed up her chest proudly.

"It was a nice tattoo," she said, "but it needed that color."

Sylvia did it. I took a deep breath and counted to ten.

"Didn't she tell you she was allergic?" I finally asked.

Sylvia made a face at me. "Look at me, a hundred tattoos and I never keeled over, did I?"

It stung a little that Sylvia had been able to talk Daisy

into the color, and I hadn't even been successful in the
discussion about organic inks. I turned to Jeff. "Didn't
you know about this?"

"Don't go blaming him for any of this," Sylvia admonished. "He went away for a weekend, remember
that?" She turned to Jeff. "You and that nice girl, you
said you needed a weekend away. So I opened the shop
while you were gone. No big deal."

I had never seen Jeff Coleman blush before. I should
take note of the date and time, so I could tease him
about it occasionally. In fact, it would be very nice am-
munition for when he decided to pick on me.

And then I wondered who the "nice girl" was.

I shook the thought aside. Sylvia had done Daisy's
color. Without asking about her allergy. But she was
right, at least about this one. Daisy didn't keel over
from it.

"She came to your shop?" I asked.

Sylvia nodded. "She said you'd done the flamingo,
but she'd seen the koi that Jeff did on your arm and she
loved the colors and the design. She was disappointed
he wasn't there, but I convinced her that an old lady
could do just as good a job."

Looking at the picture, I had to agree. The color was
impeccable.

"So you didn't know about this?" I asked Jeff.

"Not till right this moment," he said. "Not till I saw
the initials. I hadn't looked that closely before."

I remembered how Flanigan had asked if I could ask
around to see if anyone I knew would know anything
about Daisy's tattoos. And how I hadn't, because I'd
been too distracted by my own problems.

"We should tell Tim and Flanigan about this," I said,
turning to Sylvia. "You've got paperwork, right, to prove
when you did this?"

The look on her face made me realize that maybe

they weren't exactly up to date on their paperwork over at Murder Ink. And the look on Jeff's face told me that he'd been having issues with that.

"Let's go," I said, not wanting to get into it.

Jeff logged off the computer, and the three of us went back through the glass doors.

A flash blinded me as we rounded the corner.

Chapter 45

I had a flashback from the other night with Harry, when all those flashes kept going off. My heart leaped into my throat as I blinked, trying to see who had the camera. Jeff was one step ahead of me, though. He grabbed a woman's arm and whirled her around.

I couldn't believe it.

"Melanie?" It was Melanie Black, Daisy's bandmate, the one who'd invited me to the concert last night.

She held a small camera, and she did not look happy with Jeff.

"Let go of me," she demanded; then she saw me and tried an awkward smile on for size. "Brett, can you tell him to let go of me, tell him who I am?"

"Did you just take my picture?" I asked, ignoring her question.

Melanie seemed surprised to see she was holding a camera. "I was taking pictures," she admitted. "I don't think I took one of you." But her blush told a different story.

"Let's see," Jeff held out his hand for the camera, and she frowned, but she handed it over.

He had to let her go to look at the last picture she took, but she stayed put. Probably because she didn't want him to keep her camera. Jeff studied the camera screen and then held it up for me to see.

It was a picture of me. Jeff and Sylvia flanked me, but they were partially cut off.

I looked up at Melanie. "Why did you take my picture?" She couldn't deny that she had now.

Her face clouded over for a second; then she forced a smile. "I didn't realize. But it's a good picture."

"Good enough for your blog?" I sneered.

Melanie frowned. "What are you talking about?"

This could not be a coincidence. Melanie had been the one to invite me to the arena last night. She had invited me backstage. I had wanted answers about Daisy, and then Jeff and I found ourselves locked out. She had fed me the story about Sherman Potter and Daisy. Maybe it was to deflect any possible suspicion from her.

Although I hadn't thought any of the girls in the band would be suspect. Daisy was their bread and butter. Why would any of them kill her?

And then I knew. Because Daisy wanted out. Because she was leaving the band. Because she *was* their bread and butter, that wouldn't set well.

Melanie knew about me. Knew about the tattoos. Knew Daisy was allergic. Anyone could get a tattoo machine and all the equipment online for a do-it-yourselfer. The picture of the tattoo that Flanigan had showed me indicated it was the work of a scratcher, someone who didn't know what she was doing. It would be easy to set up a real tattooist, too.

Melanie was almost as tall as me. With a wig, she could impersonate me. She could be the woman who'd left that hotel room. She could be the woman Jeff met in the bar.

Now she was here. At the Golden Palace. Where

Sherman Potter's body lay upstairs. And she was taking pictures of me.

Maybe she killed Sherman Potter because he figured it out.

Like me.

Jeff was toying with the camera. "There aren't any other pictures," he said, then looked at Melanie. "If you were being a tourist and taking pictures, then why is this one of Brett the only one you've got in the camera? And why are you taking pictures here? It's a hotel front desk. Not exactly something for the photo album, is it?"

She looked decidedly uncomfortable. Good. But before she could respond, I heard a familiar voice.

"Brett?"

I turned to see Tim walking toward us, confusion crossing his face. He had a couple of uniforms and crime scene investigators behind him. They all stopped when he did.

I went over to him, knowing Jeff would hold on to Melanie so she couldn't get away.

"I think this is her," I said softly to Tim when I reached him. I told him about the picture and my theories about her.

"Did Jeff ID her as the woman he met?" Tim asked as he checked Melanie out.

Like I said, she was almost as tall as me, and her hair was short, too, but it had been dyed midnight black and the ends were purple. Her face was round and she had an upturned nose and pouty lips. Her eyes were on the small side, but she attempted to make them look larger with dark eye shadow and thick mascara and black eyeliner. It was a sort of goth look but fit the Flamingos' updated punk look to a T.

"She's not exactly incognito," Tim pointed out, and I grudgingly agreed. She would be noticeable in a crowd.

But maybe she didn't wear all that makeup all the time. I said as much.

"If her purpose was to come here, kill Sherman Potter, then take your picture, why would she make herself up like that? And how did she even know you'd be here?" Tim was playing devil's advocate, and I couldn't blame him. He had unraveled my theory with that last question. "How did you come to be here and find Sherman Potter, anyway?" he asked.

I told him how Jeff had followed Potter and how the room had been reserved in the name Wainwright.

"But she's dead," Tim said, his expression telling me he thought I might have gone over the deep end on this one.

"It's got to be her twin sister, Ann." It was like on those soap operas, when someone ended up having an evil twin.

"How do you know her sister's name?" Tim's face grew dark.

I quickly explained how the woman at the hotel desk had said that the Flamingos' new lead singer's name was Ann Wainwright, not Ainsley, as she'd presented herself.

Tim's frown deepened, but he turned and approached Melanie. Jeff wasn't holding on to her, and she hadn't tried to take off.

"My sister says you took her picture. What for?"

I could now see Melanie assessing Tim, deciding what she should say.

"Someone asked me to."

She could've just told me that before. At least she was coming clean with the cops.

"Who?" Tim prompted.

Melanie shrugged. "She asked me for an autograph, I gave it to her, and then she gave me her camera, asked if I could do her a favor. She said Brett Kavanaugh was in the business center, could I get a picture of her. When

I said she should do it herself, she said because I knew her, it would be better if I did it. She said she wanted a candid shot, so I should be discreet, not let on what I was doing."

Sounded plausible, but I still wasn't willing to give her the benefit of the doubt. Neither was Jeff.

"How did she know you knew Brett?" he asked before Tim could. "Did you ask her how she knew Brett?"

Melanie seemed confused by the questions, by the fact that someone other than Tim was asking.

"What did she look like?" I asked, throwing her off a little more.

But she recovered enough to say, "She looked a little like you. Red hair, tall. Maybe not as thin as you, though."

My impostor strikes again. And the description could easily fit Ann Wainwright.

"Where did she go?" I asked, looking around and not seeing anyone matching the description.

Melanie shrugged.

"Maybe you should come with me and answer some questions," Tim said to her.

"Kavanaugh?"

Tim and I both turned to see Detective Kevin Flanigan coming toward us. The uniforms and CSIs parted like the Red Sea to let him through.

"What's going on?" Flanigan asked.

Tim gave it to him in a nutshell. Flanigan was nodding. "You take her and talk to her," he said, meaning Melanie. "Get a description of the woman who asked her to take the picture. I'll go upstairs."

"Where should we go?" I asked.

All eyes landed on me. It was not a comfortable feeling.

"You found the body?" Flanigan asked.

Jeff and I both nodded.

"Then you come with me."

Sylvia stepped forward, her cheetah-print bag swinging from her shoulder. "And where do I go?"

Flanigan's mouth twitched, as if he wanted to smile. "Mrs. Coleman. I remember you." From a couple of months before. "You might as well come with us, too."

I was glad we didn't have to leave Sylvia behind again, and Tim looked relieved that she wasn't going to be his responsibility.

Flanigan took me, Jeff, and Sylvia up in the elevator with him, along with the hotel manager, who had to let us in the room, and sent the others up in a separate elevator. No one said anything as we went up.

We arrived at the same time the uniforms and CSIs did. Guess there wasn't too much elevator traffic today.

We all made our way down the hallway maze to Sherman Potter's room.

We watched as the manager slipped the key card into the door, and it swung open. Flanigan went in first.

I knew we were in trouble by the look on his face when he came back out right away.

"There's no body in here. Can someone tell me what's going on?"

Chapter 46

No body? I craned my neck to see between Flanigan and one of the uniforms. Flanigan noticed and stepped aside, waving his hand and giving permission for me to enter. Jeff was right behind me.

The bed was made. The pillows plumped. At least as much as they could be. There were no clothes scattered on the floor. The room was tidy. A glance in the bathroom told me the wet towels were gone.

Jeff and I looked like the boy who cried wolf.

"He was here," I insisted.

Jeff was nodding. "We both saw him."

We heard a squeaking sound in the hall and turned to see a maid's cart making its way past the room. Jeff sidled past me and asked the maid pushing the cart: "Did you just make up this room?"

The little Hispanic woman in the ill-fitting white uniform got a deer-in-the-headlights look about her.

Flanigan stepped forward, flashing his badge. "It's all right, ma'am," he said politely. "Did you just make up the room?"

Not sure the badge was a good idea, because she looked even more scared. She probably thought she was going to get deported.

"Did you see anyone in the room?" I asked softly.

A quick shake of her head and then, "The sign was gone." She indicated the doorknob.

The DO NOT DISTURB sign. It had been there when Jeff and I left. Someone had taken Sherman Potter out of here, taken the sign, and the maid had cleaned up. All while we were downstairs in the business center checking out that blog and then talking to Melanie, who had taken my picture. A great distraction.

If Melanie were the one behind all this, then she would have to have an accomplice.

Ann Wainwright.

It seemed as though it was all falling into place.

I told Flanigan about Ann and how the woman Melanie claimed had asked her to take my picture fit her description. Jeff added that he'd seen a woman with red hair go into Sherman Potter's room with him. Flanigan listened, to his credit, and then folded his arms across his chest and stood with his feet apart. He wasn't sold.

"Do you think a woman could carry a big guy like Sherman Potter out of here undetected?" he asked.

"Maybe," I said. "She's tall, too, like me, and bigger than me. Maybe she lifts weights or something. Lots of women do." I didn't, but I did hike and swim. He probably didn't care about that, though.

"What about cameras?" Jeff asked, his voice piercing the long silence as Flanigan thought about what I'd said.

The hotel manager's face turned red. He was obviously embarrassed. "No cameras in the halls here," he said apologetically. "This isn't the Bellagio."

No kidding.

"Is there a back stairway?" Flanigan asked.

Good thinking. I mean, whoever pulled Sherman Potter out of here couldn't very well have taken him in the elevator to dispose of him.

The hotel manager pointed down the hall, a little farther from where we were standing. If the stairway was back in that direction and there were no cameras, then it might figure that whoever was carrying a body might not be detected. Except maybe by the maid. She didn't look as though she was following what was going on, though. I wondered if anyone in Flanigan's entourage spoke Spanish.

Flanigan indicated that one of the CSIs should go into the hotel room to see if there were any clues left after the cleaning up. It was possible, since we hadn't been downstairs all that long, and it should take more time to clean a hotel room than that. Another strike against that poor maid. I hoped she'd still have a job after this.

Flanigan brought the other CSI and the hotel manager with him to check out the stairway. He didn't say where Jeff and I should go, so we stayed put outside the hotel room with the maid.

Jeff turned to her and started talking to her in Spanish. Really. He was just full of surprises these days. The maid's face brightened as their conversation went on, then darkened, looking pointedly at me, then abruptly away; then her face lightened again.

Finally, Jeff turned to me. "She says she was coming down the hall and saw a woman go in there. A redhaired woman, like you."

Great.

"That's when the DO NOT DISTURB sign went on the door."

Exactly what Jeff had said, but then he came downstairs to meet up with me and Sylvia. Between then and the time we went upstairs, the mysterious woman—who I was convinced was Ann—had killed Sherman Potter. She was likely hiding out, waiting for us to leave, before she dragged him down the stairs.

I thought about that picture text. She may have sent it in the hopes that it would lure us away. It worked. Once we were gone, she got down to business.

Like I said, I had it all figured out.

We heard a door open somewhere, and Flanigan appeared. He was alone. His forehead was knit in a frown, his hands clenched at his sides as he strode toward us, looking as though it were my fault that Sherman Potter and his abductor had disappeared.

I worried that he thought it really *was* my fault.

"Besides that room, were you anywhere else?" he demanded.

My heart began pounding as the panic set in. What was he looking for?

I shrugged. "We were on the elevator," I tried.

"But you were in that room," he said, and there was something in his tone that made me wonder if he thought I was lying. This was so not good. And then I remembered.

"Jeff has the room key. It was on the desk."

Jeff totally did not want me to give that one up. I could tell from the glare he shot me, but to his credit, he produced the key and handed it to Flanigan.

"We wanted to get into the business center, and we couldn't if we didn't have a room key," I explained.

Flanigan studied the key card a second, then gave me a long stare. "Why did you need to get into the business center?"

"There's a picture on that Ink Flamingos blog. Of Sherman Potter." Uh-oh. It really wasn't of Sherman at all, but the tattoo on his arm. I quickly explained what we had seen and what was in the picture.

"You didn't give Mr. Potter that tattoo?" Flanigan asked.

"I never saw Sherman Potter before the other day. He certainly had never been in my shop. The tattoo, though, was older," I said, trying to offer up something useful and looking at Jeff for backup. He nodded, but didn't say anything. So much for us having a thing. If we

246

were really having a thing, he'd pipe up right about now and get us both off the hook.

From Flanigan's expression, though, I knew I wasn't off the hook. Something was up, but before I could ask, he spoke.

"We found strands of red hair in the stairwell."

Chapter 47

"Ann Wainwright has red hair," I said. "Ainsley's twin sister. She's been using her sister's name. I don't really know why. But she must be the woman who went into the hotel room with Potter. The room was in her name."

Flanigan looked at me with a sad expression, like I was suffering from some sort of dementia. I think it was that whole evil twin cliché. But there really *was* an evil twin. Why didn't he get that?

Sylvia and Jeff were still quiet. Had they become mutes when I wasn't paying attention? When I was trying to talk my way out of this one?

My butt was on the line, and my impostor was again trying to implicate me. The fact that the Ink Flamingos blog was set up in my name and now sported a picture of Sherman Potter's flamingo tattoo could hammer yet another nail in my own coffin.

"Brett didn't do anything," Jeff finally said. "I was with her the whole time." I couldn't help but hear the implication: If he hadn't been with me, would I have dragged Sherman Potter down the stairwell, leaving my hair behind?

I was feeling rather paranoid. Was it justified? Maybe. Because Flanigan didn't seem sold on my alibi.

"I have no reason to do anything to Sherman Potter," I insisted. "I mean, I didn't even know the guy. I met him once." I was totally protesting too much.

Flanigan asked the hotel manager if there was a room he could use to take statements. The manager's head bobbed up and down as if he was going for an elusive apple, and he produced a master key card, saying Flanigan could use the room next door to the one Sherman Potter had been found in. As he spoke, he opened the door.

It was identical to the one next door, except everything was reversed, a mirror image. Flanigan ushered me and Jeff and Sylvia in.

"I didn't have anything to do with this," Sylvia argued, forgetting that Jeff was her ride and she couldn't get home without him.

"It shouldn't take too long," Flanigan said with a kind smile. I wished he'd given me that smile. Instead, he cast a narrow eye at me and asked me if I would allow one thing.

"What?"

A crime scene investigator hovered over me. I wanted to shove him aside, but figured that might not go over well.

"We'd like a strand of your hair," Flanigan said flatly, as if he were merely asking me to sit down.

They wanted to match my hair to the hair found in the stairwell. He really didn't believe me.

"It's a formality," he explained. "We need to remove you from any suspicion."

Because until they realized my hair didn't match the one found in the stairwell, I would most definitely be one of those persons of interest they're always talking about. I wasn't born yesterday.

I nodded and felt a tug. The CSI apologized and stuck the two strands he'd managed to yank out of my head into a small plastic bag.

"Is it going to take a long time to make sure it's not a match?" I asked, my voice sounding about a million miles away. I blinked a couple of times to keep a tear from escaping. It wasn't that it had hurt; it was just everything. The whole thing. The impostor, Daisy, Sherman Potter.

I felt a hand settle on my lower back, and Flanigan's eyes flitted from me to Jeff as if he knew Jeff and I might have a thing after all. He *was* a detective.

"It shouldn't take too long," Flanigan said, although he wasn't forthcoming with a specific date. "Let's get started."

An hour later, Jeff, Sylvia, and I were free to go. Tim had showed up about fifteen minutes in, with Melanie in tow so she could get subjected to even more questions by Detective Flanigan. She was still there when we left. Tim came into the hall with us.

"Going back to the shop?" he asked, and from his tone I could tell he didn't want me to go home yet. Maybe my room hadn't been completely cleaned up from the night before.

I did have another client coming in about eight, and it was already seven o'clock as it was. "That's right," I said. "I should be done about ten or so."

"I'll come by and pick you up and take you home then," he said, giving me a quick hug. He motioned something to Jeff, but I couldn't really see what it was. I was so pathetic.

When he'd gone back inside, I rubbed my head where they'd taken those hairs.

"You okay, Kavanaugh?" Jeff asked when we got into the elevator.

"Of course she's not okay," Sylvia answered for me, slapping Jeff on the arm. "Someone's playing around with her head, pretending to be her. Be nice."

"I thought I was being nice," Jeff said teasingly, with a wink at me. "I'm being nice, aren't I?" he asked me.

I rolled my eyes at him. At least some things never changed.

The elevator doors slid open to the lobby, and we stepped out.

"Am I glad that's over," Sylvia said loudly. "But I wonder whatever happened to that Sherman fellow."

I'd been wondering the same thing. While I suspected Ann of being the culprit in all this, did she really have the strength to carry Sherman Potter's body out of a room, down a hall, and down the stairs and then hide him somewhere?

We'd left the hotel and were crossing the parking lot toward our cars. I could see my bright red Mustang next to the orange metallic Pontiac. The cars piqued my memory, however, and not in a good way.

Panic bubbled up in my chest, but by now I was used to the feeling.

I stopped, grabbing onto Jeff's arm and cocking my head toward my car. "It's been used as a coffin before," I said, referring to that time a couple months back when the body of a Dean Martin impersonator had been found dead in the trunk of my car. What if I'd find Sherman Potter in there, too? It had leaked to the news stations that I'd had that misfortune. If my impostor wanted to really freak me out, putting Sherman in my trunk would totally do it.

"Give me your keys." Jeff held out his hand, and I gave them to him. "Stay here," he said to both of us.

"What's he doing?" Sylvia asked.

"He's checking my car."

"For what?"

I shrugged, not wanting to say it out loud again.

She made a face at me. "You're much too paranoid, dear," she said, hooking her hand around my elbow.

No kidding.

Jeff had rounded the back of my car, and the trunk hood lifted. I closed my eyes, not wanting to know. Then I heard, "Come on!"

Slowly, I opened my eyes again, and Jeff was beckoning us. Sylvia and I made our way to the car, our arms still linked.

"Nothing here," Jeff said, showing me the empty trunk before slamming the hood down. "It's okay."

Was it really? I had no idea.

"I'll follow you to the Venetian," Jeff said as his mother climbed into the passenger seat of the Pontiac. "And if you need anything later, call me. You know where I am."

The ride to the Venetian was uneventful, and I was thankful for that. I gave Jeff a wave as I turned in to the lane that would take me to the self-parking garage. Being back on familiar ground, I relaxed a little.

The security guard held up his hand, and I stopped, smiling at him. I leaned out my window and said, "I'm going to the shops," anticipating his question as to whether I was a hotel guest or going to the casino. I pulled back into the car, ready to move on, but he stepped out in front of the Mustang, studying it.

"I'm sorry, ma'am, but we've had a report."

I moved the gearshift so I could take my foot off the clutch and it wouldn't lurch forward and stop, then put on the parking brake. I opened the door and stepped out. "A report?" I asked. "I own The Painted Lady; it's in the shops. You can check."

He shook his head. "I've been told to detain you."

Chapter 48

My first instinct was to make a run for it. Hightail it out of there on foot and see how far I could get. And then my more sensible side told me that was ridiculous: I'd look more guilty that way. But guilty of what?

"What's wrong?" I asked.

He had a clipboard with a sheaf of papers and started flipping through the pages, finally jabbing his finger on one. His eyes met mine, and I could see something bad was on that page. But after all the things that had been going on the last few days, what could be worse?

"Could you please stand over there?" the guard asked, indicating I was to move toward the little guard-house. I was acutely aware that another guard had appeared out of nowhere and was standing behind me now. So much for sprinting.

"I think I have a right to know what's going on," I said loudly, with much more bravado than I felt.

At that moment, a familiar Toyota Prius was turning the corner to exit. Joel spotted me, his face lit up, and he pulled into a handicap spot near the guardhouse. As he emerged from the tiny car, the guard who'd approached him seemed a little taken aback by his size and gave him a wide berth.

"I'm sorry, sir, but you can't park there," the guard admonished.

Joel shrugged. "What's going on, Brett?"

I sighed. "They're 'detaining' me," I said, making little quote marks with my fingers. "I have no idea why."

I noticed now that a third guard had joined us and opened the driver's side door. The motor was still running, since I hadn't shut it off. I had a crazy thought that it was a good thing Sherman Potter's body wasn't inside the trunk.

Joel came closer, a frown on his face. He was considerably bigger than the first guard, who seemed very intimidated.

"I think you need to tell the lady what's going on," Joel said sternly.

"We need to search the car," the guard said, as the other two guards were now doing just that.

"What do you think you'll find?" I asked, hearing a familiar siren in the distance. "Did you call the police?" This was too much.

Joel gave a quick nod at me, indicating I should sidle over toward him. I did. As all three guards were now hunkered down in my car with flashlights, Joel took my hand and we began to slowly back up toward his car.

"I'm breaking you out of here," Joel whispered.

Sounded like a plan.

The guards were clearly not very good at their job, because they barely noticed what we were up to until we were already in the car and Joel was backing out and then pulling toward the exit. The little Prius didn't have a lot of oomph, but it had enough, and the guards were too startled to move quickly. They weren't exactly high-end rent-a-cops.

We passed a police car with its lights flashing as we turned out onto Koval.

"We'd better get lost and quick," I said, indicating them.

Joel knew his way around the back roads, and soon we were a couple miles away, no sirens anywhere. The guards had not taken his license plate down, hadn't really paid much attention to his car, because they'd concentrated on him. I had told them, though, where I worked, and I said as much to Joel.

"They probably already knew that. You might want to call Tim," he suggested.

I'd left my bag in my car, not even thinking. Could this day get much worse?

Joel handed me his phone, and I punched in Tim's number, knowing I'd be interrupting the interrogation over at the Golden Palace but not caring at this point. The good news was, Tim answered right away because he didn't recognize the number.

"Kavanaugh," he said.

"Tim, it's Brett."

"Brett?"

"I'm going to tell you what happened, but you can't interrupt me and you can't yell at me," I said, then quickly added, "The security guards at the Venetian stopped me, said they had to detain me, started searching my car, and Joel came, we took off, and now I think the cops are after us."

He was quiet for a couple of seconds, most likely digesting this new bit of information.

"Did they say why they had to conduct a search?" he finally asked, the restraint remarkable.

"No."

"Let me see what I can find out. Where are you?"

I glanced around at the street outside and didn't recognize it. "We're just driving around," I said. "I don't want to go back."

He must have heard the desperation in my voice, because he said, "Have Joel take you to Murder Ink. But stay put there, okay? I'm worried about all this, that someone's targeted you for some reason, and until we find out who and catch her, you could be in danger."

I gave a deep sigh of relief, tears springing to my eyes because he believed me. And then I pounced on the one word that came through loud and clear. "Her. You said her. You think this is Ann Wainwright, don't you?"

He didn't confirm anything, just said, "I'll call you later when I know something," and then he hung up.

I turned to Joel. "Tim says you should take me to Murder Ink." Jeff would be surprised to see me, but considering his criminal tendencies, he would be perfectly willing to harbor a fugitive.

Joel gave me a sly smile and pointed the Prius in that direction.

"What?" I asked, when the smile wouldn't go away.

"You and Jeff. It's cute."

Cute? What was cute? Oh, right, that *thing*. "There's nothing going on," I insisted.

Joel's smile grew into a full-fledged grin. "There's always been something going on with you two."

That was for sure, but not the way he thought.

"I don't want to talk about it," I said.

"Ace is gone," Joel said, completely switching gears.

I sat up straighter in my seat, the belt pulling against my chest. I stuck my thumb underneath it and loosened it slightly. "Gone for good?" I remembered how he hadn't been in his room when I left, but it was as if he'd just gone down the walkway to the oxygen bar. It seemed as though he really meant it when he said he quit.

He hadn't even said good-bye.

"He'll be back," Joel said confidently.

"How do you know?"

"He did this once before."

This was the first I'd heard about that. "When?"

"Right before you took over. Flip told us about how he was selling the business to you, and Ace wasn't thrilled with the idea of working for a woman." Joel shot me a look. "I had no problems with it."

I touched his arm. "Thanks. But what happened with Ace?"

"He left. Said he was never coming back. But he left his paintings. The day before you started, he was there again, never said a word, acted as though he'd never left."

I mulled that a few seconds. "But this is different."

"No. It's not. He didn't take his paintings."

I didn't see the significance of that, but Joel was satisfied, and he knew Ace better than I did. Maybe Ace would be back, after all.

We'd been closer to Murder Ink than I'd thought. Joel pulled into the alley behind the shop, the scent of the Chinese food from the take-out joint next door hanging in the air. He gave me a smile. "You'll be okay here."

"I have a client later."

"Don't worry about it. I'll take care of it. I'll tell Bitsy everything." He leaned over and gave me a peck on the cheek. "Everything's going to be fine. Your brother's going to catch the bad guy; you can get back to normal. You always do."

He was right. I smiled back. "Thanks for everything," I said, climbing out of the car. It felt good to stretch my legs. I was too tall for that car, and I couldn't imagine how Joel felt, all three hundred pounds of him squished into that little Prius.

I didn't see Jeff's Pontiac, but the back door was slightly ajar, so maybe he parked in front today.

I waved at Joel and started to push the door open, but something was jamming it from the inside. I peered around the door and saw what was obstructing it.

Another pink flamingo.

Chapter 49

They were breeding like rabbits.

Plastic rabbits.

This one wasn't wearing a tiara, though, and I couldn't see any red paint, so obviously whoever had left it did not feel as much animosity toward Jeff as she did toward me. Maybe she'd seen us together at the Golden Palace, before or after she disposed of Sherman Potter. Maybe she knew about our *thing*.

Joel hadn't pulled away yet, and I heard his door open.

"What's wrong, Brett?" he asked when he got out.

I sighed. I felt like I was in a Fellini movie, where everything was in black and white except that pink flamingo.

Joel came over and stood next to me. I pointed around the door. He craned his neck so he could see, then straightened up again.

"Whoever's doing this is nuttier than a fruitcake."

He'd just described Sylvia to a T, but it wasn't her. It was crazy Ann Wainwright, who had some sort of personal beef with me.

Where was Jeff? I wondered, pushing a little more forcefully on the door now so I could squeeze inside. I was halfway in when Joel asked, "You sure you want to go in there?"

He was right. What if whoever had put this flamingo here was still there, in the front of the shop or lying in wait in a corner or the bathroom or something? I came back out.

Time for Plan B. As I poked my head through the door opening, I shouted, "Jeff? Are you there?"

All I heard was the rattle of the old air conditioning unit.

"He's not here," I said, remembering that he had Sylvia with him when we left the Golden Palace. He was probably taking her home.

"Call him," Joel said, handing me his phone.

I punched in his number, but there was no answer. I shrugged at Joel and said, "I probably should call Tim."

I didn't wait for Joel to agree; I just dialed. Tim picked up on the first ring.

"Someone called the Venetian and reported that you were a suspect in a murder," he said without saying hello. "That's why they detained you." He snorted. "Rent-a-cops. They should know better than to listen to an anonymous caller."

"So is it all straightened out?" My hopes rose. Maybe I could go back to work now; Joel and I wouldn't have to be fugitives.

"Stay where you are," he said. "I'll call you when it's okay. You're at Murder Ink?"

"That's right, but Jeff's not here yet. I think he might be with Sylvia. I tried to call, but he didn't answer." I paused, then added, "But someone's been here. Left Jeff a little present. A pink flamingo, like the one in our house."

"You didn't touch anything, right?"

"No. It was wedged in the door, so I think I might have crunched it a little when I pushed the door open, but I didn't go in, I didn't touch it."

"I'll send someone over there to dust for prints. We

found a fingerprint at our house. Maybe whoever it is was as careless there."

"Whose print was it?" More hopes.

But then he dashed them. "No one we know yet. But we're still looking. Wait for the cops; wait for Jeff." And he hung up.

I handed the phone back to Joel and shrugged. "He says to stay here." As I looked around the alleyway, the Chinese food smells mixing with those in the Dumpster, I realized it was the last thing I wanted to do. I felt like a shark: If I stopped moving now, I might die. Well, that was an exaggeration, but you get what I mean. I needed something to do, something that made me think I was being helpful. Sure, Tim would think otherwise, but he wasn't here.

Neither was Jeff.

Although as we turned, a familiar orange car swung into the alley. He slammed on the brakes, parking right behind Joel's Prius. Jeff got out of the Pontiac with a frown.

"What's going on?" he asked.

I quickly told him about being detained at the Venetian, but adding the stuff Tim had said about how someone called saying I was wanted for murder, then went on to include how Joel had helped me escape. I must have been going on a little too long, because Jeff held up his hand to interrupt.

"Get to the point, Kavanaugh. Why are you outside my shop?" He noticed the door was open, and he went over to it, pushing against that pink flamingo, just like I had. "What the hell is that?" he asked, spotting it.

"Tim said I should come over here," I said, "but I found that flamingo in your door. You weren't here. He's sending someone over to take fingerprints."

Jeff was shaking his head, running a hand through his buzz cut, the tattoos on his arm flexing with each movement. Joel and I exchanged a look, but neither of us said anything. Finally, Jeff looked at me.

"You're full of trouble, you know that, Kavanaugh?"

"I thought you liked that about me," I quipped before I could stop myself.

A smile spread across his face. "And you are way too sensitive." He paused. "I guess the cops aren't exactly treating a plastic flamingo like an emergency."

"It's not like it's going to walk away," Joel piped up.

Somehow that struck me as really funny. Guess you had to be there. But within seconds, the three of us were laughing so hard it hurt. In retrospect, though, it wasn't so much funny as it was a chance to let off some steam.

A lot of steam.

I realized Jeff had stopped laughing and was studying the door to his shop. Joel and I stepped forward, and I could see it then. The scratches on the dead bolt, the deep grooves in the side of the door.

"Someone jimmied the lock," Jeff said. "And did a damn poor job of it, too. I'm going to have to fix that." It was a casual statement, as though he had a drawer full of locks in his office and he'd just have to replace this one with one of those. "What I don't get is this thing with the pink flamingos. I mean, I understand the symbolism and all, but do they really think a pink flamingo is going to scare anyone?"

Scared the daylights out of me. I tried to look non-chalant.

"I'm going around the front," Jeff announced. "See if anything's up over there."

He started down the alley, then looked back at us. "Aren't you coming?"

I hadn't realized it was an invitation, but I didn't have to be asked twice. Joel and I trailed Jeff around the edge of the building and along the alley between it and Goodfellas Bail Bonds. I wondered if Sonny was over at the police station trolling for celebrity clients. When we reached the front entrance to Murder Ink, it didn't seem as though anyone had tried to get in this way. The door had no marks on it at all. Jeff reached into his pocket for his keys and pulled them out.

"You can't go in," I said. "The police are coming."

Jeff snickered. "It's my shop." He put the key in the lock and pushed the door in.

The front of the shop was dark; blinds had been pulled down over the big front windows. He yanked on them and they snapped up, letting in light from the streetlamp that struck the flash on the walls and illuminated it. Joel perused the designs, nodding. He was comfortable in a shop like this; my shop was the most upscale he'd ever worked in. The chain hanging out of his pocket jingled slightly as he absently toyed with it.

A glance around told me nothing seemed out of place, although at the same time, something wasn't right. I couldn't put my finger on it, but it wasn't just the flamingo in the back. Jeff's back straightened, tense. He sensed it, too. But so far it was eluding both of us.

Until Joel spoke up.

"I didn't realize you picked up Brett's flamingo design."

Chapter 50

It was there, on the wall, right out in the open. It had been tacked over the flash on the far wall: My flamingo stencil for Daisy Carmichael.

It couldn't be the exact one, but it was close enough that it sent a shiver down my spine. It even had the little flowers in the tips of the wings.

"I've never seen that before," Jeff said softly.

All three of us stood and stared at it, as if it would magically tell us who had put it there.

"Someone is totally messing with us," I said. "I mean, besides the breaking in, this isn't really criminal stuff: putting a plastic flamingo in your office, putting this stencil here. This is some sort of head game."

"Doesn't scare me," Jeff said, going over to the wall, reaching up, and pulling the stencil down. It tore a little where it had been taped up, but otherwise it was intact. He brought it over to me, and I took it, studying it.

"Someone could've done this from the picture on that blog," I said. "It's not that hard to do a stencil. You can get instructions on the Internet." You could get mostly everything having to do with tattooing on the Internet, except experience and talent and common sense.

A flash of red hit the wall, illuminating the flash designs. We all turned at the same time to see the police car pulling up out front, an SUV behind it. Showtime.

The uniformed cop knocked on the door, and Jeff motioned that he could come in. To my dismay, it turned out to be Willis, a cop I'd come across a couple of times before and who didn't like me much. From the scowl on his face, I could tell that hadn't changed.

"We got a report," he said, eyeing me as though I was the culprit.

A couple of crime scene investigators followed him in, and Jeff led them to the back of the shop to see the flamingo. Joel and I lingered where we were. I was tired of making statements to the police and knew I wasn't out of the woods on this one yet, either, but the longer I could delay the inevitable, the better. Especially since it was Willis.

"We have to find Ann Wainwright," I said.

Joel shifted from one foot to the other, his fingers still toying with the chain at his waist. "How?"

I had no clue.

"Maybe we could go back to her sister's apartment. Talk to that neighbor again. Terri." And then a light bulb went off over my head. "Her sister worked for a dentist." I struggled to remember what it had said on that paycheck stub. "Carruthers? Columbia? Something with a 'C.'"

"Corinthian." The word slipped off Joel's tongue easily.

"What, are you psychic or something?" Joel hadn't been inside with Bitsy and me; he'd been out in the hall with Terri the whole time.

"Bitsy made me make an appointment for a cleaning. I'm supposed to go tomorrow. See what I can find out." He made a face. "I don't like the dentist."

"No one likes the dentist," I said. "So why don't we go now? Pretend that you thought the appointment was today. We could ask questions." Sounded like a plan, except for one thing: Jeff and Willis were still in the back of the shop. My eyes strayed in that direction.

"It's too late," Joel said. "It's after seven."

"Sometimes dentists stay open late. It's a Thursday. Maybe they're like banks and they're open late on Thursdays." I was grabbing at straws, but I didn't want to stick around here, and I had no other ideas.

I took a few steps toward the door.

"We're parked in back," Joel reminded me.

We could be stuck here all night. But I underestimated how much Willis disliked me, because he came storming through the sixties beads that hung between the back of the shop and the front, his face all scrunched up, a little notebook in his hand.

"You didn't touch anything?" he barked.

I shook my head, then quickly told him how the door had been ajar, the flamingo wedged behind it. "That's when I called Tim."

Jeff was standing behind Willis. I could tell he wanted him out of here, too. The crime scene guys were shuffling out now, past us and toward the door. One of them had put the flamingo in a plastic bag and he carried it with the tips of his fingers. They didn't exactly stand on ceremony, since they didn't bother to say good-bye, just left. I glanced up at where the flamingo stencil had hung, but then Jeff caught my eye and gave a quick shake of his head. For some reason he didn't want to tell them about it. Hmm.

Willis jotted a few notes down, then turned to Jeff. "You can pick up the report tomorrow afternoon." He handed him a card. "The case report number's on that. Just go to records and ask for it. Maybe you can get your insurance to pay for the damage." And with that, he took off out the door and into the street without even a nod in my direction.

We watched as the police cruiser slid away from the curb and down the street. When it was out of sight, Jeff stuck the card in his front breast pocket and said, "What a jerk."

I could think of more colorful words than that, but "jerk" would do, too.

We didn't have much time.

"We'll get out of your hair now," I said quickly, tugging on Joel's sleeve.

Jeff frowned and held up his hand. "What's your hurry?" He looked from me to Joel. He knew we were up to something.

I wasn't going to tell him. I didn't need him tagging along everywhere I went. I had Joel; he was enough. But Jeff didn't seem to agree. He stared Joel down, until Joel broke down.

"We're going to check out that dentist office where Ainsley Wainwright worked. See if they knew anything about her sister."

"Your car or mine?" he asked, adding, "Oh, we'd better take mine. More room." And without waiting for a response, he went toward the back of the shop.

Joel gave a short shrug. It was a lost cause. I wouldn't be able to talk Jeff out of coming with us. I'd just have to resign myself to the fact that he was.

The back of the shop was covered in fingerprint dust. I didn't much blame Jeff for wanting to take off right now; it would take a little work to clean up. I felt as though there should be a white chalk outline where the flamingo had been.

Jeff slammed the door shut after us and went over to the back door of the Chinese place. A Hispanic man wearing an apron came out, and they talked for a couple of minutes before Jeff came back over.

"They're going to watch the back. Make sure no one else shows up and tries to get in," he said.

"Did they see anyone here before?" I asked, kicking myself for not thinking about asking them in the first place.

Jeff shook his head. "No."

"Did the cops talk to them?" Joel asked.

"You kidding? That Willis guy wanted out of here right away." He chuckled. "You are not his favorite person, Kavanaugh."

Tell me something I didn't already know.

"What about your shop?" I asked. "Can you afford to shut down?"

Jeff snickered. "Don't worry your pretty little head about me, Kavanaugh." And he opened his car door and climbed in.

We followed suit. I let Joel sit in the front because of his size, and I squeezed my long legs in the back, angling them so I wouldn't feel too squished. Joel told Jeff where we were headed.

"Dentist, huh?"

Joel just grunted, clearly put out that Bitsy had put it on him to handle this unpleasant undercover operation.

We drove in silence. My head was spinning with everything that was going on: flamingos, pictures of me and Harry, Sherman Potter dead, Colin Bixby. Hey, how did he end up there? Oh, right. He broke up with me. And that led right into thinking about that kiss again. The one Jeff and I shared.

I felt the car slow, and I forced everything out of my head. I needed to be at the top of my game, because I was sure that there would have to be some fancy footwork to find out anything about Ainsley Wainwright at her former place of employment.

But as the car turned into the parking lot, it became obvious that this was not going to be our final destination after all, even though my suspicions about the office staying open late were on target.

Ann Wainwright was scurrying out of the building and through the parking lot, the lights of a nondescript white Toyota flashing as she hit the key fob.

Jeff slowed to a stop. I held my breath as we watched her get into the car and pull out. If she'd seen us sitting in this bright orange car, there was no outward sign. The Toyota moved out of the exit on the other side of the lot.

I told myself the metallic orange wasn't obvious because it was dark now, and we wouldn't stand out unless we were under a streetlight. Jeff really needed to get a car that was more incognito, although I couldn't talk, since I owned a bright red Mustang Bullitt convertible.

Blame it on living in the desert. We needed those splashes of color amongst all the desert browns.

Slowly, the Pontiac moved forward until we were on the street, a couple of cars back.

"You won't lose her?" Joel asked.

"Jeff was in the Marines," I said.

Joel nodded, the answer satisfying him.

Jeff said nothing as his hands tightened around the steering wheel. I saw his biceps flex, the skull tattoo looking as though it was clenching its jaw. I absently touched my chest, where my Chinese dragon poked out of my shirt.

Ann turned down a couple of side roads and then came back up to the main drag, and I started to wonder if she didn't know we were behind her, but then she maneuvered around again, and I realized she'd pulled into the parking lot at her sister's apartment house. Jeff eased the Pontiac against the curb on the street, and we watched as Ann got out of the Toyota and went toward the building, disappearing inside.

I thought about the picture I'd found. Something was gnawing at me. What if this really was Ainsley, and it was her sister who was murdered instead? I mean, she had been at the dentist office where she worked and then gone to her apartment. What if the murder had been a case of mistaken identity? What if whoever killed her sister had meant to kill her instead?

But that would mean that the Ainsley I met was leading some sort of double life. Dental hygienist by day, sex kitten for Sherman Potter by night. But maybe she'd had a dream. A dream to sing with the Flamingos. A dream she couldn't pass up.

I was grabbing at straws. Or was I?

We sat and watched the building for any kind of movement, until another car swung into the lot. A woman got out, staring at the Toyota, which was bathed in light from the streetlamp. She moved toward it, her head down as she tried the driver's side door. It was locked. She lifted her face toward the light, and I recognized Terri.

Jeff sat up a little straighter in his seat.

"That's her neighbor," I explained. "The one we talked to this morning. Her name's Terri. She's having Joel do a tattoo for her."

Jeff didn't seem to hear me.

"That's the girl I saw at Cleopatra's Barge," Jeff said. "The one who was pretending to be you."

Chapter 51

All my senses were on overload. "How do you know?" I asked. "She was in disguise, right?"

Jeff nodded, his eyes still glued to Terri, who was now holding a cell phone to her ear and watching the building, her face totally illuminated.

"She's the one. I saw her come out of that ladies' room without the disguise," he said. "I noticed her. It was her."

My brain was somehow stuck on the words "I noticed her."

Terri stuck the cell phone back in her pocket and went toward her car. She climbed in, and the brake lights came on before she started to pull out.

"Okay, guys, here's the problem. She's still in there," Jeff indicated the apartment house. "But *she*"—he indicated the neighbor—"is leaving. What do we want to do?"

"Follow Terri," Joel said without thinking.

Jeff sensed my hesitation. I wanted to see what both of them were up to.

"You want to stay here and confront that chick yourself, Kavanaugh? Because I agree with Joel. Let's follow that girl who pretended to be you."

They both needed to be watched. But we only had

one car, even though there were three of us. I said as much.

"I can stay here if you want to drive," Jeff offered.

"I can't follow anyone like you can," I admitted.

"I can stay," Joel said. "I've got a phone; I can call if anything happens. If she goes anywhere."

"But you don't have a car."

"Don't worry about me. I'll think of something." Joel scrambled out of the car. "You better get going." He indicated Terri's car stopped at the light at the next block before stepping onto the sidewalk.

I barely got out a "thanks" when Jeff peeled away from the curb. I fell back against the backseat, the passenger door shutting on its own with the force of the car.

"Hey!" I said.

We took a couple of turns, and I peered out the front window to see that we were only three cars away from Terri. How did he do that? I looked out the back window to see Joel lumbering along the sidewalk toward the apartment house. I hoped he was going to be okay. But there are definite positives to being his size and looking the way he did. He also knew a lot of people in this city, and I knew he'd have people to call on if he got into a jam.

I didn't want to sit in the backseat like a kid.

I folded myself up and squeezed my way into the front seat, shifting a little so at one point I felt Jeff Coleman's hand on my butt, steering me in the right direction. I wasn't sure how I felt about that.

As I settled into my seat, though, I didn't have time to ruminate about where his hand had been. Because Terri was slowing down. In front of Murder Ink.

"Do you think she's the one who left the flamingo?" I asked.

Jeff shrugged, said nothing. When Terri started to move again, he made sure we were well behind her but close enough so he wouldn't lose her.

I didn't want to boost his ego by telling him how good he was at this. He knew it, anyway, didn't need me to tell him, and if I did, he'd take that as more proof of our alleged *thing*.

"What if she's the one who's behind all this?" I asked, unable to shut up. I couldn't explain my sudden need to voice my thoughts. But the silence was killing me. Not to mention the intense way Jeff was watching that car. I'd never seen that expression before, and it scared me a little. Made me wonder if I shouldn't have been the one staying behind with Ann rather than Joel.

"She's pretty, isn't she?" I now said, disgusted with myself.

Jeff's head snapped around and he barked, "Kavanaugh, I get it. You're jealous. Okay. But if this is the chick who's been impersonating you and leaving flamingos all over the place, then maybe you need to refocus."

It was a really good thing it was dark, because he couldn't see the deep flush I felt move through my face and down my neck. Jealous? Is that what he thought?

"I'm just nervous," I tried.

"And I'm just going to throw you out of the car if you say anything else."

Was this our first fight? We'd never really fought. He teased, and I got upset, and then we went back to our familiar banter.

But before I could think about that further, I realized something. He really did think this girl was the one behind it all. And he was angry. Really angry. Probably more angry than I'd ever seen him.

I settled back in my seat. I thought about the rather benign conversation we'd had with Terri earlier, how Joel had offered to tattoo her at a discount. How she'd stayed outside the apartment while Bitsy and I were poking around inside. How she'd then shown up at the shop and given me the once-over that was so intimate I thought maybe she was coming on to me. Now I knew. She was studying me. Seeing how accurate she'd been when pretending to be me.

We never actually saw her go into or come out of an apartment, either. Maybe she didn't really live there. I had an idea.

• "What's her license plate number?" I asked Jeff, my voice tearing into the silence, and I worried he'd blow up at me again.

But without question, he reached into his pocket and pulled out his cell phone and handed it to me before reciting the plate number. He knew I was calling Tim. That was the eerie thing about us. I decided to stop reflecting on it as I punched in Tim's number.

"Tim, it's me," I said when he answered. "I've got a license plate you need to run down." I gave it to him, and then I told him what was going on.

Instead of scolding me for not "staying put" at Murder Ink, he merely asked, "Where are you?"

We were on the Strip, and Terri's car suddenly swerved. I saw now where we were going, and the irony didn't escape me.

"We're at the Flamingo," I said.

Chapter 52

Terri pulled up into the circular drive under the tiny white lights in the ceiling of the entryway. Jeff had pulled the Pontiac over to the side of the driveway, just out of sight, but we could see the front of her car.

"Should we follow her?" I asked Tim.

"Yes. I'll be right over there." He hung up.

I wasn't quite sure how he'd find us; it was a big place. But he was a detective, after all, and it was his job to find people, so I was sure he would, eventually. And then it struck me: He'd given me permission to follow her. Had aliens taken over my brother?

When the valet drove her car past us, Jeff pulled the Pontiac into the driveway.

"Where do you think she went?" I asked. She had at least five minutes on us and could be anywhere by now.

"Keep the faith, Kavanaugh," he said, but his voice was tight.

I didn't like it that we were handing over the keys to the valet. What if we needed to get to the car quickly? This was why I liked the self-parking so much better. The only comfort was that she'd also left her car with the valet, so she wasn't making any sort of quick escape, either.

Jeff was already at the door. I scrambled up to

him, and he held the glass door wide. We went up the escalator.

We scooted around the hotel "lobby," which was really just a long counter, passing a few people waiting in line with their suitcases. We stopped next to the familiar bronze flamingo statue—I didn't want to see any more flamingos, but it was inevitable here—as we scanned the casino, and I spotted her, over on the far side, near the doors that led out to the aviary and gardens.

"There she is," I said, pointing.

Jeff grabbed my hand, and we moved through the casino, bypassing the slots and the table games and cocktail waitresses balancing trays of drinks. As we slowed a little, I yanked my hand out of Jeff's. He glanced back at me with a sly smile. I rolled my eyes at him, because I knew what he was thinking. About that *thing* again.

She'd pushed the glass door open, stepping outside.

We'd been here before: when we'd seen Harry and Ace meeting before their tattoo party. There had been a girl here then, too. Was it the same one?

"Remember, we couldn't see her. There were too many people," Jeff said when I asked the question out loud.

Everything had started to blur into one big memory. It was all happening so fast that I was afraid I wouldn't be able to make any sense of any of it after all, even though there had been so many times over the last couple days that I'd thought I'd figured it out.

Should've known better.

She was walking briskly through the gardens, not even paying attention to the flamingos, ducks, and other birds that wandered freely along the pathways. The waterfall backdrop for wedding pictures was straight ahead, but she didn't stop there.

She veered around the path and went underneath a

fuchsia canopy, some sort of statue or something at the end.

"What's that?" I asked out loud.

"Bugsy Siegel," Jeff said. "You do know who that was, right?"

I rolled my eyes at him. Of course I did. Bugsy Siegel was the mobster who built the Flamingo back in the 1940s.

"When they renovated in the early nineties, they tore down Bugsy's suite and put up this plaque instead," Jeff said flatly.

We'd stopped just beyond the start of the canopy. Terri was pacing in front of the plaque, like she was waiting for someone. I remembered her on her cell outside the apartment building. Apparently her date was late. She reached into her pocket and pulled out a phone.

I felt like a voyeur. Spying on her like this, hiding behind this silly canopy.

I hadn't noticed how close Jeff had come toward me until I felt his hand on my arm and I was suddenly facing him, his other hand on the back of my neck, and he was leaning toward me and again he kissed me. This time it wasn't as tentative as it had been before; from the start it was as though he wanted to consume me. I let him. I couldn't think. I couldn't do anything except lose myself in that kiss. I forgot about Terri, about Ann Wainwright, about flamingos. I forgot everything except how I wanted that kiss to go on forever.

When he let me go, I couldn't catch my breath at first. My face was flush with heat, my heart racing, my lips bruised.

For a second, he smiled, his eyes full of smoky passion; then it was gone. "Let's go."

I couldn't wrap my head around it. Go where? What were we doing? Oh, right, following the girl who'd pretended to be me. Where was she? She was no longer standing by the plaque. No one was there. Except us.

And then I saw her, walking across the grass.

"Stop gawking, Kavanaugh," Jeff said. "Come on."

How could he kiss me like that and then act as though it never happened?

He'd gone a few steps before he realized I was still planted right where he'd left me.

"You can analyze it later," he said. "But for now, we've got to see where she's going."

Okay, right. My feet seemed detached from my body somehow, but I was moving forward.

"You did that on purpose," I scolded when we fell into step together, Terri heading toward the pool area.

"That's right," he said, grinning. "She almost saw us."

I felt like he'd hit me in the gut. "It was so she wouldn't see us?" I asked.

Jeff chuckled. "You really don't think it's because we've got a thing?" he teased. "Because we don't. You said so."

So maybe I was wrong, but I started to seethe. This was totally why we *couldn't* have a thing. Because I hated him. Because he drove me crazy.

Right. That kiss had driven me crazy.

He wasn't my type. And he was too old. He had to be at least ten years older than me. He smoked. Or at least he had smoked. His lungs must be black from all that smoking. His nose was a little off-kilter, as though it had been broken at some point, his smile crooked, his eyes a bright blue. So maybe I'd noticed his eyes. How kind they could be. How they flashed when he was angry. How intense they'd been when I'd given him that tattoo under his bullet scar.

His fingers snapped in front of my face.

"I know I swept you off your feet, Kavanaugh, but you've got to stay with the program here."

I made a face at him and swatted his hand away. "Get over yourself," I said sharply, surprising myself—and him.

Something akin to hurt flooded those blue eyes, but they quickly cleared and he said, "Look over there."

I looked where he was pointing, and my heart fell.

Terri was giving Ace a kiss on the cheek.

Chapter 53

So maybe I hadn't been so off on my original assessment that Ace had something to do with all this. He had access to me and my appointment book. He knew Daisy, how she'd only come to me for a tattoo. Except when she'd gone to Sylvia. Had he known about that, too? Is that why that stencil was tacked up to the wall at Murder Ink?

The question was why. And how was Terri caught up in it? Had he coerced her to do the things she did? Had he romanced her into it?

But why would he kill Daisy? Why would he kill Sherman Potter?

"He's involved somehow," Jeff said softly. "I'm sorry."

I was sorry, too. "He quit, you know."

Jeff's head moved so fast, I thought he'd get whiplash. "Why?"

I shrugged. "Said the shop was impeding his creativity. Wants to get his paintings in a gallery."

"He won't sell those paintings," Jeff said. "They're weird."

"But galleries like weird," I countered. I knew that for a fact. From my college days, when I shopped my work around and was told it was too conventional, I should branch out more, experiment a little. That's when I hooked up with Mickey over at the Ink Spot and started tattooing.

Jeff's cell phone rang, and he plucked it out of his pocket. "Hello?" he asked, then listened. Finally, he said, "Okay," and hung up.

"That was Joel. Ann hasn't left the apartment. He said she's cleaning it out, bringing stuff down to the Dumpster in the back."

"So she's clearing out her sister's stuff," I mused. "I wonder if I've been wrong about her from the start."

"But she was with Sherman Potter in that hotel room," Jeff argued. "And then he was dead. I don't think she's completely off the hook."

It was all too much all of a sudden. My brain flashed on bits and pieces from the last couple of days, and I sank down to the ground, crossing my legs, my head in my hands. I felt Jeff Coleman's fingers massaging my neck. I didn't push him away.

"This is a touching scene."

I lifted my head; Tim was walking toward us. I indicated Terri and Ace, who were now sitting on the edge of a chaise lounge down at the pool, facing away from us. Tim's eyebrows rose slightly. "Ace?" he asked.

I nodded, wishing fervently it wasn't so, but with it right there in front of me, I couldn't deny it.

I scrambled back to my feet. "So what now?" I asked Tim.

"You really think Ace is involved?" he asked, his voice laced with doubt.

I sighed. "I don't know. I don't want him involved. But the whole thing about clients saying I was canceling appointments, well, he has access to that."

"He quit," Jeff said.

Tim frowned. "What?"

I told him how Ace had quit, his reason.

"Those paintings are awful," Tim said.

Everyone's a critic.

I don't know why, but I felt the need to defend Ace's work. "He's sold some," I said.

Ace and Terri got up then. I could sense Tim and Jeff tense up.

"You're sure that's the girl you saw at Cleopatra's Barge?" Tim asked Jeff. So far Terri and Ace were merely standing poolside.

"She came out of the ladies' room like that. She had to be the one who was dolled up like Brett."

He said my first name. I stared at him, but he just frowned back at me, like he didn't realize.

The world was totally spinning in the wrong direction.

Tim took a step forward. "Stay back here," he instructed. "I'm going to pretend I ran into them by accident. See what they've got to say for themselves." He looked around. "You might want to hang out by those trees over there."

Jeff and I sauntered over where he'd indicated as Tim went down to the pool. He approached Ace and Terri, who were clearly surprised to see him. He was good, though; his expression was just as surprised, his face animated with a grin as he shook Ace's hand like guys tend to do sometimes and listened as Ace introduced him to Terri.

"When this is all over, what do you say, Kavanaugh?" Jeff asked, distracting me.

"About what?"

"You and me. Our thing."

"We do not have a thing."

"You're back to that? That wasn't just a peck on the cheek back there."

"You said it was a ruse."

"Ruse or not, well . . ." His voice trailed off.

"You caught me by surprise." I hoped he couldn't sense that I'd blushed.

"You caught *me* by surprise," he whispered, moving closer.

I totally did not have time for this right now. I let my eyes drop, and when I lifted them, I meant to tell him that I wasn't ready for this. That I didn't know if I wanted a *thing*.

Instead, I heard a splash, and we both looked over to the pool. Ace and Terri were dashing toward us; Tim was flailing in the pool. Oops.

Jeff stepped out in front of Ace and Terri, who knocked him to the side, and he fell with an "oomph" at my feet. There was no time to say anything, though, before he jumped up and took off after them.

I stood still, uncertain which way to go. Should I go see how Tim was, or should I go with Jeff after Ace and Terri?

My instinct told me to go after Jeff and Ace. That was where the answers lay.

But I'd hesitated too long.

I felt a hand wrap itself around my arm.

"Fancy meeting you here."

Chapter 54

I looked up to see Harry standing over me, a grin spread across his face.

I stammered something like, "Hi, hello, I've got to go," but he held tight on my arm, and I couldn't leave.

"I was coming over here to meet up with Ace, but I see him taking off with Terri, and then I see you standing here." The smile was, despite him holding my arm, infectious. I found myself smiling back.

Sad thing was, despite how Jeff's kiss had made my toes curl, Harry was more my type. At least what I'd always thought my type was. And I remembered his kisses, too, although they were different than Jeff's.

I shook off my thoughts. I couldn't be standing here analyzing kisses from two men while Jeff was off chasing Ace and the girl who was impersonating me.

"She pretended to be me," I explained, then had another thought. "How do you know her name?"

Harry's eyebrows rose. "She pretended to be you?"

"Yeah, Jeff met her at Cleopatra's Barge, you know, the night you and I . . ." My voice trailed off, and I was back to those kisses again.

"She doesn't look anything like you," Harry said.

"I know, but she had some sort of disguise, and she

left it in the ladies' room, and I found it the next day." It all sounded rather ridiculous.

"Where did they go?"

We whirled around to see a sopping wet Tim standing next to us. Harry finally dropped his hand.

"That way," I said, pointing.

Tim lingered for a second, staring at Harry.

"This is Harry Desmond," I said, "and this is my brother, Tim."

Tim nodded, no handshake this time. "I recognize him," he said, and I knew he meant from the pictures on the blog. More blushing on my part, but I was sure no one could see. I hoped.

"Watch her, okay?" Tim asked Harry. "I'll be back." And he took off after Ace, Terri, and Jeff.

"Nice to have the brother's permission," Harry said jovially.

"No," I said, "that's not what he meant." Was I going to have to deal with another guy who thought we had a *thing*? I had to change the subject. "Why were you meeting with Ace? Are you doing another tattoo party?"

"You know about those?" Harry asked, and while I couldn't see his expression because of the darkness, his tone was more serious now.

"You could've told me," I said. "Why didn't you? You let us all think you were out of work."

"I didn't want you to think I was competition or anything."

"That wouldn't be competition," I said. "You don't have a shop."

"Ace said I should ask you for a job. You've got an open room now that he's gone."

"Is that why you encouraged him to quit? You wanted a job?" I didn't point out that I had four rooms total, and even with Ace, only three tattooists, leaving one open. He didn't need anyone to quit.

"It's good for him," Harry said lightly. "He can concentrate on his art."

I found myself looking past the fountain with the flamingos toward the building, wondering where everyone had gone.

Harry indicated the wedding chapel entrance. "We can go in through there and get to the casino. It's a short cut, if you want to catch up with them. I'll show you."

The last time I'd been to a wedding chapel had been with Jeff under false pretenses. It felt like bad karma to go into another one with another guy I had no intentions of having a relationship with. But he looked so earnest, now that he'd stepped under the light from a lamppost.

I hated that I was missing something, so I nodded. "Sure, Harry. That would be fine." I didn't have my phone to check in with Jeff or Tim, but I saw Harry's phone clipped to his belt. I could use that if we didn't find them inside.

We crossed the lawn and went toward the chapel, but the door was locked. Great. Harry indicated we could go down to the pool and through the pool entrance just a little ways away.

"We could just go back through the gardens," I suggested.

"We're already over here," he said, and he had a point. I allowed him to lead me down the steps and then through the doors inside.

The area was crowded with resort guests. I'd started to feel a little nervous with Harry—I wasn't trusting much of anyone these days—but when the casino came into sight, I breathed a sigh of relief, even though I didn't see anyone I recognized anywhere.

"Do you know that they tore down Bugsy Siegel's

suite when they did the renovations here?" Harry said, turning into tour guide.

I nodded.

"Do you know all the windows were bulletproof in his suite?"

Okay, that was semi-interesting.

"And that even though there was only one way in, there were five ways out?"

Even more interesting. "Too bad they tore it down," I said. "It would be such a cool tourist thing now."

"Too bad Bugsy didn't do those things at his house in L.A., where he got gunned down," Harry said. "He would've been safe here." He turned to me. "You're safe here, you know that?"

I nodded, even though I hadn't felt safe in days. I just wanted to find Tim and Jeff and hope that they'd caught up with Ace and Terri.

"Who's Terri?" I asked, trying to make lighter conversation. "How do you know her?"

"She's my wife."

Chapter 55

_____

I stopped short. This was not what I expected. "Your wife? What do you mean?"

Harry took my arm and pulled me along. "This way," he said without answering my questions.

My head was spinning, and I felt my heart begin to pound. Something wasn't right, and it didn't exactly take a rocket scientist to figure that out. I kept my eyes peeled for any sign of Tim or Jeff or both, but I didn't see either of them anywhere in the sea of the casino that spread out before us. I tried to shake off Harry's hand, but he gripped me tighter as we sidestepped the gaming tables, the slot machines. The *ding-ding* of the machines rang in my head, the wheels turning to show no one was winning any jackpots. I certainly was a big loser today.

"What's your angle?" I asked Harry, but either he didn't hear me above the din or he chose not to answer. Probably the latter. I frantically tried to figure out how to get away.

As we went up the steps, that bronze flamingo in front of us, I yanked quickly on my arm, hoping to break free.

No dice. He merely gazed down at me, a smile on his face.

"Trust me," he said. "I'm taking you somewhere safe."

I screamed. At the top of my lungs. Harry's hand was so tight I wondered if I would lose circulation.

"Shut up," he hissed. "What is wrong with you?"

I continued to scream as I swung around with the arm he wasn't holding, and my fist slammed into his face.

I hadn't even noticed he'd let go of me.

"You're crazy, you know that?" Harry asked as he turned around and ran down the hallway, past the little shops. I'd stopped screaming now but began hyperventilating. Out of nowhere, Tim and a security guard appeared, and then Tim's arms were around me as I heard him explaining to the security guard that he was my brother.

I couldn't speak to tell him to go after Harry; had he even seen Harry? I struggled to catch my breath, taking in air in large gulps and then hiccupping.

I was a total mess.

"What's wrong, Brett?" Tim was asking over and over.

I willed myself to calm down, to take a few long, slow breaths until my heart began to settle down. Finally, I said, "Harry."

Tim frowned. "What?"

"Harry Desmond. He had my arm. He wouldn't let me go. I punched him, he took off, and then you showed up."

"Where did he go?" Tim's face was etched with concern.

I pointed down the hall. "Down there."

He started in the direction I'd indicated, but I grabbed his shoulder. "Don't leave me alone here."

The security guard who was still standing mute must have felt as though he were the proverbial chopped liver, but I wasn't trusting anyone I didn't know right now. Heck, I knew Harry, and he'd been up to no good.

Hadn't he?

Doubts began to settle in. Harry had said to trust him, but then he wouldn't let go of me. He said he was taking me somewhere safe. But my instincts had screamed louder than I had.

He'd said the woman with Ace was his wife.

His wife. Right.

I told Tim what he'd said.

"Did you find her?" I asked. "And Ace? Where's Jeff?"

"You shouldn't worry about anything right now. You need to stay calm, and you need to go someplace safe."

Again I was reminded of Harry, but I pushed the thought away. "Where?" I asked. "Can we go home?"

"I can't go right now, but maybe Jeff can take you. He can stay until I get there." Tim must have seen the look on my face, the one that was saying, *I'm not sure I want to deal with Jeff alone right now*, so he added, "Or Bitsy can come stay with you, or you can go back to Bitsy's. It's up to you."

I wished Joel were there. Joel was a lot bigger than Bitsy, and while I loved Bitsy and she was one of my best friends, she was a little person, and I needed someone who might be able to protect me if I needed protecting. Although I *had* punched out Harry, hadn't I?

I rubbed my knuckles, which were red and smarting from said punch. I hated it that I needed any sort of protecting at all. I'd always been able to take care of myself just fine, thank you very much, and this was so lame.

"How about your shop?" Tim suggested then. "I can pick you up there in an hour or two."

That sounded like a plan. But I asked again, "What happened to Jeff?"

Tim shook his head. "I don't know."

Jeff had been following Terri and Ace, and now all three were missing. Great.

"Joel's still hanging out at Ainsley's apartment building, watching her sister, Ann," I said. "At least I think so."

"He called me," Tim said. "I sent a cruiser over there. That's where I'm heading, actually. To see exactly what her story is."

"Let me come along," I said. "I won't be a bother."

He didn't give me an answer, and I realized he was still wet from the pool.

"You need some dry clothes," I said, indicating one of the shops.

We found him a pair of sweats and a sweatshirt, both with the Flamingo logo on them. I made a mental note to throw them in the garbage after he was done with them. I didn't want anything reminding me of any of this after it was all over.

"You look like a tourist," I teased as we went out to the parking garage to his Chevy Impala.

He rolled his eyes at me, and we got in the car.

The whole ride over I replayed the scene with Harry. The last thing he'd said was that I was crazy. Had I imagined that he was up to no good? I'd been a tad paranoid the last few days, so maybe I *had* imagined it. But what was the whole thing with him having a wife?

I figured that Tim would take me to the shop and he'd head off to Ainsley's, but now I noticed that he was taking me along with him. I decided not to say anything, because he could change his mind.

"It's safer if you're with me," he explained as we pulled into the apartment house's parking lot.

A cruiser was waiting for us, and a uniform climbed out to escort us to Ainsley's apartment.

"Where's Joel?" I asked the uniform. "My friend."

"The big guy? He took a cab."

He probably went back to the shop.

"She lives here," I said then, assessing the building.

Tim looked at me like I had two heads. "No kidding, Brett."

"No," I said, "not just Ainsley. Terri, the woman with Ace. We saw her here this morning."

Tim stopped and stared at me. Uh-oh. I hadn't told him about our little field trip. Time to come clean.

"Bitsy and Joel and I came over here," I said quickly. "We met Terri on the stairs; she said she lived here." But as I thought about it, I wondered if she really had. I didn't think she'd actually said that; we'd just assumed it. I said as much to Tim. "Anyway, there's got to be a connection between Terri and Ainsley."

Tim was fighting back the words I knew he wanted to say: Why can't you stay out of police business? But to his credit, he pursed his lips, tensed his jaw, and merely nodded.

We went up to Ainsley Wainwright's door, and the uniform knocked.

We waited. No sound from inside.

He knocked again.

Tim assessed the door, then nodded at the uniform. The two of them slammed their bodies against it, and it swung open, the sound of the doorframe cracking ringing in my ears.

The place was cleared out.

Chapter 56

The mess we'd seen this morning was gone. The books were gone, too, probably out in that Dumpster, along with all those little kitschy tourist things. A look in the bedroom showed us that the clothes had been cleared out of the closet. Nothing personal had been left. It was merely furniture and dishes in the cabinets in the kitchen.

"She's not here," the uniform said, stating the obvious. "She was here when that guy left. He didn't leave until I got here." He was talking about Joel.

Tim stared him down, until finally he blushed and said, "Okay, I needed a coffee."

Great. A thirsty cop takes his eye off the girl, and she disappears.

"I'm taking you to your shop," Tim said. To the uniform, he said, "Stay here. Watch the place. No coffee this time. I want to know if she comes back."

As we went out to the car, I asked, "Where's Flanigan? I haven't seen much of him."

Tim grunted, and I took that as my cue to stop asking questions.

The ride to the Venetian was cloaked in silence. As we went into the entrance to the parking garage, I thought about my car.

"Where's my Mustang?" I asked.

"Impounded. After you took off earlier."

My heart sank. "What do I do to get it out?"

"I'll take care of it," Tim said as he parked near the entrance to the Grand Canal Shoppes and walked me past the kiosks and the shops, past the oxygen bar where Ace was usually hanging out, to The Painted Lady. Bitsy was sitting sentry at the front desk. She hopped up when we walked through the door.

"Joel's just back. What's going on?"

Tim waved his hand in the air, said to me, "I'll be by in a bit to pick you up," and said good-bye to Bitsy as he took off.

I had no idea where he was going.

Being back in the shop gave me an odd sense of calm. As though nothing could touch me now. I wanted desperately for someone to walk through the door and want a tattoo, because I could lose myself in the act of tattooing, go into that little Zen zone I had. But as far as I knew, no one would be walking through the door. It was late now, around ten o'clock. My stomach growled.

Bitsy grinned, even though I could see the anxiety behind it. "Joel brought back In-N-Out burgers."

My heart did a little happy dance.

"And I rescheduled your eight o'clock."

My heart sank as I remembered. "I didn't call you," I said. "I didn't have my phone."

"Joel called me. I took care of it." While I figured she had every reason to be upset with me, her voice was kind. Maybe she knew how much of a mess I really was.

We passed Joel's room, where he was tattooing a guy who was almost as big as he was. He gave me a nod as Bitsy and I went into the staff room. The aroma from the Double-Doubles made my stomach growl again. I tore open one of the paper wrappers and sank my teeth into the burger. I made a yummy sound and began to tell

Bitsy about the events of the day. I left out the bit about Jeff kissing me again. Bitsy can't keep her mouth shut, and I didn't really know how I was going to deal with that and didn't want it broadcast until I did.

As it was, she settled on the one thing I knew she would.

"Harry Desmond has a wife? That girl who was here earlier?"

I nodded. "Guess so. She was with Ace. And remember, she wanted a flamingo tattoo."

We mulled that a few minutes as we finished our burgers. I took a sip of a Coke, as if I needed the caffeine, but the way I was feeling right this very minute, well, I doubted anything would keep me up tonight. I wanted desperately to lie down and close my eyes.

"Where do you think they went?" Bitsy asked. "And Jeff? You said Jeff followed them?"

I thought about Jeff's orange Pontiac, handed over to the valet. Had he gotten his car or had he followed on foot? Maybe a cab. I thought about my car, impounded. With my bag inside. With my cell phone.

I went out to the front desk, the familiar whir of the tattoo machine emanating from Joel's room. The sound calmed me as I dialed Jeff's number.

"Where did you go, Kavanaugh?" he asked.

"I could ask you the same thing," I said. "Where are you?"

"I lost them. I've been driving around, trying to find them; then I went back to the Flamingo, but you were gone."

I quickly told him about Harry and Tim and Ainsley's apartment.

He blew a low whistle. "I'll be over in a bit. Make sure you're okay."

"No need," I said. "Joel and Bitsy are here. Tim's coming to get me. You need to open your shop." Murder

Ink was open till four a.m. most nights. I wasn't sure how he did it, except that he wasn't open as early as I was.

"You sure?" I could tell from his tone that *he* wasn't sure.

"Yes. I'm fine. I'll talk to you tomorrow." And I hung up before he could argue with me.

I half expected him to call right back, but he didn't.

Joel finished up his tattoo, and his client came out and paid Bitsy as Joel and I cleaned up his room. Bitsy said we didn't have any other clients scheduled for the night, and I began to think that maybe I would get that sleep I needed sooner than expected.

I leaned against the glass door and stared out at the canal, the gondoliers packing it up for the night, too. The mall would be shutting down soon; the tourists and shoppers would go home. Everything seemed so normal.

Bitsy and Joel watched me as I went into the staff room by myself. They hadn't initiated too much conversation since Joel's client had left. I pulled the laptop out from under the light table and opened it. I knew I shouldn't do this, but curiosity was getting the better of me.

The last picture I'd seen on Ink Flamingos had been that one of Sherman Potter's flamingo tattoo. I wanted to know if anything else had shown up.

Joel had moved into the room behind me. I could hear Bitsy with the vacuum out in the hall. Joel didn't say anything, just turned on the TV, its volume soft.

The Ink Flamingos blog popped up on the screen at the same time I heard the announcer on TV saying there was something about breaking news.

I saw the picture of Jeff kissing me in the Flamingo gardens at the same time I heard the announcer say, "Sherman Potter, the manager of the Flamingos band, has been found dead in a hotel room at the Golden Palace, the same place where Dee Carmichael was found dead just days ago."

I whirled around in my seat to see a grainy Detective Flanigan talking to a reporter outside the Golden Palace, the coroner's van behind him.

"... found in a room on the third floor of the hotel," he was saying.

So whoever had moved Sherman Potter had gotten him to another room on another floor and left him there.

"... several leads."

My red hair being one of them, probably. So this was where Flanigan was, while Tim was being pushed into the pool at the Flamingo.

"What's that?"

Bitsy had come up behind me. I hadn't even heard the vacuum cut out. She was staring at the blog on the laptop screen.

I couldn't make the screen go dark fast enough. Joel had seen it, too.

"You were making out with Jeff Coleman?" Bitsy asked, a smile crossing her face. "While all this is going on? Wow."

Wow was right.

I sighed. "I don't need any crap right now, okay?"

Maybe it was the way I said it that made Joel jump up, shut off the TV, and say, "I'll go get some truffles. I think we need truffles."

Joel always needed truffles, but I wasn't going to argue.

"Sounds good," I said, thinking about the Godiva shop just across the canal from the shop. "Get a dozen."

"Or a big box," he said gleefully.

Bitsy studied my face a minute, then said, "I'll go with him. You look like you need a few minutes to yourself."

She was right. I nodded. "Thanks."

I went out front with them and watched as they went

up the walkway and around the tip of the canal to Godiva. On instinct, I locked the door from the inside, making sure the boogeyman couldn't get me while they were gone.

Still, I could see straight into the chocolate shop from here and kept my eyes on them as they perused the glass case, looking for the perfect truffles.

I watched as they paid, then came back out, but instead of coming around the canal, they turned left. Joel glanced up at me, waved, and pointed in the direction they were walking. I knew what was over there. The gelato place. Chocolate and gelato. He might be right that that's what I needed now. A total sugar rush.

I began to feel silly. Paranoid. The door was locked. There were people in the mall. I turned and went down to my room, to see if I needed to clean anything else up before taking off for the night.

I heard the jingle of the bell on the door, which meant they were coming back in.

But I'd locked the door, hadn't I? Had they brought a key with them?

My whole body tensed as I heard the footsteps. I scrambled for the door and had it halfway closed when his hand shoved it open, throwing me backward. He stepped around the door, an angry scowl on his face.

Harry.

Chapter 57

He laughed, an ugly sound. "It's just you and me now," he said, shoving me farther into my room.

I noticed the bruise on his cheek, happy that I'd inflicted it and wondering if I could do more damage. Because while I'd had doubts before, I had no doubts now.

Harry was behind all this. It was that picture on the blog. The one I'd just seen. And the iPhone he'd had when he appeared out of the blue. "They're coming back," I said.

He snorted. "Right. But even if you're telling the truth, they didn't bring their key, did they?"

No. And I flashed on a memory. Ace telling me he'd lost his key.

Harry had found it. Or, more likely, taken it.

"You set up that blog," I said. "Why?"

He pushed me back onto my client chair, putting his foot on the pedal that made the back go flat. He was stronger than I'd thought, and as he roughly turned me over, I tried to think of how I could twist away. Before I could, however, he had my arms under the chair and was tying them with something he'd grabbed off my shelf. A tattoo machine clip cord.

I'd seen one of those used to kill someone before. My whole body started to shake as he pulled the cord tight around my wrists, then got up and stepped around and behind me.

"What are you doing?" I asked, turning my head so I could see him out of the corner of my eye. He took out some ink pots and began setting them on the low table next to the chair.

I kicked up, and he grabbed my feet as I frantically tried to move my hands, but they were bound too tight. I felt something wrapped around my ankles, then around the chair so I couldn't lift my feet.

Banging from out front indicated that Bitsy and Joel were back—but locked out as I suspected.

"Bitsy and Joel will call the police," I warned Harry, who still hadn't said anything but was now slipping a needle into my tattoo machine. He was going to give me a tattoo.

He was a scratcher. Jeff had fired him because he botched tattoos.

Something dawned on me.

"You did that tattoo on Daisy, didn't you? The one that killed her?"

Harry's head snapped up, his eyes full of anger. "That wasn't supposed to happen."

"How did you come to tattoo her anyway?" I asked.

He snickered. "I met her coming here that day. She wanted another tattoo. I told her you weren't here, that you were on vacation, but I could do it for her. I told her I worked for you, that I was new to the shop. She tried to back out, said she had to meet someone at the Golden Palace, but I told her I had my case. I said I could do it there. She finally said okay."

Harry's tone indicated that because she'd consented, everything he'd done was on the up and up.

"I knew you did all her tattoos, and I wanted a piece of that, too," he said. "I wanted to prove to you that I was as good as you."

But he hadn't even told me he was a tattooist. Harry was totally delusional.

I thought about Daisy having to meet someone at the hotel. The room was in Ainsley Wainwright's name. Was she going to talk to Ainsley—or, rather, Ann—about the band? Or was she meeting Ainsley, the blogger?

"Her friend wasn't there when we got there," Harry continued. "But I talked the girl at the desk into letting us in." Like he'd talked the girl at the Venetian into giving him Sherman Potter's room number. He was smooth.

"I didn't know she'd have a reaction," he said, still tinkering with my machine. It was as though he wasn't quite sure how to get the needle in. Not good. "And then, when she did, and she stopped breathing, I panicked. I called my wife. Well, she's my ex-wife. She sort of looks like you."

She didn't look at all like me.

"She agreed to help me."

"To set me up so you wouldn't be implicated," I said.

"Everyone knew you were the only one who tattooed her," he said matter-of-factly. "It would make sense it was you."

And no one would suspect him at all.

He'd gotten the needle in now, and he settled into my chair, wheeling it around the side of the client chair. I felt my shirt being lifted up.

"Nice tat," he said when he saw the Celtic cross on my upper back. "Needs something down below."

I didn't like the sound of that. His fingers slipped into the waist of my jeans and around the front. I tensed as he found the button, the zipper, and he tugged my jeans down around my hips. I struggled to catch my breath, my heart pounding.

"Then that blogger showed up," Harry said, his voice devoid of emotion. "We couldn't believe it. She was Terri's neighbor. What are the odds of that?"

In a city that thrived on odds, Harry was right. If anyone had placed a wager on it, he'd be a rich man today.

Harry was still talking. "Terri was pretty sure the blogger recognized her. So we had to get rid of her."

His fingers traced an imaginary outline on my skin. I forced myself not to flinch.

"You killed her," I said flatly, trying to focus on his words and not what he was doing. The tattoo machine whirred to life as he stepped on the pedal. The needle pressed into the skin of my lower back. He hadn't even done a stencil. What was he tattooing on me? I tried to follow the lines he was making, but I couldn't figure it out, the usual pain nonexistent behind my fear.

"It was easy. We knew where to find her." He snorted. "I had no idea there were two of them. Terri said she never said anything about a twin sister."

"Did you think she had come back from the dead when you saw her with Sherman Potter?" I asked, forcing myself not to flinch. I was piecing it together now. Daisy went to meet the sister who was the singer, not the one who was the blogger. But Terri hadn't known, so they'd killed the wrong girl. I remembered Harry's initial reaction to the girl in Sherman Potter's room, and then how he'd wanted to come with me to find her at the bar that night. Maybe he'd finally figured it out, too, and planned to cover his tracks. But thinking about that night reminded me . . .

"Your wife, excuse me, ex-wife, took the pictures of us," I said. And then I remembered something else. How he'd taken me home in a cab. He knew where I lived. And I found a flamingo on my bed.

I shivered when I recalled the way Terri had given me the once-over when she came here to talk to Joel about the tattoo. She wasn't here for anything except checking me out, seeing if she could impersonate me better, like I'd thought.

"So why do all that stuff?" I asked. "The blog posts, the impersonation, the flamingos?"

"Your brother, the police, needed a distraction," he said. "You were the best way to do it."

I'd suspected that, but hadn't wanted it to be true.

I couldn't hear banging anymore. Bitsy and Joel were going for help. I moved my hands under the chair and felt the cord give a little. I moved my hands a little more, and to my surprise, it gave even more. I started to work at it, hoping he wouldn't notice my muscles flexing. If he did, then I'd just say my arms were falling asleep, a little white lie Sister Mary Eucharista would approve of, considering the circumstances. The needle was moving along my lower back, horizontally. It lifted a couple of times then settled back with little pinches of pain that had finally gotten my endorphins all worked up.

"So what are you going to do to me? Are you going to kill me, too?" I asked with a little more confidence now that the cord was giving way bit by bit.

"You screamed when we were at the Flamingo. In *public*," he said angrily. "Now everyone's after me."

He hadn't answered my question. Not that I really wanted an answer. Not that I needed one.

In what felt like hours but was probably only minutes, the cord fell away from my wrists. But what to do now? I couldn't move my feet; he'd see me. And he had that machine. While he couldn't go any deeper with the needle than he already was, he could use it as a weapon, hit me with it or something. But if I moved fast, maybe I could catch him off guard.

I had no choice.

In one swift move, I swung my arms up from under the table, twisted my body around to one side, and my fist connected with the side of his face as I pulled myself up to my knees.

Chapter 58

The needle slid along my lower back, but I didn't have time to think about it. I swung my arms again and slammed my hands against either side of his face. He was so startled, the machine fell to the floor and his head snapped back.

Right at that moment, I heard a crash, glass shattering, footsteps running, and Jeff burst into the room. He barely looked at me as he grabbed Harry, swung him around and threw his fist into his face.

Harry's good looks were history.

He fell to the floor, Jeff's boot on his chest to hold him down, as Jeff turned to me.

"You okay?"

I nodded, although it was a lie. My shirt had fallen back down, but my jeans were still down below my hips. I reached down and started to pull them up when I remembered.

"He tattooed something," I whispered, indicating my back.

"I got it," Joel said from behind me, and I felt a soft cloth against my skin.

A security guard was behind Bitsy, who had her phone in her hand. "Tim's on his way."

Joel finished wiping the tattoo, and I pulled my jeans

up, looking down at Harry. Jeff still had his foot on him, but Harry wasn't going anywhere. He was out like a light.

Joel untied my ankles, and as the cord fell away, I felt myself start to collapse. Jeff caught me, his arms around me as he whispered, "It's okay."

I indicated Harry. "He killed Daisy. And Ainsley. He told me."

Jeff lifted me up and carried me out of the room while Joel stood sentry, watching Harry. Bitsy waited at the front desk for Tim.

Jeff gently put me down in a chair in the staff room, but I stood right up.

"Stay put," he said.

I shook my head. I had to see what that tattoo was. I went out to the back of the shop, where we had a long mirror, then lifted up my shirt and lowered my jeans.

It was half an outline of a flamingo, with a long black line from the beak to the wing. That had probably happened when I leaped up so fast.

I choked back a sob as I stormed up to my room and shoved the door open. Joel had used the cord that Harry had used on me to tie Harry to the chair. Harry's eyes were open but unfocused, and he licked his lips.

"How does that feel?" I shouted at him. "What was the point of this? Didn't you realize you'd get caught?"

His head lolled to one side as he stared up at me. "I thought they were gone for the night."

He'd seen Bitsy and Joel leave but didn't know they were just across the canal. He'd seen me lock the door.

"So you were going to tattoo me and then what? Were you going to kill me?"

He shook his head, then winced with pain. "I wanted to leave you something to remember me by."

He'd certainly done that.

Before I could ask anything else, I heard glass

crunching, and I turned to see Tim come in with three uniformed cops and Flanigan. I pointed at Harry. "He killed Daisy. And Ainsley Wainwright."

Tim nodded. "We found Ann Wainwright tonight in a bar across the street from her sister's apartment, having a drink after she cleared out her sister's stuff. Ann was the one who saw Harry and Terri leaving the hotel room. After they were gone, she went in to find Daisy dead. She didn't know what Daisy was doing there, but we can probably figure it had something to do with the Flamingos. She panicked and took off because she didn't want to be implicated in Daisy's death, especially since she was taking her place in the band. She left the door open a little, though, which was how the room service guy found the body. Ann didn't know Harry and Terri knew her sister; she hadn't seen her sister in a long time. When she saw Harry with you in Potter's hotel room, she realized who he was. And then she found out her sister was dead, put it together that they must have mistaken her for her sister, so she decided to lie low, hoping they wouldn't go after her."

So she'd recognized Harry, not Terri, as they'd suspected. And that was why she didn't show up for the Flamingos' concert. No one had seen her, until Jeff spotted her meeting up with Sherman Potter at the Golden Palace earlier. I wondered who the redhead was at the arena, but then realized I'd probably jumped to conclusions. I hadn't seen her face. As I'd said to Tim at one point, there are a lot of redheads in Vegas. Unless it had been Terri, after all, like Jeff had suspected. And then I remembered the plastic flamingo with the tiara on my bed. It must have been Terri. She must have been there.

"Why didn't Ann go to the police?" I asked.

Tim sighed. "That's what Potter told her to do when

she told him everything in that room at the Golden Palace after Potter was released. But then Potter was killed, and she ran." He anticipated my next question. "She says she left Potter alive in that room, and I believe her. The red hair in the stairwell? It was from a wig."

"Where is Terri?" I asked Harry.

"Out in the car. It was her idea, all this," Harry said quickly, waving his arm around to indicate the shop.

Flanigan motioned to the uniforms that they were to go find Terri before asking Harry, "Why did you kill Potter?"

"That was her idea, too," Harry said. Pretty convenient, blaming everything on his ex-wife. "We found out the sister was staying at the Golden Palace, and we were going to take care of her." He flinched a little, but I wasn't buying his story that it was all Terri's idea. "Sherman was there instead. He had figured out what was what, and we had no choice."

Tim was nodding. "Ann told us she'd gone to get ice, but the ice machine was broken so she had to go to another floor for it. When she came back, she saw Brett and Jeff going into the room. Sherman was dead."

I remembered seeing Harry in the casino. We must have surprised him and Terri, and they had to wait until we went downstairs to the business center to move the body. My suspicion that the picture text of Sherman Potter's flamingo had been a ruse to get us to leave was spot on.

"Why was she using her sister's name?" I asked Tim.

He shrugged. "She said she thought it sounded more like a celebrity name than just plain Ann."

Had to agree.

"If she was worried about Harry and Terri finding her, why did she go to her sister's tonight?" I asked.

"She didn't know about Terri, didn't know Terri lived

there, too. She wanted to make sure she got a couple of family heirlooms that her sister had and ended up cleaning out the whole place."

I hadn't seen anything that had seemed to be worth something, but what did I know?

I had another thought. "Why did Terri leave, knowing Ann was in there?" I left it unspoken that it was Terri's chance to get to Ann; she didn't know that we were watching.

Harry squirmed a little. I stared him down.

"She wanted me to take care of the sister, said she was a loose end," he said. "I was over at the Flamingo. I was supposed to meet Ace, but she called me, said she was coming to get me. She didn't want to do it herself." Harry stared at me, his gaze unnerving. "Terri is jealous of you," he said in a complete non sequitur.

I couldn't hold back my surprise. "Why?"

His familiar smile flashed for a second. "She knows how I feel about you. You know I would never really hurt you, right?"

The guy was certifiable.

"She said we could leave and start over, that I didn't have a choice. She said I should use the key first, though, take care of you, too, and no one would find you till morning."

I started to shake, and Tim slipped his arm around me, steadying me.

"But I wouldn't do it, you know that, don't you?" Harry asked again. "I only wanted to tattoo you."

Like that made it all better.

But it reminded me of something. "What about that stencil and flamingo at Murder Ink?" I asked.

Harry's eyes skipped behind me. I turned slightly to see Jeff leaning against the wall, his arms crossed, his eyes dark with anger as he stared Harry down. Harry bit the corner of his lip, then said, "He fired me. And you're in love with him."

Seems he wasn't the only one who was jealous. But still, I wouldn't meet Jeff's eyes as I felt the flush crawl up my neck.

Tim frowned as he went over to Harry and pulled him up, taking note of the bruises on his face before slapping a pair of handcuffs on him. Flanigan turned to me. "We need—"

"A statement," I said. "I know the drill."

Chapter 59

Jeff's fingers traced the outline of the unfinished and marred flamingo on my lower back, causing goose bumps to rise, but not in a bad way.

"I've got an idea, but you've got to trust me, Kavanaugh," he said.

I couldn't see his expression. I was facing away from him, holding up my shirt, my jeans back down around my hips.

Suddenly his fingers were dancing along the tiger lily on my side, and then the dragon tail that curled around my torso.

"This is good work," he murmured.

Mickey, my old boss at the Ink Spot, had done them. They were beautiful. This was the first time Jeff had seen them.

"Do you have any others?" he asked.

I shook my head. "Just the sleeves and the one your mom did on my leg," I said, referring to the Napoleon on horseback.

"You need more," he said, still tracing the dragon.

"Let's get this one fixed up first, okay?" I had asked him to do the repair work on the tattoo Harry had started. Ace had said he could do it, as a sort of peace offering. He was back at work here, just as Joel had said he would be, and was feeling pretty guilty about his friendship with Harry. I didn't hold it against him, though. It wasn't his fault.

Joel had offered to fix up the mess, too, but while I admired Joel's work, it wasn't as delicate as the koi that Jeff had done on my arm. Jeff's style, when he wasn't doing flash, was more my style.

I was acutely aware of his touch; now he was back to the lily, his fingers moving up along the stem toward the flower, which touched my breast. I shivered, and his breath whispered against the nape of my neck.

I arched back and felt his lips brush my skin; then he moved away.

"Let's get started," he said, all business.

I lay face down on the chair, which was a little too reminiscent of when Harry had tied me down. I thought about how Tim had told me Terri wanted to make me afraid, how she'd called the Venetian to be on the lookout for me and to detain me, how Harry had sneaked peeks at my schedule when Bitsy wasn't looking, and Terri had called my clients to cancel appointments. This was all more than just making me a distraction for the police. Terri was obsessed with me—and with the way Harry felt about me. She'd impersonated me at the bar, and when Harry texted her that he'd gotten me drunk, she relished taking those pictures of me and posting them on Ainsley's blog. Ainsley had all her passwords written on a notepad in her desk drawer, which was how Terri had been able to do it. She'd even tracked down Colin Bixby's e-mail so she could break us up. She wanted to ruin my life.

It was too bad for her it didn't work, and now she'd end up in jail.

Jeff put the stencil to my lower back. He hadn't asked me if I wanted to see it, and I hadn't said I did. I trusted him.

When the machine started, I closed my eyes and let myself become a part of the work.

It was magnificent. Pink and red and purple plumes stretching along either side of my lower back, the beak raised upward slightly, a little haughtily. The black rogue line blended in with the lines of the bird's body. It didn't look like a flamingo now, but a phoenix rising from orange and yellow flames. As much as I loved Joel, he couldn't have done this. He couldn't have turned something so ugly into something so beautiful.

I held the mirror and stared at it, unable to tear my eyes away from it.

I hadn't said a word.

"You don't hate it, do you?" Jeff asked, a nervousness in his voice that I'd never heard before.

I reached up and touched his cheek, leaning forward. "I love it," I said, and kissed him. On the lips. In the middle of my shop.

When we finally broke apart, we stared at each other for a second; then he grinned as he put his hands on my waist and pulled me closer so our bodies were pressed against each other. He moved in to kiss me again, but pulled back abruptly and said, "So I guess we've got a thing, huh, Kavanaugh."

I rolled my eyes at him.